WHITEWATER
RENDEZVOUS

Reviews of Kim Baldwin's Fiction

Force of Nature

"...filled with non-stop, fast-paced action...Tornadoes, raging fire blazes, heroic and daring rescues...Baldwin does a fine job of describing the fast-paced scenes and inspiring the reader to keep on turning the pages."— Lynne Jamneck, *literature.l-word.com/*

"Likeable characters with plausible problems and concerns, imaginative settings, engrossing events, and a well-tailored writing style all contribute to an exceptional novel."—Arlene Germain, *Midwest Book Review*

"Nature's fury has nothing on the fire of desire and passion that burns in Kim Baldwin's *Force of Nature*! Filled with passion, plenty of laughs, and 'yeah, I know how that feels...' moments, *Force of Nature* is a book you simply can't put down. All we have to say is, where's the sequel?!"—Sherry Stinson, *Outlookpress.com*

"After wowing readers with last year's thriller, *Hunter's Pursuit*, Kim Baldwin's follow-up is a romance. But it's a romance book-ended by scenes with thriller qualities, starting with a twister...great action scenes throughout with just the right balance between plot tension and the character's internal thoughts. Highly recommended to all who enjoy a good romance with rescue/action interspersed."—Lori L. Lake, *Midwest Book Review*

Hunter's Pursuit

"'A riveting novel of suspense' seems to be a very overworked phrase. However, it is extremely apt when discussing...*Hunter's Pursuit*. Look for this excellent novel."—R. Lynne Watson, *Mega-Scene*

"A...fierce first novel, an action-packed thriller pitting deadly professional killers against each other. Baldwin's fast-paced plot comes ...leavened, as every intelligent adventure novel's excesses ought to be, with some lovin'."—Richard Labonte, *Book marks, Q Syndicate*

"Clever surprises and suspenseful drama resonate on each page, setting the wheels in motion for an exciting ride. Action sequences fire rapidly in succession leaving the reader breathless. Once you pick up *Hunter's Pursuit*, there is no putting it down."—Cheri Rosenberg, *The Independent Gay Writer*

Visit us at www.boldstrokesbooks.com

WHITEWATER
RENDEZVOUS

by

Kim Baldwin

2006

ISBN 1-933110-38-4
THIS TRADE PAPERBACK IS PUBLISHED BY
BOLD STROKES BOOKS, INC.,
NEW YORK, USA

FIRST EDITION: BOLD STROKES BOOKS, INC., MAY 2006

CREDITS
EDITORS: JENNIFER KNIGHT AND SHELLEY THRASHER
PRODUCTION DESIGN: J. BARRE GREYSTONE
COVER PHOTOS: LINDA HARDING AND VICKI MCMURROUGH
COVER GRAPHIC: SHERI (graphicartist2020@hotmail.com)

By the Author

Hunter's Pursuit

Force of Nature

Author's Note

This book is mostly set within the Arctic National Wildlife Refuge. While the Odakonya River and the village of Winterwolf are fictional, I tried to be as accurate as possible in my descriptions of the ANWR. This vitally important wilderness is under constant threat of being opened to oil drilling.

For more information on ways in which you can help to safeguard this national treasure for future generations, contact:

The Wilderness Society at:
http://action.wilderness.org/

The Sierra Club at:
http://www.sierraclub.org/arctic

The Natural Resources Defense Council at:
http://www.savebiogems.org/arctic/

Defenders of Wildlife at:
http://www.savearcticrefuge.org/

Two other sites of interest are at:
http://www.arcticwildlife.org/home.htm
http://www.alaskawild.org/

Acknowledgments

It's taken three books, but I'm finally starting to think of myself as an author. I have a lot of people to thank for that. For encouraging my efforts, for making the whole process a joy, for inspiring me.

First, to my partner, M., for great ideas when I need them, for teaching me to kayak, and for convincing me that I had to see Alaska.

I am so deeply indebted to Radclyffe: publisher, author, friend, and inspiration. I could not imagine a more positive and wonderfully nurturing environment for a writer than at Bold Strokes Books. Thank you for making my dreams come true.

I'm extremely fortunate to benefit from the expertise of two incredible editors, Jennifer Knight and Shelley Thrasher. Their contributions to this book cannot be measured.

For Sheri, for yet another dazzling cover. Your artistic wizardry is unmatched, mate.

For Connie Ward, and Sharon Lloyd, Co-Owner of Epilogue Books, my wonderfully supportive and insightful beta readers. Your feedback is always promptly returned and spot-on, and I'm very grateful.

Thanks to Linda (entourage) Harding and Vicki McMurrough, for providing the photos for the cover, and for being the best friends and cheering section an author could hope for.

For my dear friend and contributor, Xenia, many thanks for the invaluable suggestions, unflagging enthusiasm, and for constantly pestering me to see the next page. Hope we get to meet one day.

To the circle of friends who support me in all of my endeavors—Kat and Ed, Marsha and Ellen, Felicity. And especially Tim and Scott—I'm so glad we're family.

And finally, to those wonderful and generous readers who buy my books and email me with words of encouragement. I'm eternally grateful.

DEDICATION

For M.
And her marvelous trained cats

CHAPTER ONE

Chicago, Illinois

Megan Maxwell pressed the first two fingers of her right hand firmly against the throbbing in her temple, as she pushed open one of the thick glass double doors that led from the World News Central newsroom to the executive offices. As soon as the door whooshed shut, blissful quiet enveloped her, the first respite in a stressful and very long day. It was 7:15 p.m. and the management wing was dark, but for the light spilling out from under her office door at the end of the hallway.

She made it halfway there before the BlackBerry on her left hip vibrated. Sighing, she reached beneath the tailored jacket of her navy pantsuit for the handset. The display read *911 control room.*

"Maxwell," she answered in a clipped voice as she returned to the newsroom.

"A small plane has entered the restricted air space around Camp David." The voice belonged to the executive producer of the sportscast currently on the air.

"Page Shelley to the studio," she told him. "Extension 7892. She's probably in makeup. I'm headed your way." Shelley Vincent and Ted Gilliam were her 8 p.m. anchor team, and of the two, Shelley was by far the better ad-libber with breaking news.

Megan strode briskly past the noisy assignment desk and the four large U-shaped communal writing pods where teams of writers, editors, and producers were preparing for upcoming new shows. She made a point of appearing oblivious to the eyes that glanced her way as she breezed through toward the control room, but she was well aware of the effect she had on her staff. No one had better appear to be idle when the vice president of news was around.

As soon as she entered the dimly lit control room with its intimidating array of monitors and switchboards, the executive producer she'd just spoken to wordlessly vacated his chair so she could slip into it. There were two rows of seats in the futuristic control center, both facing a wall of monitors. The operations personnel who controlled the massive switchboards, a mind-boggling array of lighted buttons and switches, occupied the front row: audio operator, technical director, robotics camera operator, Chyron and graphics operator.

In the second row, set on risers, were seats and computer terminals for the producer, executive producer, and director. The wall behind them was made of glass. On the other side was the studio, with its wide mahogany anchor desk and blue chroma-key wall for weather.

Megan quickly scanned the Associated Press bulletin on the computer in front of her. It said only that a small plane had violated the no-fly zone and was approaching Camp David, and that the Air Force had dispatched two F-16 fighters to intercept it.

"Two minutes out," the director announced.

Megan glanced at the monitors to make sure the other networks hadn't beaten them to air with the story, then swiveled around in her chair to see her anchor just entering the studio.

She punched the button that would key her mike to the studio speakers. "Less than two minutes, Shelley," she informed the anchor. "Get your IFB in so I can brief you."

The anchor took her seat and fumbled for her earpiece. The interruptible feedback system allowed on-air talent to hear both program sound and instructions from the control room.

Megan, meanwhile, keyed her mike to a small speaker on the assignment desk. "Nick, do we have confirmation?"

The disembodied voice of the evening desk manager answered, "Yes, but nothing beyond what AP has."

"What about a live shot?" she asked.

"From the Pentagon, roughly ten minutes away," he answered.

"One minute out," the director announced. "Camera two, tight on Shelley."

Megan keyed her mike to the anchor's IFB. "Another small plane has entered the restricted air space around the nation's capitol," she told Shelley, glancing at the monitor where the anchor's image was being framed up and brought into focus. "This one is approaching Camp

David, where the president is spending the weekend. Two F-16 fighters have been sent to intercept. We'll have a live shot from the Pentagon shortly."

The anchor nodded and began jotting down the information.

"Thirty seconds," the director said. "Coming back on camera two."

"Since nine-eleven, hundreds of small planes have violated Washington's restricted air space," Megan spoke quickly into the anchor's IFB. "Such incidents have become so routine that most go unreported. Four, however, have forced evacuations of lawmakers and others, the most recent of which was just two weeks ago, on April 18th. The so-called Air Defense Identification Zone comprises some two thousand square miles around the three D.C. area airports."

"Ten seconds," the director announced. "Ready camera two. Shelley's mike."

"Toss back to sports when you're done," Megan told the anchor as the floor director counted down the seconds.

The cut-in went smoothly, the anchor reciting the information Megan had fed to her as effortlessly as if it had been typed on the teleprompter.

They met two minutes later in the hallway outside the control room.

"Nice job," Megan said. "You should stick close. That live shot should be up soon."

"You know, it never ceases to amaze me," Shelley responded, as she plucked a dark brown hair from the front of her taupe designer suit with a frown.

"What does?"

"How you can recite off the top of your head the background information on just about any story that crosses the wires. Names. Dates. Places. Context. And you're *never* wrong."

Megan shrugged. "I've always had a pretty good memory."

"Phenomenal is more like it. I bet you can recite the names of every teacher you ever had, can't you?" Shelley studied Megan's face, clearly awaiting a response.

She considered the question a moment. "Honestly? I could probably name every classmate, too, if I had to."

"We really should do a story on *you*."

"No, what we *really* should do is get back to work. You have a newscast to prep for." She started to leave, but Shelley's voice stopped her in her tracks.

"By the way…" The anchor was looking at her with an impish smile and a sparkle in her pale blue eyes, like a child with a secret. "You…have some ink…" She pointed to Megan's right cheek.

"Ink?" Megan touched two fingers to her face as though she could feel the mark. "Is it bad?" She glanced around for a reflective surface: glass, chrome. Nothing.

"You have a blue Sharpie…" Shelley drew a short jagged streak in the air with a perfectly manicured index finger. "Kind of like that Harry Potter—Lord Valdemort scar thingie."

"Sharpie?" Megan asked, aghast. "I haven't had a Sharpie in my hand since…" She trailed off as she focused inward, remembering. *Since my department head meeting.* She knew immediately what had happened. She had nearly fallen asleep listening to the head of the sales department drone on and on about the latest ad revenues. Had sat at the conference table with her hand propped against her cheek, fighting back a yawn. Taking notes. *Oh, crap. That meeting was at four and it's after seven.*

"Since…?" Shelley's voice interrupted her mental recounting of everywhere she'd been and everyone she'd seen in the intervening hours.

"Never mind," she grumbled, but she felt her expression soften when she looked at the anchor. "Thanks, Shelley."

"Don't mention it."

She took the long way back to her office to avoid the newsroom and to make a stop in the expansive ladies' lounge adjacent to the bookings unit. Designed for visiting celebrity guests, it was the nicest of the restrooms on the floor, and, best of all, it was deserted at this hour.

The faint floral scent of hair spray assaulted her nostrils as she flicked on the lights and headed toward the long mirror where the hair and makeup artists worked. Her green eyes narrowed as she winced at her reflection. In addition to the three-inch-long jagged Sharpie tattoo, her normally impeccable façade was marred by an errant blond strand of hair that stood straight out of the side of her head.

"And no one bothered to tell me," she griped aloud. *No one* dared *tell me. Grace had already gone home.* Her assistant certainly would have told her how foolish she looked. *And maybe a handful of others.*

The fact irritated her greatly. When she'd moved up the corporate ladder and starting making six figures, she began spending a good bit of money on her appearance, and as with everything else in her life, she paid attention to the details. Nice jewelry. Understated makeup. A $400 salon stop every five weeks for a trim from Ritchie and a touch-up to the blond highlights she added to her straight, shoulder-length medium brown hair. A pedicure, manicure, and massage twice a month. A designer wardrobe of suits—twenty-four in all—size eight, except the pants always needed to be shortened slightly to fit her five foot six height because she refused to wear heels.

Not a single person said anything. Megan had learned to have a thick skin in her position, but it rankled to think that no one cared enough about her personally to spare her the embarrassment. *At least no one you ran across in the last couple of hours,* she tried to console herself. *Whose fault is that?* The question came and went like a whisper. She didn't dwell on such things.

It took a large dollop of cold cream, a couple of squirts of liquid soap, and vigorous scrubbing to erase the marking pen. Her cheek was beet red, like someone had slapped her, but that would pass. A spritz of hair spray tamed the unruly tuft of hair, and she felt almost presentable again. *Not too shabby. Back to business.*

A loud groan escaped her lips when she opened her office door. The chaos awaiting her was far worse than she'd expected. Her massive oak desk was piled high with anchor audition tapes, employee contracts awaiting her signature, the latest ratings, reports from her department heads, and a vast number of other scripts, tapes, documents, and letters. *Great. Just great. I'll be lucky to get out of here by midnight.*

She slipped off her shoes and sank into her high-backed leather chair, automatically reaching for her remote to turn on the six monitors set into the opposite wall. The one tuned to WNC she left barely audible; those showing the competition were muted.

It was only then that she noticed a space carefully cleared in the center of her desk so that her eyes would be drawn to the travel brochure placed there, isolated from the bedlam surrounding it—an enticing island in a hostile sea of paperwork. A yellow Post-it note on top relayed a message penned in the familiar backhand slant of her best friend Justine Bernard, a reporter with WNC.

Give it up, already. You are coming along.
I'm going to nag you until you do.

Megan smiled for the first time that day. Justine was so damn persistent. *But that is why you're such a good reporter. Never take no for an answer.*

She started to toss the brochure into the trash, but stopped herself when she caught the picture on the back. It was breathtaking, a wide-angle photo of an endless caribou herd, tens of thousands of animals, set amidst a landscape of snow-topped mountains and lush, vibrant green valleys. She turned the brochure over and pulled off the Post-it note, revealing the words *Discover Alaska, Land of Endless Adventures.* Surrounding the header was a collage of happy tourists enjoying all the possibilities: dogsledding, whitewater kayaking and rafting, backpacking, fishing, whale watching.

Opening the brochure, she saw that Justine had circled the trip she'd been chattering about for the last several days. *Kayak the remote and scenic Odakonya River as it cuts through canyons in the Arctic National Wildlife Refuge and journeys across the coastal plain to the sea. Witness the magnificent spectacle of the annual migration of the Porcupine caribou herd. Fish for Arctic char and grayling. Explore the grandeur of the last great American frontier. An unforgettable experience that will change your life.*

There was a quote from Supreme Court Justice William O. Douglas about the refuge that read, "This is the place for man turned scientist and explorer; poet and artist. Here he can experience a new reverence for life that is outside his own and yet a vital and joyous part of it."

Those are some pretty hefty promises. She had to admit they really were striking photographs. And as a child, she had dreamed about traveling through an untamed wilderness, like the early explorers she had read about. But that had been too many years ago, and she'd long since given up her childhood fantasies. And her only real experience with the out-of-doors had been a nightmare. *Besides, there's no way in the world this place could get along without me for two whole weeks. Even one week would be disastrous.*

The phone on her desk rang. She snatched it up. "Maxwell."

It was the evening assignment desk manager. "I wanted to let you know the plane turned out to be nothing, as usual. Just a guy with a new pilot's license who was showing off to his girlfriend. She, apparently, was not amused."

"Okay, Nick. Thanks."

Almost as soon as she'd hung up the phone, it rang again. *I'm never going to get out of here.* This time she put the call on speakerphone.

"Why aren't you here?" Justine's usual velvet-smooth, reporter-trained voice was strained—she had to shout to be heard above the cacophony of raucous laughter in the background.

"Can't make it tonight," Megan said, her eyes skimming the mayhem of work on her desk, looking for a place to start.

"You haven't made it in weeks. We're going to revoke your membership card."

A chorus of voices chimed in. It sounded like a goodly number of the gals had managed to make tonight's impromptu gathering of Broads in Broadcasting. Megan could picture them tucked into one of the big circular booths at the Cool Breeze Tavern, a popular spot for local journalists and politicians.

"C'mon, Meg!"

"Party pooper!"

"Don't make us come kidnap you!"

"There's a cute brunette here that's just your type!"

She couldn't help smiling. It *had* been a long time since she'd seen most of the "Broads." After the marking pen incident, she could use some time with her friends. And the thought of maybe hooking up for a quickie wasn't altogether unpleasant, either. Maybe she *had* been working too hard.

"All right, already. I'll be there in a while. Someone keep an eye on the brunette for me—and don't let Elise anywhere near her!"

Fairbanks, Alaska

Chaz Herrick was having an impossibly difficult time keeping her mind on the pile of paperwork in front of her, despite the fact that it was the only thing standing between her and her liberation for the summer—her return to the wilderness that fed her soul and enriched her spirit.

The halls outside her office were empty, the students scattered. She'd traded in her professorial khakis and button-down oxfords for the flannel shirt and jeans that comprised the bulk of her wardrobe. Already, in spirit, she was far from this place.

Her gaze kept straying to the fully loaded backpack in the corner of her office and then to the wall above it, crowded with photographs she'd taken during previous excursions into the backcountry of her adopted state. Some were of trips she'd taken with her parents: cross-country skiing near Denali, kayaking in Glacier Bay, hiking in the Brooks Range. Many solo adventures were represented as well—along with a number of more recent photographs taken during her summers as a senior guide with Orion Outfitters. One particularly striking picture she'd taken of the caribou migration had been chosen for Orion's brochure this year.

Gareth Rosenberg, the head of the Biology and Wildlife Department at the University of Alaska, stuck his head in Chaz's door. He was a big, barrel-chested bear of a man, with an untrimmed beard and long hair, held back in a braided ponytail. "I can't believe you're still here. I thought you'd be long gone."

"Well, I would've been, if it wasn't for all this administrative shit you give us to fill out. I swear you come up with a dozen new forms every year solely to irritate me."

He laughed. Although he was technically Chaz's boss, they were close friends, and they both knew he had been offered the job only after Chaz had turned it down.

"Boy, do you ever get antsy these last few days." He glanced up at her wall of photos. "So where's it to be this year? You doing your guide thing again?"

"Yeah, I'm leading a couple of backpack trips at Denali, and some kayak trips. One on the Odakonya River, and a couple on the Kongakut."

"The Odakonya? Where's that?" he asked.

"It's within the Arctic National Wildlife Refuge. Doesn't get much river traffic except us, because it's pretty inaccessible along a good portion of it."

"Sounds like your kind of place."

She smiled. "Yeah, actually it's the trip I'm most looking forward to. I went there by myself at the end of the season last year, to scout it out. Beautiful stretch of river. Great views. Lots of wildlife. We can do a day hike from there and have a pretty good chance at seeing the caribou herd."

Gareth heaved a great sigh. "Every year I understand a little better why you didn't want this job," he said, sounding envious. "Take lots of pictures?"

"You got it. Now get out of here and let me get back to it. You know I'll go crazy if I have to spend another night in the city."

"The *city*, she says, like it's New York or L.A." He studied her quizzically. "You can drive five minutes out of Fairbanks and be in the wilderness."

"Not wild enough for me," she said.

Chicago, Illinois

They had lied to her. There was no cute brunette. It wasn't even a bona fide gathering of the Broads in Broadcasting, though all those present were members of the group.

No, this was just her and the five of them. They'd lured her to the Cool Breeze for the sole purpose of getting her drunk and ganging up on her so she'd go on this wilderness thing with them. After a few too many tequila shots, they had produced another one of those damn brochures with all the pretty pictures and a sign-up form already half filled out for her, with her name and address and the other stuff that Justine knew off the top of her head.

"You've been promising for years that you'd go with us," Linda Ferris, a photojournalist with WNC, said from Megan Maxwell's left. "Fearless" Ferris, they called her, for her award-winning footage under fire from a variety of war zones.

"Last year, as I recall, you swore you'd *absolutely* go this year, no matter *what* the destination," Justine reminded her from across the booth. Although she appeared in millions of homes every evening on the news, the WNC reporter was rarely recognized in public. Without makeup and with her flyaway auburn hair untamed by network stylists, she looked like a distant cousin of her on-air persona.

"At the time you were all talking a lot about seeing Paris next, as I recall," Megan mumbled.

"You're always bragging about how good your staff is," Pat Palmer reminded her. Pat was Linda's lover and a photographer as well, with TV station WGN. "Don't you trust them enough to leave everything in their capable hands?"

"Well, of course they're very capable, but—" Megan began.

"When's the last time you took a vacation, anyway?" Yancey Gilmore interrupted. "You're like...living in workaholicville, girlfriend. You need to chill." Though her vocabulary and blond, pinup girl appearance seemed to belie the possibility, Yancey was a highly regarded researcher with the Oprah empire.

"Oh, I don't know. Some say the Royal Ice Bitch is pretty frosty already," Justine said, which touched off a gasp of shock and then a chorus of snickering among the group clustered around the plush booth. Only Justine dared to bring up the nickname that the malcontents in the newsroom had assigned to Megan.

Megan glared at her. "You're lucky you're not in my department," she warned with a gruffness that was not at all convincing.

"You have only yourself to blame that I'm not," Justine responded warmly, leaning across the booth to place a hand on Megan's forearm. "I'd still be in the writing ranks if you hadn't given me a shot in front of the camera."

"Oh, shut up. You belong there. I had nothing to do with it." Megan's vision began to swim from the tequila. She closed her eyes and slumped against the thickly cushioned booth.

"Back to the trip," Elise Webber reminded them, pointing to the sign-up sheet that lay on the table in front of Megan. "We have to get this in by tomorrow to get the group discount." The youngest of the group, Elise was a graphic artist with the Discovery Channel. She was also Megan's biggest competition if there were any prospective bed partners about—both of them liked to prowl for new faces when they went out with the group.

"Right you are," Justine agreed. "So you're gonna come, right, Meg?"

"I have never even *seen* a kayak, much less *been* in one. Besides, camping and I don't mix." Megan cracked open an eye, but the room began to tilt, so she quickly shut it again.

"You're athletic," Pat said. "You'll pick it up in no time. And I guarantee you, it's a blast! You'll be so glad you did!"

"It'd be all bugs and snakes, and bad food, and sleeping on the ground, and no way to take a shower..." Megan grumbled on, as if she hadn't heard.

"Look at these pictures." Yancey thrust the brochure at her. "The last great frontier. Unspoiled beauty. How can you miss this?"

Megan ignored her.

"You'll come back a new woman," Linda promised. "Relaxed, refreshed, rejuvenated."

"I think she's afraid," Elise volunteered.

Afraid? That cut through the haze of the alcohol. "Am not," Megan said, rousing herself.

They were all staring at her, totally united in their task of getting her to sign that piece of paper she was having trouble bringing into focus.

"Prove it," Elise said. "I *dare* you to go."

"*Double* dare you," Yancey chimed in.

"Triple-*dog* dare you," Pat added.

"What are we, back in grade school?" Megan said. Her defenses were beginning to crumble.

"Rather make it a *bet*?" Justine asked.

Megan perked up a little. There might be a way out of this after all. "I'm game for that." She blinked several times, trying to clear her head. "How about...movie trivia. Or...current events. You ask me a question, and if I miss it, I sign on the dotted line."

"Oh, no, you don't," Linda said.

"No *way* are we going to take a sucker bet," Yancey agreed. "No trivia. It's got to be left totally up to chance. A flip of the coin?"

"That's fair," Pat said.

"A fifty-fifty chance? That's *not* fair." Megan never played those odds. She only bet on a reasonably sure thing.

Justine leaned forward again to claim her undivided attention. Her gray eyes grew serious, and she used her most convincing tone of voice...the one that audience focus groups characterized as "highly trustworthy." "You *need* this, Megan. Leave it up to fate this one time?"

Leave it up to fate. It was an alien concept to her. Despite the fact that her workday was ever changing and unpredictable—often dependent on breaking news—she had established an orderliness and routine to her life that she was reluctant to relinquish. She never left any important decisions to fate.

You once dreamed about exploring some place like Alaska, she reminded herself. She had to admit she did find the whole idea intriguing. Exciting, even. And not much excited her any more.

"I'm not afraid," she repeated to no one in particular, swaying as she tried to sit up straight in the booth. "Flip the damn coin."

CHAPTER TWO

Winterwolf, Alaska

One corner of the conference room was cluttered with the remnants of the trip they'd just led. Flaccid packs and sleeping pads and unused food packages had been dumped in a heap by the clients, eager to catch the noon charter home. Elsewhere was a hint of the organization that was a hallmark of every Orion Outfitters expedition.

On two long tables lay neat groupings of supplies destined for their upcoming whitewater kayak trip. There were eight piles of food and gear in all: six for the clients and two for the guides, who were, at that moment, neglecting their preparations in favor of two steaming bowls of moose chili and two bottles of Kodiak Brown Ale. The cook at the Stony Creek Lodge had become good friends with Chaz Herrick and Sally Travis during their frequent stops in Winterwolf, and sent over a busboy with some chow whenever they had a short layover between trips.

It was obvious both women spent a lot of time in active outdoor pursuits. Their bodies were tanned and fit, and their clothes were designed for their lifestyles, made of quick-drying fabrics and with ample pockets. But the similarities between the two guides ended there. Chaz was dark and lean, while Sally was all blond curvaceousness.

Sally glanced at her watch as she took a long pull of the ale. "Jeez, where has the time gone? I've got less than an hour before I have to get ready to go."

"Don't worry about it," Chaz said from across the table. "I can finish this up. Why don't you brief me on the clients?"

"Sure." Sally reached for a file folder that contained the registration forms. "You know, I *am* sorry I can't be here for the welcome and briefing. I know you hate that part."

"I suppose I can manage this *once*," Chaz replied, rolling her hazel eyes. "You do have a relatively good excuse. It's not every day your daughter graduates from college."

"Chelsea will be glad you approve." Sally pulled the top form off her pile and perused it, refreshing her memory. "Looks like a good group. All women, and all friends from Chicago."

"All women?" Chaz repeated, leaning forward and trying to read the form upside down across the table.

"Yeah, I thought you'd like that."

"Well, it'll be a nice change after this last nightmare." Chaz glanced over to the pile of discarded backpacks. "I got tired of fending off Mister Can't-keep-his-hands-to-himself."

"Why didn't you just tell him you're gay?" Sally asked.

"Because that rarely discourages them. Remember that pilot who went kayaking with us last summer? I told *him*, finally, and he only got more determined to hit on me. Said he viewed me as a challenge. What a creep."

"Oh, yeah, that big guy with the bad comb-over. Followed you around like a dog in heat."

"Don't remind me. Okay, who have we got?" Chaz gestured toward the registration forms.

"The good news is they all can swim. The first two have good whitewater experience. Linda Ferris, forty-four, who's been kayaking for fifteen years…" Sally gave her form to Chaz. "And Pat Palmer, forty-seven, who's got about the same." She handed over a second sheet. "They have their own boats and have done a lot of class III and IV."

Chaz glanced over the two registration forms. No physical limitations for either woman. No special dietary restrictions or allergies. Both said they had extensive previous camping experience, and both listed themselves as expert kayakers. In other words, on paper, they looked like very low-maintenance clients. Her favorite kind. "Okay, next?"

"Two more with *some* previous paddling experience," Sally continued. "Yancey Gilmore, thirty-eight, who goes canoe camping with her family a couple of times a year, and Justine Bernard, twenty-nine, who went on a ten-day sea kayak trip to Glacier Bay last summer with another outfitter." She tossed two more forms to Chaz. "I've talked to Justine at length a couple of times—she's the point person for the group and made all the arrangements. I like her a lot. Good sense of humor, lots of enthusiasm."

Chaz scanned the papers. Like the other two, there were no red flags on these forms, warning of potential problems. "Can we be lucky enough not to get any Muffys on this trip?" It was the word they used to describe the occasional woman client who griped from the get-go about the lack of modern amenities. "Muffys" were usually talked into coming along by a boyfriend and had no idea what primitive conditions they were in for.

"Don't celebrate too soon," Sally cautioned, perusing the forms of the final two clients. "Elise Webber—she's twenty-eight—*has* done some canoeing, but it was a long time ago, and the only camping she's done has been in an RV." She tossed the woman's form to Chaz. "And then there's Megan Maxwell. She's thirty-two."

Chaz didn't like the tone of Sally's voice. She reached over and plucked Megan's form from the other guide's hand. "How bad is it?" she asked, even as she began reading.

"No previous experience on the water," Sally said. "And no outdoorsy experience at all either, except for two-and-a-half disastrous days at summer camp when she was seven."

"She actually wrote that down?"

Sally shrugged. "Seemed kind of odd to me, too. But at least she claims to be a fast learner, and physically active—golf, tennis, racquetball. Might not be too bad."

"I hope you're right." Chaz scanned the form, trying to picture the woman who'd filled it out. The handwriting at the top of the sheet—name, address, phone, and so forth—was clearly legible, the backward slant indicating that Megan was probably a lefty. But the questions beneath had been answered in an almost childish scrawl that canted in the opposite direction, and each answer was given in painstaking detail, almost to the point of absurdity.

What intrigued her most were the words Megan had written after the disclaimer at the bottom of the registration form. All adventure trips required them; it was standard practice among the industry, and Chaz had never had a client comment on it before.

**I acknowledge that the trip I am undertaking involves
hazardous activities in a remote area, with a risk**

of illness, injury or death. I also acknowledge that
medical services and facilities may not be immediately
available during the majority of the trip. In order
to participate, I am willing to accept the risks and
responsibility for any and all risks of illness, injury,
or death due to the negligence (but not the reckless,
willful, or fraudulent conduct) of Orion Outfitters
and its employees.

I verify this statement by placing my initials here.

Megan had initialed it all right, with a barely legible MGM that
made Chaz briefly wonder whether the woman's parents had been fans
of the movie studio. And just beneath she had scribbled, *Covering your
butts, I see. Sure does inspire faith in your guides.*

"Did you see what she wrote after the disclaimer?" Chaz asked.
What a bitch!

"Yeah," Sally responded, a smile appearing at the corner of her
mouth. "I asked Justine about it, actually, once we'd kind of gotten to
know each other through a couple of phone calls."

"And?"

"Megan was apparently somewhat reluctant to join the trip, so her
friends got her shnockered."

"Drunk? She was drunk when she signed this?" Chaz was appalled.
"Then we can't accept it!"

"Relax. I thought the same thing, but Justine says Megan really
wants to go and will be great fun on the trip. To make sure, I called
her myself while she was at work and totally sober. She's some vice
president at WNC, by the way."

"The news network?"

"That's the one. I had to go through two secretaries to get to her.
Anyway, she apologized for writing the comment, said she didn't
remember doing it. And she confirmed she wants to go on the trip."

"So she sits behind a desk all day in downtown Chicago," Chaz
summed up. "And she's a bigwig executive, so she's used to giving
orders. In other words, she's *just* the type of client who'll want to dig a
latrine and gather firewood."

"Chaz, you're not one to prejudge people," Sally gently rebuked.

Chaz hung her head and gave a shrug of chagrin. She knew that a lot of clients were nothing like what she expected from their forms. And she respected Sally and valued her thoughtful opinion of things. During the five summers they'd led trips together for Orion, Sally Travis had become the big sister Chaz had always wanted growing up.

"You're right. Of course you're right." She took a deep breath and let it out. Thought a moment. Then grinned. "What *am* I griping about? We've got an all-women trip. And we're going to one of the most drop-dead gorgeous places I've ever seen. You're gonna love it, Sal. Great water. Lots of wildlife. And *awesome* scenery."

"I can't wait. Those pictures you took are incredible." Sally looked at her watch. "I hate to say this, but I'd better get going if I'm going to catch a ride out."

Like most bush communities in the north Alaskan interior, Winterwolf was accessible only by air. There were two flights a day, at noon and five. Sally would be leaving on the same small plane that was bringing in their clients.

"No worries," Chaz said, as Sally pushed back from the table and stood. "I'll wrap this up tonight after I get everyone settled."

Sally headed for the door. "Meet you in the lobby in ten?"

"Make it out front. I'll pull the van around." Once her partner guide had departed for her room, Chaz glanced once more at the file on the table in front of her. *Will you be able to really appreciate where I'm going to take you, Megan Maxwell? I sure hope so.*

❖

Her friends all had their faces pressed up against the thick-paned milky windows on either side of the nine-seater Beechcraft, but Megan, seated in the back by the door, had her eyes closed. She hated flying, especially in small planes, and this one had done enough bouncing around that she was feeling increasingly airsick. On top of that, she was fretting about all the things she'd forgotten to tell Grace, her administrative assistant, before she left.

She attended to a million details on a daily basis. Managed a staff of several hundred people. So even *with* her incredible memory, it stood to reason she might miss a *few* things. But that didn't make her feel any better. How could she even have thought about leaving for two weeks?

To make matters worse, she hadn't learned until just before leaving that they would be totally incommunicado for a good portion of the trip. Modern technology apparently still hadn't found a way to get a radio or cell phone signal from within a steep river canyon in northern Alaska.

It's only for a few days, Megan told herself, swallowing repeatedly to try to keep her nausea at bay. *Only the three or four days we're in the canyons. The network won't collapse in three or four days.*

"Is that the Brooks Range we're coming up on?" Justine asked from her seat behind the pilot, a scruffy-bearded forty-something man.

"Yup, we've crossed over the Arctic Circle." The pilot banked the plane slightly to give them a better view.

"I knew it would all be...well, *big*," Yancey said in wonder. "But this...this absence of any civilization whatsoever...as far as you can see. It takes your breath away."

"Miles and miles and miles of absolute, utter wilderness," Linda said.

586,412 square miles, to be exact, Megan thought to herself, trying to ignore the high-pitched whistle of air that came from her left; there was a bad seal between the door and the plane. *Alaska is the last great wilderness in the United States. Civilization has only encroached on about 160,000 acres of its 365 million acres, which is less than one-twentieth of one percent of the state.*

The whistle refused to be ignored. Megan hated planes that were so small that they had to ask you how much you weighed. *The doors on big planes never whistle like this.* Megan felt her stomach lurch when the plane hit turbulence and fell several feet before recovering. Everyone else seemed to take it in stride, but her knuckles went white where she gripped the armrest. *Alaska bush pilots have the third most dangerous job in the United States. More than 500 have died in crashes.*

"Look over there. Are those flowers?" Pat pointed toward the northeast, where a dense carpet of wildflowers had painted a long valley in brilliant hues of purple and red, yellow and orange. "It looks like an Impressionist painting."

The state flower of Alaska is the forget-me-not. The plane rode another big bump of turbulence. Megan's palms went clammy.

"It's all the sunshine that does it," the pilot informed them. "The sun doesn't set up here, this time of year. From early May to early August."

Megan groaned inwardly. *Oh, shit. That's what else I forgot. The damn eyeshade.* She'd had Grace pick one up at the mall, along with several books about Alaska: field guides to flora and fauna, history, indigenous cultures, ecology. She'd devoured them all, had even gone online to read up on Orion Outfitters and this caribou herd they were going to see.

She had gotten where she was at WNC in large part because of her extraordinary research skills and attention to detail. She was nothing if not fully prepared for any endeavor she decided to undertake, and this trip was no exception. She had packed every single item listed on Orion's suggested packing list, including all the optional ones, and she'd thrown in a few of her own impulsive purchases from the L.L. Bean catalogue. It was a good thing money was not an issue—the only things on the list she'd already owned were underwear, toiletries, and a swimsuit.

But the eyeshade was still sitting in the top drawer of her desk. It wasn't like Megan to forget things, and this was a rather important item to miss, as she had trouble sleeping even under the best conditions. *What the hell's happening to me? I'm the master of going with the flow, great under fire, calm in a calamity. So how come going on vacation has me more stressed than I've been in a year?*

Megan barely heard the others after that, oohing and ahhing over the sights below. She was too busy compiling a mental list of all the people she needed to call when they landed.

❖

Chaz leaned back against the van, watching the southern horizon. She ran her hands over the front of the Orion Outfitters T-shirt she'd pulled on, trying to smooth out some of the wrinkles. The navy shirt was so faded it was hard to read the words or make out the namesake constellation drawn above it, but she couldn't bear to part with it. The rest of her clothes were made of more durable fabrics and bore labels recognizable to any serious outdoor enthusiast.

Sally was occupied digging in her duffel bag for a paperback to read on the plane. They were parked on the edge of a single long runway cut into the tundra, a short distance from Winterwolf. There was no terminal, no control tower, only a pair of well-weathered wind socks to help guide the pilot. The weather was fine this early June afternoon, with temperatures in the midsixties. The wind socks barely moved, and the sky was clear and blue.

Chaz was itching to be on their way to the Odakonya; this first day and a half of preparing the clients would drag on more than usual without Sally. They'd worked up a routine that played up each woman's strengths. Normally, after the welcoming dinner, Sally—the more gregarious of the two—would spirit the clients away and conduct the orientation, while Chaz—the more detail-oriented—would take care of getting their gear together and packing all the meals. The following day, the two of them together would conduct the individual paddling and rolling lessons.

With Sally going away for her daughter's graduation until tomorrow night, Chaz would have to attend to all their combined duties by herself, but she wasn't worried. She didn't think it would be too difficult since most of the clients had previous paddling experience.

A speck appeared on the horizon, and her heartbeat kicked up a notch. "Here it comes," she announced.

❖

"Man, we *are* out in the middle of *nowhere*," Megan heard Yancey say as the plane bumped down onto the runway. She'd been so lost in thought she hadn't been aware they were about to land.

She opened her eyes and looked around. They'd touched down in a long valley surrounded on every side by snowcapped mountains, the runway a narrow strip of asphalt surrounded by wildflowers and a few scrawny, low scrub trees. The only other signs of civilization were two wind socks and the blue van they were taxiing toward and, across the tundra, in the distance, a small settlement of buildings.

Finally. She pulled a small day pack from under her seat and began digging through it for her BlackBerry.

"Are those our *guides?*" Elise asked, with obvious delight in her voice. "I think I'm in *love.*"

The pilot turned to glance at Elise with raised eyebrows and a bemused grin.

"Down, girl," Justine said, but she was straining to get a good look at their welcoming committee, too.

"Hey, she's not kidding," Pat added, as the plane rolled to a stop some twenty-five feet from the van. "They're both certainly easy on the eyes. Check out the legs on the brunette."

"Hush, you," Linda said, poking Pat good-naturedly from the neighboring seat. "You're taken, remember?"

"Oh, I certainly remember, darlin'. No harm in looking." Pat leaned over to plant a quick kiss on Linda's cheek as the pilot got out of his seat and maneuvered through the narrow aisle to the door at the back next to Megan.

After he deployed the stairs, the women began filing out of the plane.

❖

Chaz watched the clients emerge, making no immediate move toward the plane. The first one off, a handsome and butchly older woman with a short, severe haircut, sent her gaydar pinging off the scale. Her suspicions were confirmed when the woman paused at the bottom of the steps to offer an assisting hand to a petite woman with long, curly brown hair and was given a quick peck on the lips in thanks. They waved to the guides but remained by the plane for their bags, which the pilot had begun to unload from a compartment in the wing.

The third to disembark was a striking young woman—tall and lean, with dark spiky hair, chocolate brown eyes, and the kind of androgynous appeal that could melt men and woman alike. She wore tight black jeans and a matching T-shirt, and she didn't take her eyes off Chaz as she bounded down the steps and headed directly for the two guides.

"Well, well, *well*..." Sally said under her breath as the woman approached. "See what I mean about how the registration forms don't tell you everything?"

"Elise Webber," the woman introduced herself as she extended a hand toward Chaz.

"Chaz Herrick," she responded as they shook. "Welcome to Winterwolf."

Elise's grip was firm and reluctant to immediately disengage. They looked at each other for a long moment, openly appraising each other with knowing smiles.

"*Very* pleased to meet you, Chaz." Elise gave Chaz's hand a final squeeze before finally releasing her grip and turning to acknowledge the other guide.

"Sally Travis," Sally said with undisguised amusement as they briefly shook hands.

"Hi, Sally. Well, better get my bag." Elise walked away with a sexy sway in her hips, and Chaz couldn't help but appreciate the woman's effort to get her attention.

All the clients were now busy retrieving their luggage, except for one, who stood off to the side, preoccupied with the phone in her hand, her back to the guides. *Megan Maxwell*, Chaz decided, taking in the woman's clothes. She was dressed head to foot in brand-new gear, from her North Face jacket and L.L. Bean clothes to the tips of her shiny, right-out-of-the-box hiking boots. *Those boots could be trouble. Obviously got them mail order. A good salesman would have warned her to break them in.*

"Sure looks to be an interesting group. Here we go," Sally said, as the two guides pushed off the van and headed toward their clients.

"You owe me *big* for this," Chaz muttered under her breath. "You know how I hate this schmoozing part." It wasn't that she was antisocial by any means. But she was always a bit uncomfortable in the beginning, having to make polite small talk with strangers. It was much easier once the ice was broken, and the trip got underway.

❖

Damn thing. We're not even out on the river yet. Megan frowned at the no-signal display once more before she shoved the BlackBerry into her coat pocket.

"Have you gotten a good look at our guides, Meg?" Justine's voice, subdued from behind her, alerted Megan that something was amiss.

"What? Why?" She turned and peeled off her sunglasses, glancing first at Justine, who had the oddest expression on her face—then at the two strangers who were approaching.

Both women were fit and athletic, she could see that at first glance, which was not unexpected. *The blond in the lead looks a little like Helen Hunt*, Megan thought, *and the one behind her.* Her mouth hung open in shock, and she could feel the color draining from her face. *It can't be.* She stared, disbelieving, unable to move.

"Are you all right?" Justine asked in a low voice.

Megan couldn't answer, her mind busy cataloguing the differences, no matter how small, as if to reassure herself that this could not possibly be Rita, five years older and with a shag haircut instead of the long, straight locks she'd had throughout their relationship. No, this woman was taller, at least five foot ten, and definitely had a more tautly muscled physique, especially in the shoulders and upper arms. Slightly smaller breasts, too, though well-rounded, like Rita's. *And no bra. Rita never went out in public without a bra.* And though the hair was the right shade, a deep chestnut brown, the eyes were entirely wrong. Hazel, with yellow flecks, instead of piercing blue.

Still, there was much that was the same. The high cheekbones, the almond complexion, the expressive eyebrows and full lips surrounding a perfect white smile. It was such an uncanny resemblance that Megan could not tear her eyes from the dark-haired guide, or find her voice to respond to Justine's gentle inquiry.

"Welcome to Alaska, ladies," the blond guide said in greeting. "I'm Sally Travis and this is Chaz Herrick. We'll be leading you on this adventure."

Her friends stepped forward and began introducing themselves, but Megan hung back, fighting the overwhelming urge to flee. *I should never have come. This is a really, really bad omen.*

❖

The look on the client's face was indecipherable. But something was definitely *wrong* with Megan Maxwell. Chaz could see it. And damned if it didn't look like it had something to do with *her*. The woman hadn't taken her eyes off her since the moment she'd turned around. Those expressive green eyes reminded Chaz of a deer caught in the headlights: bewildered, vulnerable. And then, something else—she looked...*angry*, almost. *What the hell?*

Chaz had no time to try to decipher what the woman's problem was—she was immediately occupied with greeting the other clients. The first to introduce themselves were the two who had been first off the plane. They looked to be a bit older than the others, though both seemed to be in excellent physical shape.

"Hi, Chaz, I'm Pat Palmer. Good to meet you." The butch shook her hand firmly, then turned to put an arm around her companion. "And this is Linda Ferris."

A compactly built woman with blue eyes and dark hair tinged with hints of gray, Pat carried herself with an athletic grace, and her muscular shoulders and forearms evidenced her many hours in a kayak. She wore a T-shirt with the words OCOEE RIVER embroidered on it, and bungeed to her duffel was a top-of-the-line, take-apart crankshaft carbon fiber paddle, expensive but extremely light and ergonomic. Chaz had one like it.

It was equally obvious that Pat's partner was the other experienced client. She'd brought along her own high-tech paddle as well, and Linda Ferris had tucked her curly brown hair under a well-worn baseball cap that read "Kayakers do it rapidly, then roll over and do it again."

Linda greeted Chaz with a big smile. "Sure am looking forward to this."

Next to introduce herself and shake hands was Yancey Gilmre, the only blond among today's clients. "Hey, there. Good to meet ya." Yancey was built like a Barbie doll, with trim hips, a narrow waist, and surgically enhanced breasts that strained against the confines of her red-and-black-checked flannel shirt.

"Welcome, Yancey," Chaz said, trying to keep her eyes from straying to the blond's ample assets. All of Yancey's gear, she noticed, from her duffel bag to her clothing—most of it Patagonia—was well-used but well-tended. This woman had also obviously spent a lot of time in the out-of-doors.

The introductions were interrupted by a shout from the pilot. "Hey, Sally! We better get going!"

"Sorry, ladies, but I have to leave you in Chaz's expert hands for the moment." Sally picked up her bag. "I'm off to see my daughter graduate, but I'll be back tomorrow night." After a nod of encouragement and a quick wink toward her partner guide, she took off toward the plane at a trot.

Ah. So that's the story. Megan caught the wink and immediately surmised that their two guides had a thing going on between them. She still hadn't recovered from the shock of Chaz's uncanny resemblance to her cheating ex. *Looks the same, probably acts the same. A slut, just like Rita was. I shouldn't be here. I should be back in Chicago.* That reminded her of the calls she needed to make.

"Where's the nearest phone?" she asked Chaz without preamble. "Or at least somewhere where mine can pick up a signal?"

Chaz pasted on her best professional smile. "There's a phone at the lodge. We'll be there in a few minutes." She gestured toward the van, and without further ado, Megan picked up her bag and headed for the vehicle. *What the hell is your problem?* Chaz wondered, watching her go.

"Hi, Chaz, I'm Justine." A slim, attractive woman with wild auburn hair and a ready smile approached and offered her hand. "I made our arrangements with Sally."

"Ah, right. Good to meet you, Justine. You're the one who's done Glacier Bay, right?"

"That's me. The rude one, by the way, is Megan." She gestured toward her sullen companion, who had tossed her bag into the van and settled into a seat. "She's not really as bad as she seems. She just hasn't yet realized she's on vacation. It'll sink in."

"Good to hear that." Chaz smiled back at the redhead. She liked this one already. "Ladies? Shall we go?" she asked the rest.

The women piled into the van as Chaz loaded their bags into the rear storage area. Megan Maxwell's duffel, she noted, was like her clothes—brand-new, right off a store shelf. And it was easily twice as big as any of the others. She had obviously well exceeded the what-to-pack list that Orion had sent to all the clients. It would be a challenge to get all the gear on the supply raft.

Soon they were underway, and the women began peppering her with questions.

"So what's this river like?" Pat inquired from the front passenger seat.

"Oh, it's a *blast* to run," Chaz replied, her enthusiasm for their destination evident in her tone. "The first stretch will take us four or five days. It's nice and easy, with fabulous scenery and all sorts of wildlife and birds. Give you a chance to all get comfortable with the kayaks, and those of you who haven't done a lot of paddling can get some experience before we hit the faster water."

"There are a couple of stretches of class IV rapids on the section we're taking, aren't there?" Yancey asked, from the second row of seats.

Chaz glanced in the rearview mirror, which happened to be pointed at Yancey's considerable cleavage. She readjusted it to aim at the woman's face. "Yes, near the end of the trip. And there's a long stretch of class III in the middle section of the river, where it cuts through some steep canyons. But those of you without a lot of experience don't need to worry—"

"I need to make some calls when we get to the lodge," Megan interrupted Chaz from the back row. "I hope we're going to get some time to ourselves before we have to be somewhere."

"You'll get about a half hour to check in and get settled in your rooms," Chaz explained, trying to keep in check her growing irritation with Ms. Maxwell. She could already see this client was going to test her normally placid and easygoing demeanor. "We'll meet in the dining room at six. During dinner, I'll brief you on the trip and answer any questions you have. Tomorrow, you'll be assigned your gear, and I'll conduct training sessions for everyone in the creek behind the lodge. I expect that some of you won't need much instruction from me, in which case you can use the time to get the feel of your gear."

"You probably don't need to spend a lot of time with Pat and me," Linda said. "We've been kayaking together a lot. We just got back from doing the Middle Gauley in West Virginia."

"That's some great water, I've heard." Chaz knew it wasn't the most difficult section of the famed river—the area with class V+ whitewater—but you still had to be a skilled paddler to make it through the Middle Gauley.

"It was awesome," Pat confirmed.

"So I understand you're all friends, right?" Chaz asked.

"Yup," Justine answered. "We work at different media outlets in Chicago. TV is a very small industry, really, and one where people change jobs a lot. So you get to know those who work in the same market you do. You cover the same stories, attend the same events and parties. Well, a few years ago, Megan and I started up a group called Broads in Broadcasting and invited a lot of women we'd met to join. I think we have a half-dozen media outlets represented. A bunch of us get together at a pub a couple of times a month to kick back and dish the dirt."

"And every year, a few of us take a trip together. Last year, ten of us went to London," Elise supplied. "We stayed at the Hilton."

"This will certainly be a change of pace," Chaz remarked dryly.

The women—all but Megan, who was staring out the window—chuckled at the understatement.

"About half the group are your typical I-can't-be-without-my-hairdryer-and-makeup gals, Pat said. "They tend to sit out trips like this one."

"The other half are more adventurous," Yancey added. "We want to get *away* from the city when we get some time off."

"So we've compromised," Justine said. "A posh trip one year, an outdoor adventure the next."

"How do you decide the destination?" Chaz inquired. *Quite an interesting concept*, she thought, glancing at Megan in the mirror. *Which type of woman are you?* Megan was staring out the window but seemed entirely self-absorbed, and Chaz wondered whether she was seeing any of the beauty of their surroundings. She sure looked out of her element here.

"When we started the group, every member wrote down a destination or type of trip, and we put them all in a jar," Linda explained. "We draw one every year. If we select a ritzy location on a year we're supposed to do an adventure trip, we put the slip back in the jar and keep drawing until we get it right."

"How many are in your group?" Chaz asked.

"Oh, gosh, close to thirty, I guess," Justine said. "Although most are in it only for the occasional socializing. A lot of the 'Broads' are married with kids and can't get away for long trips."

"So none of you fit into that category?" Chaz inquired. "Married with kids, I mean?" She noticed several of the clients exchange looks with each other—Pat and Linda, Elise and Justine.

"I've got a hubby at home," Yancey answered. "And two boys who love getting a week or two alone with Daddy each year. They get to eat McDonalds and Pizza Hut every day and stay up late." She laughed.

"What about you? Are you married, Chaz?" Linda asked.

"Nope. Never married. Never close."

She glanced up to find Elise staring at her in the rearview mirror with a raised eyebrow and flirtatious grin. Chaz couldn't help smiling. *So Yancey's straight, but Elise sure isn't. And Pat and Linda are definitely a couple. Justine might be a lesbian, too,* she thought, but her gaydar was less certain on that one. And who knew what Megan's deal was—she was still staring out the window and seemed totally removed from the rest of them.

"What about Sally?" Justine asked. "Didn't she say she was attending her daughter's graduation?"

"Mmmhmm. Chelsea is graduating from Washington State. Sally and her husband Tom also have a son named Nathan, who's a sous chef at a fancy Seattle restaurant."

"Sally and I became phone pals setting up this trip," Justine said. "She has a right wicked sense of humor, doesn't she?"

"That she has," Chaz agreed. "And a practical joker, too. I advise all of you to check your sleeping bags the first night out for rubber snakes and spiders."

"Oh, great," Megan mumbled from the back. "I'm back in summer camp." It was the first acknowledgement that she'd been paying attention to the conversation.

"Lighten up, your Majesty," Justine chided, snickering.

"Your Majesty?" Chaz repeated.

"Our auspicious friend back there has quite a reputation among her underlings at work…some of whom refer to her as the Royal Ice Bitch," Linda supplied, grinning.

"Oh, come on, guys," Megan grumbled, but the explanation surprisingly brought the first smile to the woman's face and seemed to crack her cool exterior. Chaz tried not to stare at her in the rearview mirror. She felt a flutter of something unexpected in the pit of her stomach. *She's an altogether different woman when she smiles.*

"We can kid her about it, you see, because we all know what a softhearted ol' gal she really is," Yancey added.

"Will you all stop talking about me as if I'm not here?" Megan complained good-naturedly.

"Although she *can* be pretty intimidating when she has on her I'm-a-vice-president! mask," Yancey went on.

"Before I knew you, I thought you had *no* sense of humor," Linda admitted. "But boy, when you have a few tequilas…"

"That's *enough*!" Megan rebuked, but she was still smiling. Chaz noticed a slight flush to the woman's cheeks. *There's certainly more to her than meets the eye.*

They entered the bush community of Winterwolf, a block-long cluster of buildings that included a small gas station/convenience store, a one-room school, tiny post office, and a handful of homes, and at the end of the street, their destination—a quaint log and stone building whose sign out front proclaimed it the Stony Creek Lodge.

"We're here," Chaz announced, pulling into a parking spot in front. She shut off the engine and turned in her seat to address her clients. "Sue and Paul Bartlett own the place. They'll meet you inside and show you to your rooms. We'll gather in the dining room at…" She glanced at her watch. "…six? That gives you thirty-five minutes." She said the last directly to Megan, who nodded and reached for the door handle. "There are no phones in the rooms," she added. "But there are pay phones in the lobby."

"Thanks," Megan mumbled before getting out and hurrying inside. She was so intent on her call that she left her bag in the van.

Chaz retrieved it, surprised by its heft, and followed the clients inside. She spotted Megan facing away from her on a phone in the corner of the empty lobby, and headed toward her to drop off the bag. Chaz paused when she overheard part of the conversation. It was impossible not to. An obviously exasperated Megan was nearly shouting into the phone. Chaz didn't want to interrupt.

"You're going to have to make these calls yourself," Megan was saying. "Use your best judgment." She listened for a moment. "*Stop!*" she interjected, raising her voice. "Deal with it! I'm on vacation and I'm turning my BlackBerry *off!*" She hit a button on the device and took a deep breath. Then another. She turned to find Chaz staring at her from six feet away and jumped a little.

"Eavesdropping, are we?" Megan inquired without humor.

"Sorry," Chaz stammered, embarrassed. She dropped the duffel and headed to her room. *Why did you let her get to you like that? You weren't eavesdropping.* She couldn't understand why the two of them seemed to be mixing like oil and water, but that had to change. They were going to be spending an awful lot of time together, and she wanted both of them to enjoy the experience.

As senior guide, Chaz would take the lead kayak, scouting the river and assisting the less-experienced clients as needed through the tough spots. Sally would bring up the rear, rowing their gear and supplies on a large raft.

Chaz had to figure out a way to improve her rapport with Megan, the sooner the better. *Maybe an opportunity will present itself.*

❖

Megan's stomach clenched involuntarily as she watched the guide depart. *Well, that was extremely rude of me,* she admitted, instantly regretting her words. *She was only bringing me my bag, and I nearly took her head off.* She sighed. It was just that she'd only been gone one day, and already things were going to hell at work. *Okay, and maybe it's weirded me out a bit that she looks so damn much like Rita.*

For nearly five years, she had successfully avoided thinking very much about the woman she had married. She worked sixty to seventy hours a week to fill her waking hours with distractions, and when the memories refused to be ignored—when her cheating ex popped up on TV or in a magazine—Megan escaped with sex or alcohol. But now here was Rita's twin, and she had nearly two whole weeks ahead with the woman. Far too much time to remember what she'd fought so hard to forget.

Chapter Three

Even though she'd technically been on vacation for more than twenty-four hours, Megan still felt every bit as stressed as she did in the newsroom. Perhaps even more so. For not only was she having to worry long distance about what might be happening back at WNC, she was more unsettled than she'd expected by the abrupt and radical change in her surroundings and routine.

She'd spent nearly every bit of her thirty-five minutes of getting-settled time on the phone with Grace, putting out brush fires and briefing her assistant on the few things she'd remembered on the plane. So she barely had time to drop her duffel bag in her room before she had to meet the others.

When she arrived at the dining room, she spotted her friends sipping cocktails around a long table, framed by an immense picture window. Beyond were the mountains of the Brooks Range, their snowcapped peaks cast in the golden alpenglow of the lowering sun. It was a beautiful sight, but Megan's eyes were drawn to the dark-haired guide, seated at the head of the table, who at the moment held the entire group's attention.

The guide said something that made everybody roar with laughter, and Megan frowned, unexpectedly disappointed she'd missed the punch line. *They smile the same, too,* she realized. *That easy, charming, suck-you-in, you-can-trust-me grin.* Every time she looked at Chaz, she was struck anew by the uncanny similarities. The same long legs. The same thick, silky hair. She remembered the feel of it between her fingers. A cauldron of emotions welled up and churned within her, throwing her off balance. Chaz definitely unnerved her.

She detoured to the bar to fortify herself with a double martini, downing half of it on the spot. But she still felt unsteady on her feet when she joined the others.

"Sorry I'm late," she muttered as she took the empty seat they'd left her, halfway down the table next to Justine. She was grateful she had the menu and the view to distract her. She told herself it would be a lot easier if she just didn't *look* at Chaz.

"I recommend the rainbow trout, with asparagus and roasted garlic mashed potatoes," Chaz was saying. "That's the specialty of the house. Paul gets the fish in fresh every day from local Inupiat fishermen."

Of course she has to have a great voice too. Rita had started out in radio, and Chaz could have gotten a job there as well, Megan decided. They both had bedroom voices, as they called it at WNC—that low, seductive, breathy quality that draws in viewers—especially male viewers—who happen to be channel surfing. *Okay, so I do have to listen to her. But I don't have to look at her. At least, not much.*

After they placed their orders with the waitress, Chaz outlined the next couple of days.

"After dinner, I'll pass out garbage bags and dry bags to everyone. You'll need to repack all your clothes and your sleeping bags, double bagging them first into the garbage bags and then into dry bags. Sally will take the big bags of gear and all the food and equipment on our supply raft. You'll get a small dry bag to keep with you, that you can put essentials into—snacks, camera, bug head nets, sunglasses. Oh, and you can leave your luggage here at the lodge if you like, until we get back. Just check it at the front desk."

The double martini was finally helping her to relax. But Megan kept her eyes on the scenery outside, steadfastly refusing a niggling temptation to glance in Chaz's direction every ten seconds.

"Tomorrow morning after breakfast you'll get the rest of your gear—PFDs—that's Personal Flotation Devices, or life jackets, which you *must* wear at *all* times in the water..." Chaz's mellifluous voice trailed off, as if she was seeking an acknowledgement from her audience, but Megan would not look her way. "You'll also get paddles, helmets, neoprene gloves and boots, and dry suits...and then we'll spend some time fitting you with boats."

"What kind of boats do you have?" Pat asked.

"We mostly use Dagger Crazy 88s," Chaz replied. "They're stable, responsive, adjust easily, and clients find them to be about the most comfortable. And they're good if you have to portage—they only weigh about twenty-eight pounds. But we do have a few others—a Riot

Nitro 58, a couple of Mambos for beginners, and a Necky Orbit Fish, if you're familiar with those."

"I've tried the Fish," Pat said. "They're nice boats."

"You'll get to try them out down there." Chaz pointed out the window to the wide, deep creek that ran behind the lodge. "I'll go over paddling fundamentals for those of you who need it, and you can spend the late morning getting a feel for your boat. Then after lunch, we'll have some individual training sessions to make sure everyone knows how to do a wet exit and an Eskimo roll, and I'll spend some time with those of you who need extra help on anything."

Individual training sessions. Megan's heartbeat picked up a notch at the thought of spending alone time with the guide. *I hope to God I pick this stuff up fast.*

"Sally will be back right before dinner tomorrow," Chaz told them. "We'll turn in early so we can get going right after breakfast. We'll be ferried to the Odakonya in two groups by Twin Otter. The trip there takes about a half hour."

"How far do we go each day?" Elise asked.

"We'll spend four to six hours a day paddling, on average." Chaz glanced down the table at Megan, who seemed to be off in her own little world, staring out the window. "We don't want anyone to get so sore they aren't enjoying themselves, and we want to give you plenty of time to do day hikes to get up where you can really see the surrounding scenery and wildlife. So we keep a flexible agenda. We also have a day built in to take it easy, or to stay off the water if the weather turns foul. That's the one constant up here—the weather can change in an instant."

"When do we get where we can see the caribou herd?" Justine asked.

"Three or four days in, we should start seeing them. It's a truly amazing spectacle. One you won't soon forget."

"The picture of them on the brochure was awesome," Yancey said.

"Why, thanks!" Chaz beamed. "I took that last summer when I was scouting out the Odakonya for this trip."

Megan looked over at Chaz. *You took that picture.* The picture that was responsible for her ending up here. *That brochure would have ended up in the trash, and I wouldn't be here admiring how nicely those muscles in her upper arms move when she takes a bite of food.* She forced herself to look out of the window again as Chaz continued.

"We at Orion follow the Leave No Trace principle on our trips, like every other outfitter who leads groups into the refuge. The arctic ecosystem is very fragile—easily impacted by human activities. Are any of you at all familiar with Leave No Trace?"

Pat and Linda nodded their heads.

Yancey stuck a hand in the air. "I've heard of it, anyway. It's packing out all your trash, right?"

"That's a part of it," Chaz acknowledged. "There's a lot more to it than that, though. It's about choosing the right campsites to minimize our impact on the environment. Taking care of how we wash up and how we dispose of human waste and leftover food. It's about respecting wildlife. Watching where you walk when you venture away from camp. And leaving behind souvenirs—no bringing home antlers or fossils or any artifacts we might find. And there's a distinct possibility of that, I might add. This area has been home to the Inupiat Eskimo and Gwich'in Indian people for centuries."

Another page of the field guide she'd read popped into Megan's head. *There are more than 300 archeological sites in the refuge.* That had really appealed to her. The idea that she might find some ancient relic. Her eyes skimmed over the wide expanse of tundra out the window. *You'll be walking where wooly mammoths and saber-toothed tigers once lived.*

"I'll give you handouts to read tonight that explain the Leave No Trace principles in more detail," Chaz went on. "And Sue and Paul have a number of books on the refuge if you'd like to study up on some of the animals and birds you might see on the trip. Sally and I will be pointing things out as well, of course, as we see them."

"What about fires?" Linda asked. "Part of Leave No Trace is not building campfires, isn't it?"

"We don't get a campfire?" Yancey asked with obvious disappointment. "I love sitting around a campfire."

"The rule of thumb is to evaluate the wood resources and the potential impact to the environment," Chaz said. "And if you do decide to build a fire, you leave no trace of that fire. We *will* be using stoves for all of our meals. But there *are* a couple of places on our route where there is ample dead wood and where we can have a small campfire in a fire pan that we'll bring along."

"Great," Yancey said. "That'll do fine!"

"The first stretches of the river are very mild," Chaz said. "But when we get to the canyons and the water gets faster, I'll be scouting ahead on occasion to look for obstacles or check the line."

"The line?" Justine asked.

"The best route to take," Chaz elaborated. "I'll evaluate how you're all doing as we go along, and when we get to the more challenging stretches, I'll decide who paddles and who portages."

"Portages? You said that earlier. What's that?" Elise asked.

"You get out and carry your kayak. All of the tougher stretches can be portaged, which is one reason it's a good river for all ranges of experience," Chaz said. "You and Megan will definitely portage the class IV rapids and probably some of the III as well. We'll see."

Megan bristled at the declaration. *She's already decided I'm not going to be capable of doing any of the harder stuff. I'll show her.* "You say *definitely* like it's not open to discussion," she said, glaring at Chaz.

"It's a precaution for your own safety," Chaz replied in a friendly tone, meeting Megan's eyes. "You said on your form that you'd never been kayaking before. Has that changed?"

"I might pick it up faster than you expect," she challenged, her stare unwavering.

"I have no expectations at all about your abilities, Megan," Chaz said.

There was something about the way the guide said her name that made their exchange sound more *intimate* than it was. Megan was annoyed by how much she *liked* the way it sounded.

"It's just a policy of ours," Chaz continued. "We don't take unnecessary risks with our clients. The most difficult stretches of the river also happen to be the same areas where we are the most inaccessible to outside help."

"What if I think I can do it?" Megan asked.

"That doesn't matter. This has to be my call."

Megan wasn't ready to concede. She opened her mouth to argue further, but the waitress interrupted.

"Dessert, ladies?"

❖

Over cappuccinos and raspberry cobbler still warm from the oven, Chaz touched on the chores that would have to be done at each campsite. "Sally and I will take care of the cooking. Though we won't object if anyone feels inclined to pitch in any time." She smiled.

"You'll put up your own tents and take care of your boat and gear. And everyone needs to help with cleanup and with collecting wood when we have a fire." Chaz glanced at Megan. The woman was hard to read. After their brief exchange, she had gone back to staring out the window and seemed not to be paying attention. But Chaz had thought the same thing in the van.

"We're in bear country, which means we have to take careful precautions. We cook and eat well away from the tents. All food and trash need to be put into bear-proof containers and carried at least 200 feet away from camp each night. There must be nothing left in the tents that might attract them. No candy, flavored drinks, strong cosmetics, toothpaste, things like that. If you help with the cooking, or spill food on your clothes, change before you go to bed."

"Have you ever had any problems with bears?" Yancey asked.

"No. We've seen them, of course, but if you give them a wide berth and take the proper precautions, they're usually no problem."

"I'd love to see a bear in the wild," Justine said.

"Speak for yourself," Linda chimed in. "I'd rather not get acquainted with any bears, thank you very much."

"I'm with you," Yancey said.

"Ordinarily, you want to travel quietly in a pristine area like this, to avoid disturbing the wildlife and to have the best chance of observing it. Bears included. And that's what we should try to do when we're on the river and hiking as a group to see the caribou. *But…*" she paused for emphasis. "If you're off by yourself, especially in an area with lots of brush or uneven terrain, avoid game trails and make some noise. Not that we advocate you go wandering off by yourself without letting one of us know, but keep it in mind when you make a bathroom run and may be out of sight of the rest of us. One more thing," Chaz said. "Please be careful to wear lots of sunscreen—don't forget your neck and your hands—and good sunglasses, and I hope everyone brought a wide-brimmed hat?"

There were nods or raised hands all around. Justine's WNC baseball cap was hanging behind her on a peg on the wall.

"Well, ladies, if we're all done eating." Chaz surveyed their empty plates. "Let's adjourn down the hall and I'll pass out your dry bags."

They trooped over to the conference room that Orion rented between trips, still in disarray from the aborted gear and food sorting session that morning.

"You get two of these." She held up a large dry bag. "One for your clothes and one for your sleeping bag and pad." In her other hand, she held up a much smaller one, about the size of a large purse. "This is for the essential stuff you need to have with you during the day. Both of them should be lined with garbage bags. They're on the table over there, you can help yourself."

"I'm also giving each of you one of these." Chaz put down the dry bags and held up a Ziploc bag containing a roll of toilet paper and a lighter. "When you need to use the bathroom, pick a spot 200 feet away from camp *and* away from the water. That's about seventy steps. Dig a hole, six to eight inches deep, preferably in an area without vegetation. Do your business—and try to burn the paper when you're done. Any remnants go in the hole, then you cover it and try to make it look like you were never there. Oh, and any feminine hygiene products need to be packed out with the trash. I can give you extra Ziplocs if you need them. Any questions?"

There were none. But Megan gave her a look she couldn't quite decipher when she picked up her bags. *She's unhappy about something*, Chaz guessed, *probably the lack of bathroom facilities.*

Once all the clients had retired to their rooms to repack their gear, Chaz picked up where she and Sally had left off assembling their equipment and meals. She spread out the food on the long tables, allocating perishables for the first days out and freeze-dried and dehydrated meals for the later stops. She packed the ingredients for each meal into a large Ziploc, labeling it "Thursday lunch" or "Sunday breakfast" or whatever was appropriate. She also packed individual bags that contained drink powders, candy, and energy bars for each of the clients.

She was finishing up when she felt eyes on her and glanced up to find Megan Maxwell watching her in silence from the doorway.

"I need a couple more dry bags," Megan said. "I can't fit all my stuff into the three you gave me."

"We have a limit on what we can take with us on the raft," Chaz explained patiently. "We generally only allow each client the three bags—that's why we sent out detailed packing lists of what to bring. Can you leave some of your things back here at the lodge?"

Megan frowned at her for a moment before she replied. "Well, I really don't want to do that unless I absolutely have to."

Clients had asked this before, and she and Sally had always stood firm. But despite Megan's abrasiveness thus far, there was something about her that touched a chord in Chaz, and she relented. Maybe this was her opportunity to improve their rapport. "I'll give you one more bag." She reached for one of the smaller ones she had left over on the table. "But you'll have to limit yourself to that, all right?"

"Just this?" Megan complained, taking it from the guide. "Can't I at least have a bigger one if I'm only getting one more?"

"I'm sorry. That's the best I can do. Anything you don't have room for you can leave with Sue and Paul, and they'll make sure it's safe until we get back."

Megan didn't try to hide that she wasn't happy with the arrangement. Her expression said it all. She looked like a pouting child. "Whatever," she harrumphed. Pivoting on her heel, she headed back to her room.

Peachy, Chaz sighed as the woman departed. *Royal Ice Bitch indeed. Why am I trying so hard to please the Queen of Rude?*

CHAPTER FOUR

Chaz glanced at the bedside clock as she stretched awake and was startled to find it was already seven. She rarely slept that late, but she *had* found it more difficult than usual to fall asleep the night before, preoccupied with thoughts of Megan.

She'd had rude clients before. Business tycoons who were full of themselves, spoiled rich kids who never had learned an ounce of common courtesy. She had always dealt with them easily. Kept on smiling. Killed them with kindness. But this one…this one really bothered her, and she wasn't entirely sure why.

Craving coffee, she dressed and headed for the dining room. She was surprised to find Megan already up, sipping coffee and enjoying the view from one of the big comfy chairs in the lobby.

"Good morning, Megan," Chaz greeted her, determined to break her rude client's distant coolness. "You're up early."

"Force of habit," Megan replied glumly. She glanced over at Chaz as she said it, but made no further attempt to engage her in conversation.

Chaz took the hint and continued into the dining room. *Damn. What the hell is her problem?*

Megan watched Chaz depart out of the corner of her eye, mentally chastising herself all the while. She hated being rude, but at the moment she seemed unable to respond in any other way to the guide. *Every time I see her, it all comes back.* It was like tearing the scab off the most agonizing moments of her life, exposing the raw pain of betrayal all over again.

She was also feeling particularly cranky because she hadn't slept well. The room's blackout curtains had worked well enough to keep out the midnight sun, but worries about work had kept her tossing and turning until late into the night.

And then there was the dream. Part memory and part imagination. Rita's face and body, then Chaz's. She'd bolted awake at two in a tangle of sheets, sweating though the room was cool, her mind working furiously to remember, her body as tensed up and tight as the drawstring of a bow. It had taken her ages to fall back asleep, half afraid she would have the same dream again, half afraid she would not. Even then, her body was still in a different time zone, so she was up for good at five thirty and had downed half a pot of coffee by the time Chaz found her in the lobby.

❖　　　　・

At nine, after everyone had eaten breakfast, the women all trooped back to the conference room where Chaz distributed their gear for the trip. Each client was fitted for a dry suit, PFD, helmet, spray skirt, and neoprene gloves and boots. Then each got a paddle, a water bottle, a Ziploc bag of snacks and power bars, and an emergency whistle to clip to her vest. Chaz also passed each woman a rescue throw rope, coiled into a small floatation bag.

After suiting up, they followed a narrow foot trail down to the creek behind the lodge, where their boats were lined up in a neat row. Chaz paired them up with the kayaks according to size and skill level, and spent time making minor adjustments to thigh braces, hip pads, and seats until everyone was comfortable.

"I really wanted the blue one," Megan griped as Chaz knelt down and leaned into the cockpit of a bright yellow Dagger Mambo to shorten the foot pedals for Megan.

"This is a more stable boat for beginners," Chaz said amicably. When she finished what she was doing, she leaned back on her heels and looked up at Megan. "And I like to have the lesser experienced clients in the bright colors, so I can pick you out more easily when we get in the rougher waters."

"Oh." Megan's pout began to evaporate.

"Want to get in for me, see how it feels?"

"Sure." Megan stepped into the kayak and eased into the seat, bracing her arms on the sides of the cockpit so she could slip her legs into the forward space of the boat. Chaz had set the foot pedals perfectly.

"You brace your thighs here." Chaz put her hand just inside the rim of the cockpit, and it brushed against the top of Megan's leg.

Megan could feel the heat rise to her face as she glanced down to where they had touched. Chaz had strong hands, with long slender fingers. Short nails, no polish. No rings, either. No jewelry at all, she noticed, except a necklace of some kind—a couple of inches of a thin gold chain had escaped the collar of Chaz's wet suit. And what a wet suit it was. *Oh, Lord, I hope she's not going to wear that thing the whole trip.*

The rest of them were wearing dry suits, but Chaz's red and navy wet suit hugged her body like a second skin, and at such close proximity Megan couldn't help but notice the round swell of the guide's breasts, the bump of nipples faint but unmistakable. She suddenly realized that Chaz was still talking to her.

"I'm sorry, what?"

"I *said,* you want to sit so you feel as though you're actually *wearing* the boat," Chaz repeated. "The fit should be comfortable but snug, so the boat moves *with* you, like an extension of your body." As she talked, she reached behind Megan and made a slight adjustment to her back band.

Megan leaned forward, all too vividly aware of the brush of Chaz's fingertips against her spine. "I think I get the idea," she said, anxious for the guide to move a bit farther away.

As if reading her mind, Chaz stood and took a step back. "Brace your hips and legs against the sides, and roll your hips a little from side to side. Get a feel for how the boat is balanced here on land."

Megan did as instructed and was surprised to find that with the tiny adjustments Chaz had made, the boat did indeed move with her, like an extension of her lower torso. It was more comfortable than she'd imagined, with a padded seat and thigh braces, and cushy foam knee blocks. She was anxious to try it out.

"It feels fine," she said. "I'd like to get in the water now."

"Soon," Chaz promised with a smile. "We need to go over a few paddling strokes first."

"Oh, right."

Chaz took them through an onshore lesson of the basic strokes: power strokes and sweeps, high and low braces, back paddling.

Glancing around at her friends, Megan noticed that of the six of them, only she and Elise seemed unfamiliar with all this stuff.

"Very good. How many of you know how to do a wet exit?" Chaz asked.

Four hands shot up. All but her and Elise again. *Wet exit. Power strokes. Why does every word out of her mouth seem to have a sexual connotation?*

"Great. And who can Eskimo roll?"

Only Pat, Linda, and Yancey raised their hands this time, and Yancey's affirmation was only halfhearted. "I learned how to do it a couple of years ago, but I haven't really tried it in a long time. I'm not real gung ho I could do it in a pinch."

"Kind of the same with me," Justine said. "I've done it once in a pool, that's it. I don't really remember much."

"All right, then. Well, it doesn't look as though I'll need to spend any more time with you two." Chaz gestured toward Linda and Pat. "You're welcome to spend the rest of the day as you like, getting your muscles warmed up and getting used to your boat. I'd appreciate it if you'd stay together and keep an eye on each other."

"No problem!" Pat replied, openly leering at Linda, which got all of them chuckling. The couple immediately donned their spray skirts and PFDs and headed for their kayaks, while Chaz turned her attention to Justine and Yancey.

"You two can paddle around until lunch. This afternoon, I'll spend an hour or so with each of you one-on-one, going over how to roll."

"Cool beans," Yancey said.

"I may need more than an hour," Justine said. "I had a hard time getting the hang of it, as I recall. Everything seems so ass-backwards when you're upside down."

"Whatever time you need," Chaz replied. "It's not imperative that you can do one, but it's always a good skill to have under your belt." She turned to Megan and Elise. "Now if you two would put on your spray skirts and get into your boats, I'll teach you how to do a wet exit."

"That sounds like *fun*," Elise said, cocking one eyebrow suggestively in Chaz's direction.

Chaz laughed, a low ripple of pleasure. "Not very. Not in this water."

Megan squeezed into her neoprene spray skirt without comment, trying to ignore the obvious flirtation between the two. *So maybe she's not with that other guide. Or maybe she's just with anyone and everyone.*

Once they were in their kayaks, Chaz went to sit on the back of Elise's boat, straddling it so that she was seated just behind Elise.

"Now this is cozy," Elise commented, looking back over her shoulder at Chaz before the guide had a chance to say anything.

Megan saw Chaz blush; a faint trace of rose blossomed on her cheeks. "To attach your spray skirt," the guide said, all businesslike despite the smile on her face, "first you lean back slightly…"

Elise, smiling broader now, leaned back until she rested right up again Chaz's chest.

Chaz laughed and her blush deepened. "I said *slightly*, Elise. Only enough so that the back of your skirt will hook around the edge of the cockpit."

"Spoilsport," Elise groused under her breath as she sat up.

"These fit so tight that it's easier at first if someone helps you and holds the back down," Chaz positioned the spray skirt over the curled rear rim of the cockpit, "while you lean forward and attach the front."

Elise did as instructed and stretched the front of the skirt over the leading edge of the cockpit until it snapped into place.

"Great." Chaz stood. "After a while, you'll be able to do it without help."

"I sure hope not," Elise said suggestively, eliciting another smile from the guide.

Well, Elise, just throw yourself at her right now, why don't you? Megan's irritation grew with each exchange between the two. She didn't know why she was getting pissed off. She'd certainly seen Elise in action when they'd cruised the bars together.

"Next?" Chaz said, stepping toward Megan's boat.

"I can probably do it myself," Megan said quickly, hooking the skirt around the back of her cockpit. Her tone of voice warned Chaz away, and the guide froze, watching her.

But when Megan sat forward to attach the front, the back popped out. She tried again, with the same result. And then again, and again, her frustration growing with each effort.

Before she knew what was happening, Chaz was seated behind her on the kayak.

"Like I said, it's easier at first with some help," the guide said gently, fastening the skirt into the rim and anchoring the back firmly in place with her hands. "Now get the front. Lean forward."

As soon as Megan snapped it into place, Chaz stood and stepped away. Megan felt the sudden absence of the body behind her, though they hadn't touched.

"If you happen to capsize and can't do an Eskimo roll to right yourself, you'll need to do a wet exit," Chaz explained, glancing between Elise and Megan. "First, you grab the loop there on the front of your skirt and give it a tug. That releases the skirt. Then you relax, put your hands on the side of your cockpit, and slide your legs out. It's kind of like taking off a pair of pants."

"Now *that* I can visualize," Elise said.

Megan could, too. *All too well, in fact.*

Chaz continued without pause, suppressing a grin. "You'll actually do a kind of half somersault to get out of the boat, but it won't really feel like that under water. It's pretty easy. You just need to stay calm and focused. That cold water will be a big shock when you go over." She looked out across the water. "This creek is very slow, so you should have an easy time of it today. I want to also practice wet exits once we're on the river, so you won't panic if you capsize in the rougher water. If you turn over in water over your head, get out, grab your boat—and your paddle, if possible—and try to push toward shore."

Chaz reached into a small pack she had brought with her and pulled out two nose plugs. "I recommend these when you're starting out." She tossed one to each woman and they put them on. "Who's first?"

"I'll go!" Elise volunteered.

Megan watched as Chaz pushed Elise's boat out into the water, wading out with it until the water came up to her chest.

"Any time you're ready," Chaz told Elise. "Just relax, and lean over to one side until you go over."

Elise took a deep breath and held it, closed her eyes, and with one hand on the release loop of her spray skirt, turned over. She broke the surface an arm's length from Chaz a few seconds later, gasping for air. "Damn! That's *ice water!*"

Yancey and Justine, watching from their kayaks a short distance away, broke out laughing.

Chaz tried a little better to hide her amusement. "Told you it wouldn't be much fun. Nicely done, though." She made Elise do it twice more before she let her go inside to dry off and get warm. Then she turned in Megan's direction. "Ready for your turn?"

"I guess," she answered, with no conviction in her voice.

Megan would never admit it aloud, but the whole kayaking element of this trip scared the hell out of her. She hadn't really faced up to that fact until this moment. *You don't know anything at all about boats and currents. And the water is frickin' cold as hell, and the only swimming you do is in the heated pool at the gym.*

Chaz waded in and towed Megan's boat out into the creek as she had Elise's, until the water was deep enough to do the maneuver safely. "There's a sandy bottom here," she said as they got into position. She looked directly into Megan's eyes then. "No reason to be nervous. Just relax, and you'll be back up before you know it."

"I'm not nervous," Megan lied. *Don't think about it, just do it.* But she hesitated, staring at the icy water. She started to hyperventilate. Her mind was screaming instructions, but her body wasn't listening.

Chaz's patient expression held no challenge, only encouragement. "You can do it, Megan," she said in a soft voice.

Damn right I can, Megan thought, her eyes glued on Chaz until the very last second. She closed them as she leaned left and sucked in a deep breath right before she went under. She popped the skirt and before she knew it, she was out of the boat and back on the surface, Chaz's firm grip on her arm orienting her upright. She touched bottom and Chaz released her.

"See? Cold, but not so bad, eh?" Chaz was only a foot away, smiling that damn charm-your-socks-off smile again.

Much as she wanted to resist it, Megan was finding it harder by the moment. "Not so bad," she agreed.

❖

After lunch, it was time to learn to Eskimo roll—combining leverage from your paddle with a strong hip snap to right yourself after capsizing. Chaz went through the steps on land; then she got into one of the kayaks and demonstrated the maneuver. Megan found the display something akin to a nautical ballet.

On the water, Chaz was all fluid muscle, the kayak a part of her, every movement graceful and efficient. The blades of her paddle sliced cleanly into the water with no splash and no sound. Once she got in position, she went over with a wink and a smile, like this was one of her secret pleasures. And when she came up again, easily, gracefully, shaking water from her dark hair, her face pink from the cold, Megan thought she looked beautifully at one with her surroundings. Wild. Primitive. Larger than life.

After a couple more rolls to break down the process into steps that they could visualize, Chaz paddled in, and they all took to their kayaks for their individual lessons.

Megan was up last, but she stayed close by so she could watch the others. She paddled around in the shallow water, getting used to the boat and practicing the strokes that Chaz had taught them that morning. For the first several minutes, she felt awkward and uncoordinated, but she gained confidence quickly and began to get the hang of it.

From a distance, learning to roll didn't seem that intimidating. Not at first. Chaz had made it look easy, and Yancey got it right away, rolling her kayak back upright on the first try with little apparent effort, a big smile on her face. But Justine struggled for a half hour to get it right, cursing loudly every time she couldn't manage to turn her kayak back over and had to rely on Chaz to do it for her. Freezing and exhausted by the time she was finally able to master the maneuver, she limped back up toward the lodge shaking her head.

Elise fared no better. Megan actually counted this time, recording each unsuccessful effort. She wanted to learn the technique faster than Elise, though she didn't bother to imagine why. It took Elise eleven tries to do it right. *Surely I can do it faster than that. I'm an athlete. I play tennis. Golf. Racquetball. Those all take good coordination.*

When Chaz hailed her over for her turn, Megan felt both fear and determination in equal measure.

Chaz was beginning to feel the cold despite her wet suit. *Please do well,* she thought to herself as the bright yellow boat came nearer. She wanted Megan to catch on quickly to rolling, and not just because that meant they would both be able to get out of the water and get warm. She knew, somehow, that Megan was afraid of all this—of tipping over, of learning to roll, maybe even of kayaking altogether. Chaz had seen it in her eyes that morning, and she wanted to help her get past her fear so she'd enjoy the trip ahead.

Standing next to the boat, one hand on the forward carrying toggle, she went briefly back over the fundamentals: how Megan should hold the paddle, how she should distribute her weight. When she should begin the hip snap and sweep that would turn her upright again.

They were close together, concentrating intently on each other, all businesslike but breaths apart, when Chaz first felt the sparks begin to fly. It was entirely unexpected. One minute, she was assessing with cool detachment her client's readiness to try the roll for the first time. *Good grip, good hip snap, hands the right distance apart. She seems nervous, but that's normal.* The next, without warning, she was suddenly fixated on how soft and silky Megan's hair looked. And how the sun caught the blond highlights. And how could she not have noticed before that Megan's eyes were an uncommon shade of green. *That vibrant, iridescent green of early spring. And she has the most incredibly long eyelashes.*

Chaz realized she was staring. And Megan was staring back, a smirk creeping outward from the corner of her mouth. *Oh, shit. Busted. Don't ogle the clients, idiot.* She quickly averted her eyes and cleared her throat, trying not to blush.

"Ready?" she asked, letting go of the paddle and putting some distance between them, taking up position at the front of the kayak.

She glanced at Megan. The smirk was gone, replaced by a look of grim determination. Megan nodded, her eyes glued to Chaz. She put on her nose clip and gripped her paddle firmly, took a deep breath, leaned left, and flipped over.

After a few seconds, there was a big splash as one blade of Megan's paddle clumsily broke the surface at an odd angle, then disappeared again. Chaz could see her flailing away under there, and her heart began to beat faster as the seconds ticked by. She kept a firm grip on the boat, ready to turn it back over, waiting anxiously for the sign of distress she had taught them all. *Too long*, she thought, a millisecond before she felt them through her fingertips and heard them vaguely, muted by the water—the three raps on the hull of the kayak that said *I need help!*

She flipped the boat over, and Megan came up sputtering, shaking the cold water from her hair and gasping for air. "Damn it!" she cursed.

"Everything is so turned around down there, I couldn't get oriented. It all seemed backwards."

"That was only your first try. You'll get it," Chaz said in a soothing voice. She waded a step closer and looked into Megan's eyes. "You can't *think* about it too hard. I know that doesn't make sense, but it *is* hard to orient yourself when you're upside down. It's better to memorize the action that you need to do and let your body—not your mind—take over." She held out one hand, the other on the kayak so it wouldn't drift. "Let me have your paddle."

Megan gave it to her with a confused expression.

Chaz oriented herself so the paddle was laid on the surface of the water between them, parallel to the boat. "I want you to go over again…leaning *away* from me. When you get upside down, reach up on this side for the paddle. I'll be holding it in the right position, and I'll help you get yourself back up, so you can see what it should feel like."

Megan looked like she was about to object, but she nodded reluctantly, took several deep breaths, and then went over. It was only a moment before Chaz could see her hands just beneath the surface, groping for the shaft of the paddle. Chaz clamped her hand around Megan's forearm and led it to the paddle. As Megan began to pull herself up, Chaz helped her, twisting the paddle and pulling up on it until the kayak had righted itself.

Megan sucked in air, her face pink from the cold, hair plastered to her head. "Shit, that's cold."

"That wasn't bad at all," Chaz said, trying not to stare at the rapid rise and fall of Megan's chest, only a couple of feet away and at eye level at the moment. "Did it feel better that time?"

"No! I don't know." Megan's shoulders slumped. "Maybe a *little*." She blew out a breath. "This is really *hard*."

"You have pretty high expectations of yourself, don't you?" There was no malice or rancor to Chaz's question, that was obvious in her tone, but Megan visibly bristled anyway.

"I usually catch on to things pretty quickly," she snapped. "And I don't think there's anything wrong with expecting the best from yourself."

"I didn't say there was. I just meant that I don't think you can…or *should* expect to be able to do this on the first try. It's a very tough maneuver."

"I think that I'm the only one capable of knowing what I'm capable of... doing." Megan looked a little flustered as she said this, as if she wasn't entirely sure that what she'd just said made sense. "Anyway, I want to try it again."

Stubborn one, aren't you? Chaz felt a guilty stab of pleasure at seeing her off balance. "Great. Are you doing it with or without my help?"

"Without."

There was no hesitation this time. As soon as Chaz backed off and got into position on the end of the kayak, Megan went over. Chaz could see immediately that she would never make it. She put her hands around the kayak and flipped it back upright.

Megan let all the air out of her lungs with a big whoosh of surprise, then her expression turned to fury. She slammed her paddle against the kayak. "What did you do that for?"

"Your paddle was in the wrong position. Remember? You need to put your hands—"

"I know what I did wrong," Megan snapped, cutting her off. "Just get ready and let's go."

"Not until you take a deep breath and focus," Chaz said slowly. "It's important that the setup is right—and remember, you have to have the upward blade flat on the surface of the water when you begin the sweep and hip snap. If the blade dives—if it comes down perpendicular to the water—you won't have enough resistance to pull yourself up."

"I know," Megan said, biting her lip.

Chaz positioned herself, hands on the bow of the boat. She normally had infinite patience at this procedure, even with difficult clients. Three tries at Eskimo rolling was nothing. But the frigid water had seeped deep into her wet suit, and something about Megan's princess attitude was starting to get to her. She was anxious for this to be finished. "Whenever you're ready."

Megan closed her eyes. Several seconds passed. Then she squared her shoulders, leaned left, and disappeared under the surface. Chaz counted seconds, holding her breath. Ten. Twenty. She saw the blade of Megan's paddle break the surface of the water, turn, orient itself. Thirty seconds. She took her hands away when she felt the boat begin to move. The kayak righted itself and Megan reappeared, gasping for air and shivering.

Her eyes found Chaz's. They were bright and sparkling, and a smile spread across her face. "Did I make it? Or did you help me?"

Chaz grinned back. "You made it all by yourself. Congratulations." *You look altogether different when you're happy.*

"Wow!" Megan whooped. She raised her paddle aloft in a moment of unabashed giddy happiness. But she reined herself in at once and became her usual serious self.

"That's plenty for today. Why don't we both go in and get warm?" Chaz suggested, giving Megan's kayak a shove toward shore.

Megan put her paddle in the water and started to go in, but paused a few feet away. "Thanks," she said, over her shoulder, just loud enough for Chaz to hear.

"Welcome." *Why are you so determined not to like me?* She frowned. *What's not to like?*

There was no ego behind Chaz's musings. She had always been well liked. She was an honest, and loyal, and steadfast friend, the first to remember a birthday, to show up in a time of crisis, the first to volunteer her time and energy to a worthy cause. Many of her Orion clients had kept in touch over the years with her, Christmas cards and letters updating their lives and fondly recalling their Alaskan experience.

She shook her head in puzzlement as she watched Megan beach the kayak and head to the lodge. She just couldn't fathom what could be behind the woman's prickly attitude, or why she seemed to be so strangely drawn to her despite it.

❖

Chaz went back to her room and took a long hot shower before setting off for the airstrip to pick up Sally an hour before dinner.

"Everything went well, I trust?" Chaz inquired after their hellos.

"Great. I brought some pictures I'll show you later." They climbed into the van, Chaz behind the wheel, and headed to the lodge. "So how does it look?" Sally asked. "Anybody need special handling?"

"It'll be a good group, I think. Everyone did well on the water today. Pat and Linda are really top-notch kayakers—we sure don't have to worry about them. I'd say Justine and Yancey are above average, and Elise and Megan both learned the strokes pretty well and managed to do a roll."

"So if everyone did good why are you in a lousy mood?"

"I'm not in a lousy mood." Chaz glanced over at her partner guide. Sally sat facing her in the large bucket seat, with a look on her face that said she wasn't buying it for a minute. "Okay, I'm a little…well, annoyed, maybe, at one of the clients. That's all. It's nothing. And I won't sour your judgment. You can make up your own mind."

"Oh, no, you're not getting off that easily. Give it up. What's the deal?"

"Forget I said anything."

"*Spill*, Chaz," Sally demanded in a sterner voice.

"Well, one of them is kind of…abrupt. You know—hard to warm up to. Not a lot of social skills."

"Sounds like someone I know," Sally remarked, a smirk on her face.

"Who, me? I'm not like that."

"Well, you're *great* with the clients after you get to know them a bit. But you do tend to be a bit standoffish at first. And you don't let many people get to know you *well*."

"Oh, I'm not that bad."

"No? And when was the last time you went out on a date, hmm?" Sally pressed.

"That has nothing to do with anything. And how did we suddenly start talking about me and my dating habits, anyway?"

"Doesn't matter. Now that we are, fill me in. Your love life improve any over the winter? You deftly avoided the subject during the whole last trip. Don't think I didn't notice."

"Sally, you know I'm very happy with the status quo," Chaz said.

"I know what that means."

"It means I'm not necessarily lonely just because I'm alone."

"Oh, that's crap, pardon the expression." Sally reached over and gave Chaz's shoulder a shove for emphasis. "You're scared of getting involved and you know it."

"I am not. I'm selective. How did we ever get off on this subject? We were talking about the clients."

"Speaking of which," Sally said, "I saw the way Elise was coming on to you when she introduced herself." A lot of cute women hit on Chaz, but as far as Sally was aware, her friend never took anyone up on their offers.

"Well, you know my feelings about that. It's so unprofessional. I would never get involved with a client. Kind of like sleeping with one of my students."

"*Maybe* during the trip, you could argue that, although personally I don't see a problem with it. And there's certainly nothing wrong with taking somebody's phone number and getting to know them better afterwards," Sally suggested.

"If I ever get hit on by somebody I have real chemistry with, I promise I'll think about it, *okay*? What do you know, we're here," Chaz announced as they pulled up at the lodge.

"You're not off the hook, you know. We're going to talk about this some more," Sally promised.

"Look, I appreciate what you're trying to do. I know you mean well. But we have lots of other things to think about right now." Chaz opened the door of the van, hoping it would end the discussion.

But Sally wouldn't let it go. She put her hand on Chaz's forearm to keep her in her seat. "You can handle two things at once, Chaz. You should always keep an open mind in matters of the heart. You never know when an opportunity might present itself."

Chaz patted her friend's hand. "Spoken like the true married-for-life die-hard romantic that you are, Sally. Tom is a lucky man."

"You're a good catch too," Sally said. "Smart, funny, bighearted, and cute as a bug."

"Aw, gosh, you'll turn a girl's head." Chaz sighed dramatically. "It's such a shame you're not gay."

"So…I counted at least three from your team among our clients. That couple who were all over each other—Pat and Linda, right?"

Chaz nodded.

"And Elise, for sure," Sally continued. "Any chance of anything happening there? She's cute, and sure interested in *you*, my friend."

"Get your mind out of the gutter. I told you I don't date clients."

"Translation—she doesn't make your heart go pitter-pat. What about the others? Did your gaydar give you good vibes about any of the rest?"

Megan's face popped into Chaz's head. The way she'd looked after the roll, all flushed with excitement. Chaz could feel the heat rise to her cheeks.

Sally's eyes got wide. "Oh? And what's this? Hey, wait a minute.

This client that's so…annoying. Do you mean annoying as in 'getting under your skin'?"

"Jeez, Sally. Lay off already, would ya?" Chaz got out of the van and headed toward the lodge.

"I bet I get it figured out within twenty-four hours," Sally predicted as she trotted up the steps behind her friend.

Of course Megan *would* be the only client in the lobby. She was back in the same chair she'd been in that morning, this time with her attention on a book. They had to go right by her to get to their rooms. *We can't just ignore her.* Chaz dearly hoped her blush wouldn't worsen with Sally on high alert. And even more than that, she prayed that Megan wouldn't notice her embarrassment. *Get a grip.*

Megan looked up as they approached. She glanced at Chaz only briefly before turning her full attention to Sally. She gave her a big smile. "Hi, Sally. How was the graduation?"

"My kind of ceremony." Sally paused in front of Megan's chair. "Short and sweet and all concerned straight to the nearest Irish pub after. So I heard you did an Eskimo roll today. Congratulations."

"Yes. Thanks." Megan glanced at Chaz, but when their eyes met she promptly looked away again and back at Sally. "I'm not entirely certain I could do it again, but I did manage it."

"You'll do some more," Chaz said. "I want everyone to do a few while we're in the slower water. We'll have a couple more rolling sessions in the early stretches of the river after we set up camp."

Megan glanced down at her watch. "It's nearly dinner time." As she got to her feet she shot Sally another smile. "I'm going back to my room to wash up. Looking forward to getting to know you, Sally. See you in a few minutes?"

"Yup. See you in a bit."

"Bye," Chaz added, but Megan was already heading away from them. She didn't look back, and she didn't acknowledge the farewell.

"My stuff still in the conference room?" Sally asked.

Chaz stared after Megan for several moments, bothered by the fact that she'd seemed much warmer to Sally right from the start. She was positively effervescent, compared to how she was when it was only the two of them. *What gives?*

She suddenly realized Sally was waiting for an answer. "I'm sorry, what?"

"I said, is my gear still in the conference room?"

"Yeah, do you have your key?"

Sally dug in her pockets. "Nope. Must be in my bag. Can I borrow yours?"

"Why am I not surprised?" Chaz fished for her key. Being organized was not Sally's strong point.

"So which one is the rude one that's got you all hot and bothered? You going to tell me?"

"Knock it off." Chaz handed her the key. "Please?"

"'Fraid not, chum. This is the first time I've ever seen you even mildly interested in someone. It's especially intriguing that you seemed to be repulsed by her even as you are attracted to her."

"I wouldn't say repulsed," Chaz blurted out before she could stop herself.

"Aha! I knew it!"

"Oh, shit."

Sally was laughing now. "Okay, who is it?"

"I have things to do," Chaz lied. "And so do you. I'm going to my room." She headed off in that direction.

"You can escape for now," Sally relented. "But we're not finished!" she hollered after her.

Dinner only served to reinforce Chaz's growing perception that it wasn't that Megan was distant and rude. It was that she was distant and rude to *her*. Megan was chatty and charming and animated at dinner, down there at the other end of the table between Justine and Sally. She had arrived last and had taken the farthest seat she could from Chaz. *Was that deliberate? So she could get away with not having to say a word to me all evening?*

Over the next hour while the women lingered over drinks and dessert, Chaz sat brooding, observing Megan and amazed at the transformation. The woman who had spent the previous night staring out the window seemed interested in anything and everything tonight, engaging everyone in sparkling conversation. Everyone, that is, but her. Megan ignored her all evening, ignored her so absolutely and completely that she wondered how it was possible that not a single person at the table seemed to notice.

CHAPTER FIVE

Megan stood looking out of the thick insulated window in her room, sipping coffee and berating herself for her cowardice. *You won't be able to hide from her much longer.*

There was a knock on her door. "Come on in," she called, and Justine entered, carrying her three dry bags of gear. She dumped them inside the door.

"Got any more of that?" she asked, indicating Megan's steaming mug with a tilt of her head.

"Sorry, they only give you enough coffee for four small cups, and this is the last of it."

"That's all right. I've got to get going anyway if I'm going to have time for breakfast before we go," Justine said. "Just wanted to stop and make sure you haven't changed your mind."

"No. I know it's silly. I'm going to have to spend the next eleven days with the woman. A plane ride shouldn't matter one way or the other."

"I understand, Megan. It really is eerie how much they look alike. They say we all have a twin somewhere."

"I guess. Anyway, thanks for hustling to get ready to go in my place."

At dinner the night before, Chaz had announced the arrangements for the morning flights to the river, since they all couldn't fit in the Twin Otter. She would take the first flight out at eight, along with Linda, Pat, and Megan. Sally would take the second at nine-thirty, with Yancey, Justine, and Elise.

Megan didn't object at the time, but she'd decided, after another mostly sleepless night, that she'd take any opportunity she could to avoid having to be close to Chaz. So she'd tapped on Justine's door a half hour earlier and asked if she would switch flights.

"What do you want me to say if she asks why we've changed places?" Justine asked.

"Say I overslept and needed the extra time to get ready."

"Anything else I can do?"

Megan shook her head. "Thanks, though."

"You sorry you came along?"

Megan sipped her coffee and thought about it. "Yes and no. I have to admit that Alaska is everything you said it was. And more. Spectacularly beautiful. And I'm actually beginning to look forward to the whole kayaking thing." Her expression went grim. "But every time I look at her, it tears my guts out all over again. Instead of relaxing, I'm reliving some of the worst nightmares of my life."

Justine took two steps and put her arms around Megan. After a moment, Megan relaxed and hugged her back.

"She was a shit, Megan," Justine said gently. "You need to move on."

"Oh, I moved on a long time ago." Megan disengaged from their embrace.

"Have you?"

"Oh, come on. I date all the time."

"And how many women in the last five years have you dated more than once or twice?"

Megan turned away to look out the window again, and the question hung in the air. "You better get going," she said finally, without looking at Justine.

"I didn't mean to get you pissed off at me."

"I'm not." Her tone and posture made it clear that she most certainly was.

Justine sighed. "I'll see you at the river, then." When Megan made no move to answer, Justine picked up her gear and departed.

I am over you, Megan chanted again and again to herself, as if the words could form a talisman to keep images of Rita and their life together at bay. They'd had five wonderful, perfect years together. Life in suburbia, white picket fence, exotic getaways, and exceptional sex.

But so far, Chaz had been stirring up mostly negative memories. Memories of *the day*. March 29. The day Megan's orderly life turned upside down, and everything she thought she knew went right out the window. The day a stranger told her that her loving, devoted wife was screwing someone else, probably right at that moment, in the posh hotel room the network had booked for her at the Paris economic summit.

Back then, Megan was only a copy editor, so she rarely got calls in the middle of the night, even when a major story broke. The anchors ad-libbed everything, and there was always a skeleton crew of writers and editors to cover any event. So when her phone rang at 2:30 a.m., she was instantly awake and immediately worried that something had happened to Rita, who was on assignment in Paris. The voice on the phone was unfamiliar.

"Megan Maxwell?"

"Yes."

"You don't know me, Megan. Can I call you Megan?" The caller had sounded like she was crying.

Megan's heartbeat picked up. "What is it? Is it Rita?"

The caller laughed, a hollow laugh that became a sob.

"What is it? Has something happened?" Megan gripped the phone so tight her knuckles went white.

"Yes, it's about Rita. And yes, something's happened." Megan could tell the caller was trying to compose herself. "There's no way to tell you this except to tell you. Rita is cheating on you and she's going to leave you."

The words hung there. She closed her eyes and saw them in her head, pictured bloodred letters on a black background. RITA IS CHEATING ON YOU AND SHE'S GOING TO LEAVE YOU. She thought in words and pictures, a photographic memory. Usually like a newspaper. Black letters on a white background. But not this time.

"Are you there?" The stranger's voice jarred her.

"I don't believe you." Rita had kissed her good-bye like she always did. Nothing at all different. They'd made love the night before she left. It had been wonderful, as always. At least for Megan it was wonderful. The first doubt crept in.

"You have no idea she's been seeing my girlfriend for six months?" the caller asked shakily.

Six months? It was impossible. "Your girlfriend? Who are you?"

"My name is Denise. My girlfriend is…was…Iliana Theroux."

A face sprang instantly to Megan's mind. Clear blue eyes set against lush dark eyelashes, bronze skin. Iliana Theroux was the exotically beautiful chief foreign correspondent for the Canadian

Broadcasting Company. The CBC had a reciprocal arrangement with WNC, so Iliana's reports often aired on the shows that Megan edited.

But how? Iliana Theroux was based in Washington. And Rita had been in the capital a lot during the past year, filling in for vacationing reporters in the D.C. bureau. WNC was grooming her for big things, maybe a permanent gig as one of the White House press corps, and Rita had never been happier. *She's always been ambitious. She told me that on our first date.* Megan's stomach churned.

"They met when both were covering some State Department briefing," Denise went on, her voice calmer. "The briefing kept getting delayed, so they had a couple of hours to get to know each other. Apparently it was love at first sight, or so they say."

They say. Her stomach roiled in violent upheaval, and she felt the first tears form.

"Iliana moved out last week. I knew they were seeing each other, but I thought it was a fling. It wasn't the first time." Denise wept softly into the phone. "I knew she was never in love with me, but she always came home." There was the muffled sound of her blowing her nose. "I had no idea how serious it was until she announced she was leaving. She told me everything, then. She says they're getting married in Amsterdam next month."

Married. And legally married if they're going to the Netherlands. It had been a major story on WNC and the networks that week—it was going to be legal for same-sex couples to wed there in just a few days. Megan and Rita had made private vows on a beach at Lake Michigan, promising to love each other forever. Her head swam. It was unbelievable. Unthinkable. That Rita had been pretending to love her. *How long has she been lying to me?*

"Your girlfriend's hired a lawyer," Denise said wearily. "I overheard Iliana on the phone with her. They were talking about telling you, but it sounded like Rita wasn't going to until she hired a lawyer. Something about your house and bank account, I think."

The house was in both their names. And Megan hadn't checked the account balance at the bank in a long time. Rita paid all the bills out of their joint account, took care of all things financial.

"Iliana at least was honest with me in the end and tried to make it easy on me." Denise sounded desolate. "I saw the news tonight and realized they're both in Paris at that summit. So I knew you'd be alone, and I thought you should know. That's all. I'm sorry."

There was a soft click and then a dial tone. Megan had listened to that dull drone for several long seconds, frozen with shock. She'd been on the phone for five minutes or less. That was all it took for her whole life to change.

❖

Megan lay on her back on a smooth rock the size and shape of a sports car, her eyes closed, while a short distance away, her five friends and the two guides prepared to get underway.

Seven kayaks and one large raft were lined up along the shore of the Odakonya at a place where the river was wide and shallow and flat, meandering through a long valley of muskeg and low, scrubby spruce trees. The pilot had landed in the middle of the river, the fat front tires of the plane bouncing them along on a wide gravel sandbar.

The weather could not have been more perfect for the start of their adventure: seventy-four degrees with a light breeze. In every direction, the awesome spectacle of snowy peaks starkly outlined against the deep blue cloudless sky behind.

They were all in high spirits and anxious to get underway. Everyone but Megan, who had puked her coffee and toast into her airsickness bag in the Twin Otter on the way over. The turbulence in the little plane had exacerbated a stomach already in upheaval over memories of the past.

"Are you feeling any better?"

She hadn't heard anyone approach. She was glad it was Sally and not Chaz. "Yes, a bit. Are we all ready to go?"

"Pretty much, but we're not on a schedule. If you'd like to spend more time here so your stomach can settle…"

"No, I'm all right." She sat up slowly. "I don't want to hold everyone up." The raft was loaded, all the gear tied in, and everyone was putting on their spray skirts and PFDs. Chaz was looking right at her from the water's edge, forty feet away.

"Will you help me with my spray skirt?" she asked Sally as she pushed off the rock and headed toward the group.

"Sure." Sally followed her to her boat and got her situated, and soon they were on the river.

They settled into a lazy pace, rarely paddling, enjoying the view and letting the gentle current sweep them along. Megan kept to the rear, about as far away as she could be from Chaz.

It wasn't long before they got their first glimpse of some of the wildlife they'd been promised. A bald eagle, following the course of the Odakonya, soared low over their kayaks, looking for fish, allowing them all a close-up view of his magnificent white head and tail.

Megan and most of the other clients had been talking in low voices until then, remarking on the scenery and telling stories of past vacations, but the eagle stunned them into silence. Then they could hear that the air was alive with subtle but constant bird songs—juncos and myrtle warblers, gray-cheeked thrushes and tree sparrows.

Megan spotted a couple of Arctic ground squirrels playing tag on the bank, a muskrat swimming next to the shoreline, and several hawks, flying so high she had no hope of identifying them. She drifted very near a male rock ptarmigan, starkly contrasted in its winter plumage against the brown grass alongshore. *They stay white to distract predators from the nest,* she'd read. *The females turn brown.* She was excited to be able to identify so many animals that she'd never seen before. It was an eminently satisfying use of her considerable research.

A bit farther on, Chaz, in the lead, slowed her kayak until all the others were grouped up and able to see her. Then she pointed her paddle blade at one of the nearest mountains—its base rose from the tundra a half mile away.

Megan couldn't decipher for the longest time what she was pointing at. She had excellent eyesight, but she didn't see them until one of the Dall rams took off on a run up the steep slope. Then she could see them all, a scattering of white sheep among the gray and tan granite rock behind. Specks at this distance. *How the hell did she see them?*

They stopped for sandwiches and chips at a spot on the river where a wide gravel bar offered a perfect parking spot for the kayaks and a chance to stretch their legs. Most sat atop their decks, but Pat and Linda sat side by side, leaning up against their boats.

"What's that?" Elise asked, pointing to a flash of movement in the clear emerald water.

Elise had, Megan noticed, managed to park her kayak right next to Chaz's, and had been flirting openly with the guide all through lunch. She asked Chaz what every single bird and plant and animal and tree in sight was. *And damn if that woman couldn't answer every single question, too.* Their exchanges were really starting to get under her skin.

"Those are grayling," Chaz answered, with the same patience she had every one of Elise's incessant queries. "Hopefully we'll have some for dinner one night."

"I love a woman who can cook," Elise said.

I'm going to go nuts if I have to listen to this for two weeks. How is it that in all the times we've gone cruising together, I never realized that Elise is quite so painfully, dreadfully obvious.

"We do eat well," Chaz agreed. "Menus are a high priority."

So you're deflecting her flirtations, for the most part anyway. Aren't you interested? I know you're one of us. Aren't you?

"Man, I can tell I'm going to be sore tomorrow," Justine said, getting creakily to her feet. She arched her back with a groan, then rolled her shoulders to loosen them up. "I should definitely get more exercise."

"No lie. This sure reminds me about some stomach and back muscles I don't use very much," Yancey added.

And shoulders. And arms. Megan didn't want to admit aloud that she was feeling it, too. She'd thought she was in pretty good shape, but decided tennis and golf must use different muscle groups. *And you've been working so much, you really haven't played that much the last year or so.*

"I think I'm beginning to see why you invited me along," Elise said.

"Oh, yeah! I get first dibs tonight!" Pat raised her hand.

"Me second!" Linda chimed in.

"Not fair! You two do this all the time. You don't need her like we do," Yancey said.

"Let me state right up front that I'm not doing all of you every night," Elise said.

"Maybe we should draw straws or pick numbers or something," Justine suggested.

"Can someone clue me in on what's going on?" Sally asked.

"Before she became a graphic artist, our dear, sweet, charming Elise went to massage therapy school," Pat said.

"Sucking up will do you no good. I'm still only doing two or three of you a day, max." Elise turned to look at Chaz. "You can get in on this, you know," she said invitingly. "You *and* Sally," she amended.

"I'm in," Sally said immediately.

Megan watched Chaz, waiting for a response. *Don't do it.* Picturing Elise with her hands on Chaz was not an image she liked very much at all.

Chaz neither accepted nor declined. She merely stood and stretched—slowly, languidly, a contented smile on her face. Looking every bit, Megan thought, like a pampered cat getting up from a nap, like they hadn't already been paddling three hours on the river. Like this was no exertion at all for her.

Chaz looked up at the sky as if judging the position of the sun and announced, "Everybody ready? There's a great campsite about another three hours downriver."

You're nice to watch, Megan admitted. *Much too damn nice to watch.*

After another hour or so, the river began to split into channels, some wide, some narrow—fingers separated by swampy tussocks of earth or wide, pale gray gravel bars. The group all followed Chaz like ducklings behind their mother, with Sally bringing up the rear in the raft, and eventually all the fingers of the river seemed to join up again.

Megan was halfway up the line of kayaks by then, quite a bit closer to the front than before. Not enough to have to make conversation with Chaz, but close enough to get a first-rate view of the guide. She didn't look much like Rita at the moment. Rita never looked this good from the back.

In the warmth of the afternoon sun, Chaz had peeled off her outer shirt and was wearing only a tank top under her PFD, allowing all those behind her a splendid view of her well-developed and wonderfully tanned shoulders and arms as she paddled her smooth, effortless strokes. *Poetry in motion. So that's what that phrase means.*

Several of them had been jockeying for position since the shirt had come off, none of them too overtly, of course. Megan had moved up, and so had Justine. And Elise seemed determined to keep the spot behind Chaz that she'd held most of the day.

The river led them very near a low, wide mountain with a big splotch of green limestone on the side. They saw more sheep there, close enough this time that with binoculars they could pick out the big curved horns on the rams. Chaz had encouraged them to keep their binoculars always close at hand. It was easy in this wide, gentle current to put down their paddles for a moment now and then. They began automatically reaching for theirs when she reached for hers, following her eyes, never disappointed.

The hours passed quickly, they were all so absorbed in the awesome views, in every direction, ever changing with each stroke of their paddles. Not a landscape to be rushed through. Mountains, mountains, mountains, and wide plains of tundra meadows dotted with dark pools of placid water and interlaced with a dazzling mosaic of lichens and mosses and wildflowers.

She was guessing, having only colors to go on and not the details of blossoms and shapes of leaves, but Megan thought the wide swaths of pinkish-purple flowers she was seeing must be fireweed—the guidebook said it was ubiquitous in Alaska.

It was such an immense and endless landscape of wilderness that it began to unsettle her. She was the center of the universe at WNC; the newsroom revolved around her, and she was in total control of everything. Her words moved mountains. But out here…all bets were off. *You can't control this place. Get lost out here and you're in some damn serious trouble.* It was frightening, but exhilarating too. Like she was living on the edge of danger instead of just reporting about it.

She hadn't seen any sign at all that another human being had ever been this way before. But Chaz was here, she remembered. She took the caribou picture on this river. For the first time it occurred to her. *Who was with you when you took that? Who did you share that with? Sally?*

There were more trees than she'd imagined she'd see this far north—forests of spruce and thickets of dwarf birch and alder and willow. They were coming up on one now, an area of dense conifers with an undergrowth of spongy green moss, and Chaz was pulling off, beaching her kayak.

"We're stopping here!" she called as she waved them over.

It was a delightful spot, Megan had to admit, with the soft sphagnum to cushion their sleeping bags. Through the trees, a short distance away, she could see a small lake shimmering in the sun.

Once they had shed their life jackets and spray skirts, Chaz laid out the camp: the area for the tents, where the food prep and cooking would be done, and the designated bathroom area—over a small rise for privacy and away from the water.

"We have two-person tents," Sally said, taking four identical navy blue tent bags out of a large compactor garbage bag and lining them up near the area where they would spend the night. "Since you're all friends, we're assuming you can decide how you want to divvy up the sleeping arrangements."

"Linda and I will take one." Pat plucked bag number one.

"Megan? How 'bout it?" Justine asked, glancing her way as she reached for number two.

"Sure, that sounds great."

"That leaves me with the masseuse." Yancey ruffled the spiky dark hair on Elise's head as she passed by her to pick up the third bag. "You all didn't think very smart on that choice, my friends."

Elise smiled at the compliment, but her eyes hadn't left Chaz since they'd beached the boats. "Well, we can always change the sleeping arrangements at any time, if someone wants a little variety, can't we?"

Here we go again. Though it was increasingly obvious that Chaz was not exactly jumping at the chance to take Elise up on her blatant, nonstop flirtations. More and more, Megan began to wonder why. She was fairly certain Chaz was gay. *I swear I caught you checking me out for a second during that rolling lesson. So, what is it, then? Are you involved with somebody, or just not interested in Elise?*

❖

Nearly simultaneous shrieks from the tent area 200 feet away brought Chaz to her feet and instantly alert, but the familiar laughter that followed quickly reassured her that it was merely Sally's traditional opening night prank of assorted artificial spiders, hidden in the tent folds and among the poles and stakes. She relaxed back down on the rock she'd been sitting on and resumed preparations for their dinner. Shortly thereafter, she spotted Linda and Pat approaching.

"Oh, come on, honey." Pat's voice rang with amusement. "You know there are no tarantulas in Alaska. Chaz even warned us this would happen."

"So I forgot. And you better stop teasing me about it if you want any nookie tonight." Linda tried to sound annoyed, but Chaz could see she was pretending.

Nookie in the next tent. Not that it hadn't happened before on trips; she and Sally sometimes had a hard time stifling their laughter over what they overheard a few feet away. Growing up in a commune, Chaz had thought she'd heard it all when it came to sounds made during sex. But apparently "doing it" in the wilds of Alaska brought out the beast in some people. They'd had clients growl, and snort, and howl, and one guy even yodeled a little. But they'd never overheard two women making love. Thinking about it sent an unexpected ripple of arousal through her.

"I think it's hysterical that you have no qualms at all about jumping out of an airplane or going into a war zone, but a tiny spider gets you all unnerved. I didn't think you were afraid of anything." Pat sat down near Chaz and leaned back against a large boulder. When she reached up and took Linda's hand, Linda allowed herself to be drawn down into the cradle of Pat's arms.

"So what else is Sally going to pull on us, hmm?" Linda asked, as she settled comfortably between Pat's legs and reclined back against her lover's chest. Pat ran her hands slowly through Linda's curly brown hair, and Linda closed her eyes and groaned in approval.

"She'd kill me if I told you all her tricks," Chaz responded with a smile, as she made up a rub of fresh tarragon, thyme, and garlic for the night's main course.

"Anything we can do to help with dinner?" Linda offered.

"Got it covered, thanks. So how do you like everything so far?"

"Amazing place you've got here," Linda said. "Breathtaking."

"I'll second that. We're already planning to come back. Do you live in Alaska?" Pat asked.

"Yes. Outside Fairbanks," Chaz answered.

Elise joined them, taking a seat on a rock next to Chaz. "And what do you do in Fairbanks?"

"Teach," Chaz said.

"A teacher? Ah, beautiful *and* brainy," Elise remarked.

"You know, you really are incorrigible." Chaz couldn't help but be a bit flattered by the attention, even if she would never in a million years consider a liaison with Elise. The woman certainly was attractive, though.

"That's what they tell me." Elise reached over to steal a dried cranberry from a small bowl at Chaz's feet. "So, what's on the menu for tonight, mademoiselle chef?"

"Grilled pork tenderloin with an herb rub, served with a cranberry rice pilaf and Caesar salad," Chaz replied. "And for dessert, chocolate cake with bourbon chocolate sauce."

Pat whistled approvingly.

"This sure isn't roughing it." Elise stole another cranberry. "I kind of expected hot dogs or something."

"The menu is courtesy of my son, Nathan," Sally told them as she ambled up, the others not far behind. "He's a sous chef at the moment, but hoping to get his own restaurant soon."

"I'm so glad not to have to be the one cooking for a change that I'd be happy with absolutely anything," Yancey said, setting up a small portable camp chair.

"I could eat cardboard with this view," Justine agreed. "The light is so wonderful here. It seems altogether different than in Chicago."

Linda smiled. "I noticed that, too. It's got this soft glow to it. Kind of…ethereal."

"Very romantic, I think," Pat said, nuzzling Linda's neck.

"You two find everything romantic," Megan groaned. "It's the angle of the sun, that's all."

"Come on, Megan. You don't find this to be the most romantic setting on earth? Are you blind?" Linda looked disbelieving. "Surely you haven't been cooped up in that office so long that you're not appreciating all this?"

"It's great, it's great," Megan hastily agreed. "I'm only saying that when you're newly in lust, like you two, everywhere is paradise."

"*Love*, Megan," Pat corrected her with only a gentle hint of reproach. "Newly in *love*, though I'll readily admit that my whole world and everything in it got brighter when I met Linda."

Pat hugged Linda tightly to her as she spoke. At the look of such pure bliss and devotion that passed between them, Chaz felt a momentary pang of envy over the glimpse of what she might be missing. She glanced at Megan. *You sound like such a cynic about love. Why is that? And why does it seem to matter to me?*

She kept trying to tell herself that she was imagining things. But by the time they finished cleaning up the supper dishes, Chaz was convinced that Megan had something against her personally. It was like last night's dinner back at the lodge. Around absolutely everyone else, she was fine. Relaxed. Talkative. *But the moment I get within earshot she goes all quiet. And she seems to go out of her way to avoid sitting close to me or interacting with me in any way.*

She tried to tell herself it shouldn't matter as long as Megan was enjoying herself, which she evidently was. But her pep talks to herself weren't helping. Megan's behavior was starting to really drive her crazy. *Got to find some way to get her to warm up to me.*

The clients turned in early, beat from the day's exertions. Elise gave massages to Pat and Linda in their tent after much pleading and begging, but all was quiet about the campsite by nine thirty. Feeling restless, Chaz climbed a nearby hill and sat with a cup of decaf, watching the landscape turn pink in the alpenglow effect of the midnight sun. She thought Sally had also retired for the night, but her partner guide appeared with a mug of her own and reclined comfortably beside her.

They enjoyed the view for several minutes in companionable silence before Sally spoke. "It's Megan, isn't it?" she asked gently.

"Don't go there."

"Why is she giving you the big chill?" Sally asked, refusing to be deterred.

Chaz sighed. "Beats me." There was a long silence. "She did kind of catch me…looking at her…you know, maybe a bit inappropriately… when I was teaching her how to roll." She could feel a rush of warmth rise to her cheeks. "I didn't mean to. And it was only for a few seconds. I didn't think much of it then, but maybe she was offended."

Sally put her arm over her friend's shoulder. "I doubt very much whether you offended her just by looking at her. What can I do? Extol your virtues to her? In a very subtle way, of course."

"Subtle? You?" Chaz laughed. "Please, Sally, promise me you won't say anything."

Sally withdrew her arm and playfully punched Chaz. "That's not fair. I can be subtle."

Chaz laughed harder. "If you say so. But I still want you to promise me you won't try."

"All right," Sally agreed. "But if you change your mind, say the word."

"I know your heart's in the right place," Chaz said. "You're always trying to play matchmaker, and bless you for that. But don't meddle in this. I had a momentary lapse in judgment, that's all. Okay, so she's attractive. But even if she wasn't a client, which she *is*...she is still *not* my type. We have *nothing* in common. It just bothers me that she doesn't seem to like me much."

"If you say so." Sally got to her feet. "I'm going to turn in. You coming?"

"Soon," Chaz answered. "'Night, Sal. Sleep well."

"You too. 'Night."

We have nothing in common at all. And you apparently can't stand the sight of me. So why is it, Megan Maxwell, that I can't stop thinking about you?

CHAPTER SIX

Megan was so groggy from lack of sleep that she took no note of what time it was when she decided to get out of her sleeping bag. She just knew she had to get away from that appalling racket. She couldn't take it one minute more. Justine might be one hell of a good friend and an exceptional reporter, but she could sure snore the paint off a wall.

It was bad enough that she didn't have an eyeshade. The tent helped to mitigate the light a little, and she'd rigged a half-assed blindfold out of a bandanna she'd brought along because it was an "optional and recommended item" on Orion Outfitter's suggested packing list, God bless 'em. But she had nothing to combat the cacophony of noise vibrating through her tent.

First she'd flipped her sleeping bag around, so her head was at Justine's feet. Then she'd stuffed rolled-up tissue in her ears and, over that, her fleecy hat. Then she wrapped her pillow around her head and burrowed into her sleeping bag. All for naught. She only got uncomfortably warm and claustrophobic. Justine's particularly quirky snore—a long raspy wheeze, followed by a megadecibel snort, reverberated through her body regardless of how many layers she used to cushion her ears. It was like the tent was equipped with a surround sound system.

Finally, when she could stand the Dolby snore no longer, she got up and went in desperate search of coffee. To her amazement, though apparently no one was up and about, a large thermos sat on a rock outside their tent, next to their steel mugs. She was delighted to find it contained hot coffee. And not just any hot coffee. A smooth Jamaican Blue Mountain, if she was any judge. And she was.

She poured a cup, walked up the nearest rise to sit and admire the view, and began to feel better immediately. It was impossible not to.

Such a vast and varied expanse of terrain spread out before her, it was hard to know where to look first. *How far can I be seeing? Fifty miles, easy, in this direction. Maybe more. Nearly all of it unexplored.*

She quickly decided to institute the routine that she would use whenever they set up camp. First she took a couple of minutes to check all around her for anything *moving.* If something moved, it got a close-up look with the binoculars for identification. Then she sat down and studied the view in front of her with the naked eye. Big picture first. The whole landscape. Then in small parts, very systematically. Close in first, surveying for insects, wildflowers, birds. *Siberian phlox. Ivory anemone.* Then farther out. *Oooh, that's a peregrine falcon. Gray-blue above, kind of a cream color underneath. Definitely a peregrine. Very cool.* Next, the horizon. She'd admire the sharp delineation of blue sky against the white mountain tops. Now and then she'd go for her binoculars if something struck her fancy.

When she'd completed her meticulous inspection of everything she could see, she'd turn ninety degrees and do it all again. *Those are sure some big birds over there.* She adjusted her binoculars. *Bald eagle! Two bald eagles! Three! Three!* Many minutes later, she'd turn another ninety degrees. *Oh, wow. Look at him go. That's an arctic fox, I think. Big tail. Dark face, lots of brownish-blue fur. Yeah, that's an arctic fox, for sure.* She couldn't remember the last time she'd gotten so much pleasure out of her uncanny memory.

She whiled away an hour and a half and drank three cups of coffee studying the view from their first campsite, and by the time she was done, she had decided it was a damn fine thing she'd come to Alaska, regardless of the bad memories it was dredging up. This really was a unique and unforgettable experience.

She stood up and brushed herself off and only then glanced at her watch. It was just a bit before six thirty. No wonder nobody else was up. She knew she'd had too much caffeine to try to go back to sleep. *Well, I really could do with a bath after all that paddling yesterday. I'm probably a little ripe, and my hair is not fit to be seen in.* She refused to think about whom it might be that she needed to look good for. Arching her back, she groaned loudly. Her back, arms, and shoulders were still sore. *I'm not in shape for this. I sit behind a desk too much.*

She was amazed to realize she hadn't thought of work once since they got on the river yesterday. *Grace will never believe it when I tell her.*

She went back to the tent for a towel and a change of clothes. Justine was still sawing logs so loudly that Megan didn't worry about accidentally waking her. She scribbled a note that said she'd gone to the lake to wash up and left it on her pillow. There was one stop she had to make first. She detoured to the area where they'd left their food and some of their personal items in bear-proof cylinders and picked up her toiletries kit.

Yancey and Justine had spent an hour at the lake the night before and reported it was too cold for bathing unless you were a polar bear or masochist. But they both managed to tolerate it enough to wash their hair. At least it was unusually mild, with temperatures that felt like the upper sixties.

It was only a short walk, and she could see the lake through the trees the whole way, so her mind drifted as she trod slowly along on the soft moss. She inhaled long and deeply. *The air is so clean here. The colors so vivid. Is that the angle of the sun too?* Whatever it was, she felt more *alive* in Alaska, like all her senses had been enhanced.

Before she knew it she had stepped out of the tree line and was at the lake. The water was deep and clear, and so absolutely calm it reflected the enormous mountain behind it in a perfect mirror, taking her breath away.

"Wow." The word escaped like a reverent sigh.

"Awesome, isn't it?"

Chaz's voice, so near and so unexpected, startled her so much that she dropped the bundle of clothes and toiletries she was carrying. As she picked it all back up, she glanced around but didn't immediately see the guide.

"Up here," Chaz drawled lazily.

She was six feet in the air, lying atop a large black rock, face up to the sun, as if she was on a beach in Florida instead of the Arctic Circle. Her head turned slowly toward Megan, her eyes concealed behind sunglasses. It was the only thing about her that was hidden. She was otherwise completely and utterly nude.

Megan's jaw dropped and her brain short-circuited for a moment, as she tried to fully grasp what she was seeing. She was unable to speak. She couldn't bring herself to look away.

"Megan?" Chaz's demeanor changed from languid torpor to concern, her brow furrowing above her dark glasses, her rosy lips pursed in worry. As she roused herself from her semislumber, she seemed to become aware that Megan, who was *not*, unfortunately, wearing sunglasses, was staring at her breasts, not at her face. She half sat up, reached for her towel, and draped it across herself.

"I'm sorry. I wasn't expecting anyone to be up this early. Does nudity bother you?" She turned to lie on her side, facing Megan, propped up on one elbow.

Bother me? Hell, yes, it bothers me. But she certainly couldn't say *that*. Her mind struggled to come up with a suitable reply while her eyes, of their own accord and totally without her permission, burned the image she glimpsed of the naked Chaz into her memory. Legs that went on forever, athlete's legs—with firmly muscled thighs and calves that complemented the buff upper body she'd been staring at the prior afternoon. A flat plane of stomach, not a tan line in sight. Her breasts were not too large, but they were round and firm and inviting, the dark areolas standing out like the center ring on a target, pulling her eyes to them. The triangle of dark hair below testified that Chaz had indeed been born with that rich, vibrant chestnut brown everywhere.

Photographic memory indeed. She was doomed.

"I'm fine. Just fine," she managed after several moments.

She forced herself to look away—at the lake, at anywhere else. It really made no difference. She was still seeing that absolutely delicious body in her mind's eye, and she knew she would for a very long time. But at least she might hope to appear outwardly a bit more composed. No way did she want Chaz to have any idea what effect she was having on her. *What the hell is the matter? I've certainly seen naked women before. Lots of naked women, as a matter of fact.* She took a deep breath. Then another. *Yeah, but not like her,* some part of her whispered. *Even Rita. In the nude, they look nothing alike, really. Rita never looked this good.* She realized her hands were trembling. She gripped her bundle of clothes and towel tighter to herself to hide it.

"I can't believe it's this warm." Chaz lay back down, face up to the sun. "Wind's from the south." She kept the towel draped across herself. "I went for a run and then I had to take a swim, I got so hot."

Stop with the double entendres, Megan wanted to say, but she knew they were unintentional. Frankly, she didn't think it was *that* warm, not *let's-sunbathe-nude* warm, but maybe anything above freezing was balmy to an Alaskan.

"Did you find the thermos of coffee?" Chaz asked.

She'd forgotten all about that. *So you're my secret caffeine benefactor. Gotta give you points for that.* "Yes, I did, thank you. Excellent blend."

"Glad you approve." Chaz smiled. "Personally, my morning coffee is my most important meal of the day."

"I was a bit worried about that part," Megan found herself admitting. "I was absolutely expecting terrible burned coffee, or instant, or something."

"I use a French press out here, with beans I roast myself. The results aren't bad. I also brought an old-fashioned stove-top espresso pot, any time you're interested."

So she's a coffee connoisseur too. "Thanks. I may take you up on that."

Megan began to relax a little as silence fell between them. *This isn't so bad. I'm fine now. As long as I don't look at her.*

On the one hand, the more time she spent with Chaz, the more she saw the differences between her and Rita. She was thinking less about Rita by the day. *But now I'm thinking about Chaz, instead. And seeing her naked sure isn't gonna help that.* She had absolutely nothing in common with this woman. *Well, except for coffee, maybe.* She stole a glance up at Chaz.

Her face was relaxed and her body still, except for the slow rise and fall of her chest. Megan thought she'd fallen back asleep, but it was hard to tell with those damn sunglasses on. She felt suddenly reluctant to bathe as she'd planned. The thought of Chaz perhaps watching her from behind those shades was a bit disconcerting. *Later. I'll come back later.*

Backtracking quietly the way she'd come, Megan returned to their campsite. She could hear Justine's snoring from thirty feet away. *I bet everyone else will have heard her, too. No one will want to switch tents.* Perhaps she'd start sleeping outside the tent. They'd been warned the mosquitoes could be ferocious in Alaska in June, but she'd seen hardly any at all thus far.

❖

The swarm from hell arrived an hour later, just as they were getting ready to eat breakfast. Sally had cooked bacon and eggs and fresh muffins, and they were all just sitting down to enjoy them when a cloud of hungry mosquitoes found them, enveloping them and biting at every inch of exposed flesh, which was abundant on this unusually warm morning. The skeeters flew into their ears, buzzing their torment as they raised welts in a hundred places at once.

Guides and clients ran to their tents and dove inside. They'd all been complacent about the mosquitoes. None of them had their head nets with them, and the few who'd bothered applying repellent had done so in much too cursory a fashion to impede the little buggers at all, so no one escaped unscathed. The sound of zippers rang through the air, along with a litany of cursing as all eight of them sought sanctuary.

"Bastards!"

"Damn it! Get *off* me!"

"Nasty bloodsuckers!"

Then there was the frenzied clapping of hands, as they all sought to eradicate the tiny beasties who'd snuck in and were trapped inside the tents with them.

"They got me *everywhere*," Yancey moaned. It was so pleasant out, she'd gone to breakfast in what she'd worn to sleep: loose-fitting shorts and tank top.

"Join the crowd," Pat hollered from the next tent. "I am *so* going to itch."

"I hope somebody else brought a lot more hydrocortisone cream than I did," Elise yelled. "I'm going to go through this tube I brought in about three hours!"

"We've got plenty," Sally called back.

"What do we do now?" Justine asked. "Our breakfast is getting cold!"

"Sorry, ladies, I'd bring your breakfast to you, but we can't have any food in the tents," Chaz's voice rang out. "Not in bear country. Cover up your arms and legs and dig out your head nets and repellent."

"Oh, shit," Megan groaned. "I left that stuff in my toiletries kit, out by the cooking area." She turned to Justine, who was digging through the contents of her small dry bag. "Do you mind getting it for me while you're out there?"

"Soon as I find my head net," Justine said. "And my gloves. I'm not leaving any skin exposed for a *second*. I was going to spray my hands, but I put my repellent in with the bear-proof stuff." She found the gloves immediately, but the head net was more elusive. She hadn't unpacked it yet. It was still in its wrapper, and she didn't immediately notice it had gotten lost between the pages of her book at the bottom of the bag.

Megan could hear someone moving around outside the tent, but it was opposite the opening so she couldn't see who it was. "Whoever's out there, would you mind handing me my red toiletries kit out by the food?"

Chaz appeared at the entrance to Megan and Justine's tent a minute later. She wore a head net, draped loosely over a navy felt hat to keep the fabric away from her face. The hat looked quite dashing on her, Megan thought, netting notwithstanding. The rest of her body was entirely covered. The hand that held up her toiletries kit wore thin deerskin gloves that had been so long used they had conformed themselves to the shape of her fingers.

That melt-your-heart smile that Megan was becoming increasingly fond of made its way across Chaz's face, and a twinkle came to her hazel eyes, now blessedly free of the shades. "This is yours, too, right?" She held up the towel and clothes Megan had carried to the lake in her other gloved hand.

Megan nodded. "Yup."

"Pretty bad out here," Chaz said. "Let's coordinate this, to minimize enemy infiltration. On three—Justine unzips, I do a quick handover to Megan, Justine then zips back up. Ready, me hardies?" she added with the right touch of pirate inflection, her hands poised outside the zipper.

Despite herself, Megan had to smile. "Aye, aye, Captain."

"Ready when you are, Gridley," Justine added, getting into position.

They completed the handover with mercifully few invaders getting in. "Thanks!" Megan hollered after Chaz as she headed back to the cooking area.

"She's not really very much like Rita when you get to know her, is she?" Justine observed in a low voice.

"No. Not very," Megan agreed.

"Is it getting any easier to be around her?"

Megan shrugged. "A little, I guess." She dug in her bag for a long-sleeved shirt and long pants to change into, as Justine resumed searching for her head net.

"She sure knows a lot about all the birds and flowers and everything else around here," Justine said. "Both of them seem to really know their jobs."

"I wonder if she does this year round," Megan mused aloud as she changed. "Doesn't Orion take out snowshoeing and dogsled trips in the winter?"

"Not Chaz," Justine replied, pretending not to notice that Megan's question only referred to one of the guides. "She's a teacher."

"A teacher? Really?"

"That's what she told Elise."

Megan felt a tiny twinge of jealousy that Chaz was sharing details of her life with Elise, but she brushed it aside. "What age does she teach?"

"Haven't a clue. Aha! There you are!" Justine held up her head net in triumph.

"What else did she tell Elise?"

"I don't know. You'd have to ask Elise."

Megan frowned. That idea wasn't very appealing. "Never mind. It's not important." She pulled on her head net and gloves and scooted to the tent entrance. "Ready to face the bloodthirsty scavengers?"

"Lead on!"

In no time, they were all back to their breakfasts, which Megan was surprised to find didn't seem to have suffered too badly from their lengthy absence. Or maybe it was only that everything seemed to taste better in the out-of-doors. Like the fresh air had blown away the urban pollution that clogged her lungs and nasal passages and taste buds.

"Okay, so who's the buzz saw who kept me awake half the night?" Pat inquired as she took a bite off a slice of bacon.

Linda snickered.

"Oh, *man*! No lie!" Yancey added. "Some set of lungs!"

"I didn't hear anything," Justine said.

Megan groaned so loud that all eyes turned first to her, and then at her tent mate.

"What's everyone looking at me for?" Justine asked, the picture of innocence.

"I thought it was your tent," Pat said to Megan. She frowned sympathetically. "Poor kid."

"I don't suppose anybody would be willing to consider trading tent mates tonight?" Megan asked, trying not to sound too desperate. When there were no takers, she added, "Twenty bucks a night 'till we get home? Thirty?"

There was laughter and smiles all around, but no one raised a hand.

"I can't be that bad," Justine protested.

"You're worse," Pat said.

"You beat out my husband, and I thought he had a corner on the market," Yancey said. "Fortunately, he only snores when he sleeps on his back, so I make him sleep with one of those antisnore-ball thingies pinned to the back of his pajamas. Works like a charm."

"Wouldn't help even if I had one. She snores on her stomach, her back, her sides, you name it," Megan told them.

"Megan! Some friend you are!" Justine reached over and punched her lightly on the arm.

Megan laughed. "Justine, you know I love you, but you're a record-class snore bucket, and I'll take drastic measures if I have to, to get in another tent tonight." She turned toward the rest of her friends. "Do I hear any takers at forty dollars a night?"

Sally hoped that Chaz would forgive her for what she was about to do. "I'll swap with you," she volunteered. "My husband snores. I'm used to it. You can stay with Chaz."

It was hard to say which of them looked more shocked at her suggestion, which told Sally all she needed to know. Megan looked aghast, her eyes as big as saucers, and Chaz looked taken aback too, for a moment—though she regained her composure much faster.

"Or *I* can stay with Chaz, and Megan can stay with Yancey," Elise offered, before either of them had a chance to say anything.

Megan turned to stare at Elise. *Like hell you will.* "No! I'll swap with Sally."

It was out before she could think about what she was saying. She just knew she didn't want Elise staying with Chaz, that's all. She looked toward Chaz for confirmation and only then really realized what she'd done.

Chaz was eyeing her with a bewildered expression, as if her

acceptance of the arrangement was the last thing she'd expected. Which of course it was, since Megan had been treating her like shit. Suddenly the mental photograph she'd taken of Chaz in the nude roared up out of nowhere and implanted itself on her eyelids. *Oh, shit. What the hell have I done?* She looked away, her brain scrambling to find a way out of this mess she'd somehow gotten herself into. *She turns my brain to mush. I can't be held responsible for my actions.*

"Whatever you like," Chaz said. "I'm fine with it."

"It's settled then," Sally said. "We'll swap beginning tonight."

"Sure I won't keep you awake, too?" Justine asked sheepishly.

"Nah, I can sleep through anything. This'll be fun," Sally said. "I'll get a chance to hear some great inside stories about TV news."

And I'll get the chance to see how well I can hide the fact that she's really getting under my skin, Megan thought, glancing at Chaz.

The guide was watching her with an unreadable expression. "All right, then," Chaz said. "If we're all done eating, why don't we pack up and get ready for another day on the river."

❖

Despite the breathtaking scenery and abundant wildlife they spotted, a good portion of the hours passed in a blur for Megan. Oh, she got out her binoculars when Chaz pointed out the snowy owl, his white feathers starkly contrasted against the gray-green spruce tree he was perched on. And she thrilled with the rest of them at the first caribou they spotted, a small group of eight adults far in the distance. But she got totally lost in thoughts of Chaz for great long periods of the day.

She was comfortable and confident now in the kayak, and able to daydream as they mostly drifted in the wide, slow current. Over and over again, she replayed the small loop of images she'd captured of the handsome guide. Her sculpted back, as she dug her paddle into the water. That brief look of attraction and desire that had crossed her face as she stared at Megan's breasts during the rolling lesson. *I didn't imagine that. I know I didn't.*

And of course it was impossible to keep that mental picture of the naked, relaxed Chaz at bay. Megan was tortured relentlessly by those round breasts and dark nipples, the glimpse of hair at the apex of those long legs.

There were other mental snapshots, and as she reviewed them in her mind, she saw new differences between Chaz and Rita. Chaz was a lot more nonchalant about her body, for one thing. She seemed to have not an ounce of pretension about her perfect physique and smoldering good looks. No makeup at all, and always dressed in clothes so faded and comfortable-looking that Megan suspected Chaz couldn't bear to part with them.

I haven't seen her look in a mirror once. She combs her hair by running her hands through it. Megan had to admit she found that habit kind of sexy. It was almost as if she was totally unaware of how great she looks. Though she must get hit on all the time.

Rita, on the other hand, had been obsessed about her body. She went to the gym religiously and weighed herself twice a day, morning and night. She was always on weird diets, Megan recalled. And she wouldn't be caught dead without her makeup and hair just so. For her, appearance was everything. Megan had gotten a little that way herself, since she'd become a vice president. She didn't particularly *like* getting all gussied up. But she knew how to play by the rules.

She had to admit, though, she really liked the *au natural* look on Chaz. *Perhaps a little too much.* Now that she'd begun to see Chaz as someone completely different from Rita, *the thought* crossed her mind for the first time. The possibility of maybe flirting with Chaz herself. *Why not? What's holding me back?* She'd never been shy about going after a woman who interested her. *Nothing's stopping me. She's not Rita. She's just one deliciously hot woman, and I'm on vacation, after all.*

A niggling of her conscience tried to warn Megan she should not be so cavalier about this one, but she ignored it. She really hoped she hadn't only imagined the way she'd caught Chaz looking at her. *I'll find out soon enough if we're sharing a tent, won't I?*

The thought of sleeping beside Chaz made her heart skip a beat, and a thrill of anticipation skittered up her spine. *Oh, God, I really hope I'm not wrong about what I saw in your eyes.*

CHAPTER SEVEN

Chaz scarcely noticed the scenery during the first couple of hours after breakfast. She was totally thrown by the prospect of sleeping next to Megan that night, and equally baffled by the sudden thaw in her client's frosty attitude toward her. It almost seemed like Megan jumped at the chance to stay with her, rather than one of her friends. What was up with that?

Chaz was even more perplexed by the way her mind and body were reacting to the turn of events. Whenever she pictured them lying side by side in the tent she felt a sharp twinge of arousal.

Okay, so you're really, really attracted to her, she admitted, paddling along on autopilot, her eyes seeing only the way Megan had smiled at her that morning from the other side of the tent screen. She'd felt something warm her from within when Megan smiled at her that way.

But nothing is going to happen, she reminded herself. *Even if she is warming up to you. She's a client, you have nothing in common, and she lives on the other side of the country. Besides, you're not even really sure she's gay. It's your hormones talking.* She kept telling herself that, but it was doing nothing to stop her overactive imagination from wondering what the pale skin of Megan's neck would taste like, what the press of Megan's body would feel like against her own. What the network vice president might be like in bed. *Do you always have to be the one in control?*

She felt both tremendous anticipation and profound dread when she thought about the nights ahead of them. Sharing a tent with Megan might test the limits of her resolve. Though she hoped that no one had noticed how distracted she was all morning, she wasn't too surprised when Sally sought her out soon after they stopped for lunch.

Chaz had taken her sandwich and gone to sit on a rock next to the river, her back to the clients.

"You're not mad at me, are you?" Sally asked as she settled beside her.

"Now why in the world would I be mad at you?" Chaz answered calmly. It took some effort, because in all honesty she *was* a tad peeved at what was blatantly a misguided effort to play matchmaker. *It's all your fault I'm apparently going to have a frustrated libido the next week and a half,* she wanted to say. But she knew Sally's intentions were honorable.

"Well, I can see that I really threw you for a loop when I volunteered to swap tents with Megan. I just thought you needed a nudge. I know you like her. And I think she likes you, too, despite how she's been acting. I've seen her looking at you a lot, kind of like you've been looking at her."

"You didn't throw me for a loop, and I haven't been looking at her any more than anyone else," Chaz protested, annoyed with how well Sally could read her. She didn't want to admit how much Megan was getting to her; it would only encourage Sally's determination to hook them up.

"I guess there must have been some other reason you failed to point out a half-dozen things during this last stretch of river, then." Sally grinned.

"What? What did I miss?"

"Let's see. A golden eagle, another nice grouping of Dall sheep, and the first musk ox of the trip, among other things."

"Oh, shit, really? Where was the musk ox?" Chaz felt awful for slacking on her responsibilities. They might not see another one, she knew, and that was an animal that always made a real impression on the clients.

"There was a pair of them a good ways back, and they *were* a long distance away—I could only really see them with binoculars. But I knew that if *you'd* blown by them, Miss Eagle Eyes, there was something major going on with you."

"There's nothing going on with me," she replied, a little too defensively.

"Whatever you say," Sally said, with an inflection that said she clearly didn't believe a word of Chaz's denials.

"Okay, so your tent-swapping plan distracted me a little," she admitted. "But I already told you, I'm not getting involved in any one-night stands with a client."

"Well, I think you're limiting yourself," Sally said. "Maybe it wouldn't have to be a one-night stand. You never know." She put her hand on Chaz's shoulder, and her voice grew serious. "Maybe you're throwing away a prime opportunity for happiness. I'd hate to see that happen. Think about it, would you? Please?"

Like I can think about much of anything else. "Give it up, Sally. It's not possible. We have a job to do here, a responsibility to these women, and I'm not going to forget that." She packed up the remnants of her lunch and stood, ending the discussion for the moment anyway.

She managed to keep her mind on her duties when they got back on the river to head to their next campsite, at least for the most part. She didn't want the clients to miss any more prime wildlife sightings because of her daydreaming.

But it wasn't easy. She'd caught Megan watching her as she got back into her kayak, and Sally's words rang in her mind. *I think she likes you, too...I've seen her looking at you a lot, kind of like you've been looking at her.*

Something told her that the greatest tests of her self-control were still to come.

❖

Most of that day the Odakonya meandered lazily through a wide, flat plain of tundra, the mountains far distant and the view unfettered by trees or brush for miles in every direction. But late in the afternoon, the river turned and entered a long valley thick with trees: a forest of cottonwoods and aspen and spruce, protected from the killing winter winds by the mountains rising steeply on either side. The lush growth around them after several hours of unbroken, treeless terrain made Megan feel a bit like she'd come upon an oasis in the desert.

There were birds everywhere, and ground squirrels chattered noisily at them from the riverbank, adding to the cacophony of twitterings and chirps and snippets of birdsong. Up ahead, she could see that Chaz had pulled off and was out of her kayak. They must have reached their second campsite.

Justine brought her kayak alongside Megan's. "What a great spot."

"Beautiful," Megan agreed.

"Are you sure you're okay with the sleeping arrangements? You actually *want* to stay with Chaz?"

"It'll be all right." *I hope it will be, anyway.* "No offense, Justine, but I haven't slept well since we left Chicago."

"Sorry. I guess I should have warned you."

"You *knew* you snored?" Megan asked.

"Well, *duh.* I *am* a grown woman. And too long unattached, I grant you, but only because I've been working a lot. I do have overnight guests, you know. Although most of them are apparently too diplomatic to tell me honestly how loud I am."

"What team are you trying out for these days, by the way?" Megan asked as they drifted near the place where they would spend the night.

"I think I've had it with men. Women are way more interesting."

And some women are much more interesting than others. "You got that right, kiddo. Got any prospects in mind?"

"Well, I might have made a play for tall, taut, and lovely over there." Justine nodded in Chaz's direction. "But I hate to stand in line. You realize that Elise is out for her too, right?"

Their kayaks crunched against the gravel bank, and they both popped their spray skirts to get out.

"I never said I was interested in her," Megan protested feebly, as she got to her feet and stripped off her PFD.

"You don't have to," Justine said, following suit. "It's pretty obvious, Meg. I just want to make sure you knew that you've got some competition, and you know as well as I do that Elise has a way with women."

"Well, I don't know that *quite* as well as you do. I've seen her in action, but I've never succumbed to her charms *personally.*"

"That's not fair. It was just the once, and it only happened because I was stressed out and she was helping me to relax," Justine said.

"Yeah, right." Megan rolled her eyes. "She went to massage school to add to her arsenal of seduction tools. The sexy punk haircut, the flirtatious grin, the big pouty lips. She's butch with the femmes, and femme with the butches, and she gets them all."

"So why has she never gotten you?" Justine asked.

"Never tried." Truth be told, Megan had always been a bit irritated by the fact that Elise had made a play for virtually every lesbian in their close circle of friends except for her. Not that she had any particular attraction to Elise; it was only that she felt slighted, like there was something wrong with her.

"Well, for all her flirting, she doesn't seem to be making a lot of headway with Chaz," Justine said, as they gathered up their gear and headed toward the others, who were already unloading their bags of gear from the raft. "Are we sure she's gay?"

"I'd say that's a no-brainer," Megan replied. "But I intend to find out for sure tonight."

"Tonight?" Justine stopped short and put a hand on Megan's arm to keep her from getting any closer to the others, where they could be overheard. "You have some kind of plan in mind, hmm?"

"Not a plan, per se. But let's just say I do intend to find out who and what her type is."

"Well, good luck. She is one scrumptious-looking woman, that's for sure."

Not telling me anything I don't know, Megan thought as they joined the others.

Sally helped her put up the tent that she and Chaz would share that night, because Chaz was preoccupied with trying to catch some fish to add to their dinner.

Megan decided it was the perfect opportunity for her to do a little research. "So how long have you two been guiding together?" she asked as they laid out the tent, poles, and stakes.

"Five summers," Sally said. "I started doing this when my kids went away to college."

"So what do you do the rest of the year?"

Sally laughed. "Not much. I've been a full-time mom so long, I've kind of been at loose ends with the kids out of the house. I do some volunteer work, and I'm thinking about going back to college for my Master's degree."

"What about Chaz?"

"Chaz is a biology professor at the University of Fairbanks."

"Ah. A professor, eh? That explains her extensive knowledge of all the flora and fauna we're seeing."

"Yeah, she's much better at it than I am. I've learned most everything I know from her," Sally said.

"So…what else can you tell me about her?" Megan asked with forced nonchalance, as she fitted the tent pole into one of the narrow sleeves in the tent.

Sally stopped what she was doing and smiled a kind of Cheshire-cat smile, as if she were privy to a secret. "What do you want to know?"

"Oh, I don't know," Megan responded vaguely. *Is she gay? Is she seeing anyone? What's her type? Has she talked to you about Elise? About me?*

"Well, let's see. I would describe Chaz as…loyal and honest. Trustworthy. Sensitive and intelligent. Considerate and kind. Resourceful."

She sounds like a Boy Scout, Megan wanted to interject, but didn't. She found Sally's listing of Chaz's attributes somehow reassuring, but she didn't stop to consider why. "So she...uh…told us she wasn't married," she said, cursing her nervous stammer.

"Nope. She's had a few girlfriends, but no one recently," Sally volunteered. "I think it's hard for her to make the first move when she's interested in someone."

Bingo. Megan felt buoyed by the confirmation of Chaz's sexual preference, and very interested indeed to hear that she was the type to let others take the lead in a relationship. She was so intrigued by this bit of information, in fact, that she failed to think twice about the smug grin on Sally's face.

❖

Chaz was successful in her efforts to catch enough grayling and arctic char to feed them all. And because they were in an area with ample downed wood, she prepared them grilled over an open campfire and served them with lemon and a side of wild rice. She was grateful she had tasks to do to keep her mind occupied. But all through dinner, she couldn't help glancing in Megan's direction. She often caught Megan looking at her, in a way that made her a little weak in the knees. Once again she wondered what had precipitated the apparent change in Megan's attitude toward her, and she worried about how she might react when they were alone in the tent together.

After they had eaten, they split up into small groups. Yancey and Justine took a turn at washing dishes, while Sally and Chaz packed the garbage and leftover food into bear-proof canisters and carried them to a spot well away from where they'd be sleeping. Pat and Linda excused themselves to take a walk together along the riverbank, while Megan and Elise tended the fire.

"You know, if you'd be more comfortable staying with Yancey, I'd be happy to bunk with Chaz tonight," Elise offered.

I bet you would. "That's not necessary," Megan answered as offhandedly as she could manage. "I'm fine with things the way they are."

"Well, actually, I'd *like* the chance to get to know Chaz better, if you get my drift. She is so flaming *hot*, I think I'm going to spontaneously combust!" Elise confided, as if her intentions hadn't been patently obvious the whole trip.

"I'm sure you'll find ample opportunities to flirt with her, Elise," Megan said, cutting off further discussion of their sleeping arrangements. *Unless I have something to say about it and beat you to it.*

Elise frowned, as though she'd expected that Megan would readily swap tent mates with her once she'd expressed her interest in Chaz. But before she had a chance to protest, Yancey and Justine returned to the campfire, followed soon after by the two guides.

"Saved you a spot," Elise said, nodding her head with a smile toward a camp chair beside her as Chaz neared.

Megan was initially irritated by Elise's invitation, and Chaz's quick acceptance, until she realized that would put Chaz directly opposite her, where it would be impossible for them not to look at each other.

The sun sank low in the sky, painting the tall mountains on either side of them with that pink light of the Arctic, and casting long shadows beneath the forest surrounding them. They all settled comfortably around the fire, sipping merlot and relaxing in their camp chairs or lying half supine on their sleeping mattresses, and chatted about the sights they'd seen that day.

Megan heard little of it. She could hardly keep her eyes off Chaz, who sat with her long legs stretched out in front of her toward the fire. She was damned sexy-looking in the golden glow of the midnight sun, with the flickering firelight reflected in the dark pools of her eyes.

Before too long, Pat and Linda reappeared, their arms around each other and with their clothes and hair in enough disarray for the assembled gathering to clue in on what they'd been up to the last half hour or better. As they took seats, Linda curled within the circle of Pat's embrace, and Pat gave her a long, deep kiss.

"If you two don't give it a rest, you're going to get me way too hot and bothered…and just when there's apparently nothing I can do about it," Elise jested, looking pointedly at Chaz as she said it.

Chaz squirmed slightly at the comment and looked away, but she was smiling. Though she considered herself a nonviolent person, Megan felt like slugging Elise.

"So who's up for a round of probing questions?" Yancey asked.

"Probing questions! I forgot all about probing questions!" Elise said, a mischievous look in her eyes. "Oh, absolutely, I'm game."

"Probing questions?" Sally repeated.

"Our version of Truth or Dare, without the dare," Elise said. "Someone comes up with a probing question, like 'how did you lose your virginity?' and we answer in turn, going around the circle. The last one to answer poses the next question."

"Me first," Linda said. "Let's start off easy. Most embarrassing moment." She turned in the circle of Pat's arms and looked at her lover. "You first," she challenged, with mirth in her eyes.

"Most embarrassing moment? Let's see. As you know, I don't embarrass easily."

"Which is exactly why I asked that." Linda turned to the others. "She's almost gotten us into trouble a half a dozen times getting too amorous in public," she confided, which made them all smile.

"Oh! I know!" Pat said. "I did feel kind of embarrassed the morning I woke up in the hospital after my appendectomy, when they told me I hit on the surgeon while I was under anesthesia."

"That's doesn't sound so bad," Chaz said.

"Except that the surgeon was straight, married to the anesthesiologist, and I was apparently very explicit in what I wanted to do to her," Pat said sheepishly. "Your turn," she said to Sally as the others laughed.

"I actually have a picture of my moment," Sally said. "I tripped going down the aisle at my wedding."

"You tripped?" Chaz got up to toss a few branches on the fire. "You never told me that."

"Yup. Stepped on the dress and took a header into the nearest pew. Fortunately my dad caught me as I was going down. My mother swore it was God getting me back for playing practical jokes."

"I see it didn't deter you any," Linda said. "By the way, I thought the rubber snakes tonight were a nice alternative to the spiders. Very realistic looking."

"Thanks. We aim to please." Sally beamed. She shifted to look at Megan. "Your turn."

"Right out of college, I was a reporter for about a day and a half at a TV station in Traverse City," Megan said. *I can't believe I'm gonna tell this.*

"You were on the *air*?" Justine's eyes widened in astonishment. "Oh, I want to see a tape of that."

"There is no tape. I destroyed all copies personally," Megan huffed.

"So what happened?" Justine asked.

"Shortly after I was hired, I had to anchor the 11 p.m. show. Right before airtime, the regular guy got food poisoning. Well, I was so nervous I took several deep breaths before we went on, and I guess I hyperventilated. I fainted, midway during the first paragraph."

"Fainted?" Yancey gasped.

"Fell face-first into the desk and caught my chin on the corner of it." Megan lifted her chin and pointed to a hairline scar that ran beneath it. "Took eight stitches to close. I bled all over the desk while the director decided what the hell he should do. After several seconds, he went to commercial and then to a repeat of *Cheers* while they called the ambulance. I decided to be a behind-the-scenes person after that."

Everyone cracked up, but it was Chaz's reaction that pleased Megan the most. She felt a warm rush of satisfaction to have provided the reason for that dazzling smile and warm, rich laugh.

"Next, please," Pat said.

"Caught by the law in a compromising position is all I can say about mine," Elise said, to sniggers from around the campfire circle. She smiled at the memory and turned to Chaz. "Your turn."

"While I was still in college, I was asked to present a scientific paper I'd authored to a conference in Seattle," Chaz said. "It was in one of the ballrooms in this huge hotel, and I was really nervous—I was not used to speaking in front of groups." A smile lifted the corner of her mouth. "I hid out in one of the bathrooms until right before I was to speak, then I came out on this tiny stage and launched right in to 'How Climactic Changes Impact Musk Oxen Reproduction.'" She paused a moment, chuckling. "In my own defense, the stage was brightly lit and the rest of the room was dark, so I couldn't *see* that the audience was made up entirely of rabbis."

Everyone started laughing.

"They let me talk for at least five minutes before a nice bearded gentlemen told me he thought I might want the Arctic Wildlife conference in the ballroom next door."

They howled with laughter.

"How have you ever kept that from me?" Sally asked, wiping a tear from her cheek.

Chaz shrugged. "Next!"

They continued around the circle, swapping stories and laughter. When they finished with most embarrassing moment, they covered pet peeves and biggest crushes, then it was on to hidden talents.

"Gosh, hidden talent. That's kind of hard." Yancey stretched out on her sleeping mattress and took a sip of wine from her metal mug. "I am *so* sore, by the way. I keep stiffening up if I stay in any position for too long."

"Yeah, me, too. Speaking of which, I think I'm due to take another dose of ibuprofen." Elise reached into her pocket for a small bottle. "Anybody else?"

The bottle got passed around the circle and Justine, Megan, and Yancey also took a couple of tablets.

"Okay, I've got it," Yancey said. "At least this is what my kids would say my hidden talent is. May I have quiet, please?"

The only sound that could be heard was the crackling of the fire.

Yancey put her fingers next to her mouth, took a big deep breath, and out came the uncannily realistic sound of a taxi horn.

The women all clapped.

"Wait!" Yancey waved away the applause and got to her feet. "There's more!" She leaned over and put her hands around her mouth. After a moment, the distinctive chirp of a cricket could be heard. More applause. That was followed by the slurp of a toilet plunger, then the unmistakable blare of a foghorn.

"Very cool!" Sally said. "You'll have to teach me how to do that.

My kids would love it!"

"My oldest can do lots of sound effects. We got them out of a book." Yancey turned toward Megan. "We all know what *your* hidden talent is."

"That's not true," Pat reminded her. "Sally and Chaz don't know about Megan."

"No, we don't," Chaz confirmed, looking at Megan curiously.

"Megan has a photographic memory," Justine provided. "Virtually a walking encyclopedia."

"What shall we have her do?" Pat asked.

"Nothing mundane, like the Declaration of Independence," Justine said. "It should be something really spectacular."

"I like when she does the countries of the world in alphabetical order," Yancey suggested.

"As long as it's anything but that awful shipwreck poem that goes on forever!" Linda pleaded.

"It's only twenty-three stanzas. And 'The Wreck of the Hesperus' was written by Henry Wadsworth Longfellow, I'll have you know," Megan said.

"So it's a classic." Linda pulled a face. "It's still awful."

Megan looked directly at Chaz. "Try me," she said, with a hint of flirtation in her voice.

A corner of Chaz's mouth tipped up as she suppressed a smile. It was a long moment before she spoke. "All right. What can you tell me about the Arctic National Wildlife Refuge?"

"I could talk about it for a couple of hours. What would you like me to address specifically?" Megan answered confidently.

"How about bird life?"

"Let's see," Megan began, as she leaned back in her chair and stretched out her legs toward the fire. "There have been 181 different species of birds spotted in the refuge, most migrating here from at least four continents, at least according to the official government Web site."

"What draws them here?" Chaz challenged.

"When the permafrost melts in the summer, you have thousands upon thousands of little pools of water everywhere, the perfect breeding ground for an enormous insect population, which draws the birds."

"Very good. I'm impressed," Chaz complimented her, as though that had been her entire answer.

"Oh, she's got a lot more, I'm sure," Justine interjected. "Don't you, Meg?"

"Well, I could name all 181 species, if you like, and tell you something about each one," Megan said. "What they look like, where they can be found in the refuge, where they migrate from." She was pleased to see the look of astonishment on Chaz's face.

"Now I'm really impressed." Chaz said. "Do you remember everything you see and hear?"

"Everything important, anyway." *I won't forget any single detail of you any time soon, that's for sure.*

"I can't remember my ATM pin number half the time," Yancey complained. "At least tell me that you occasionally misplace your car keys."

"Never," Megan said, smiling.

"Bitch!" Yancey answered with a laugh. "All right, now who gets to follow that? Isn't it your turn, Justine?"

"Oh, great. This is going to be so impressive after *you*." Justine stuck out her tongue at Megan. "I used to be able to tap dance. That's my talent."

"You? Klutz Bernard? When was this?" Megan asked, not buying a word of it.

"From about age six until I was probably fifteen or so. I stopped when we moved away from the woman who had been teaching me."

"Prove it," Megan challenged. "I don't believe you have ever danced. You trip over something every time we go somewhere."

With a sigh, Justine stood up. "It's been a long time, and this isn't exactly ideal footwear," she said, holding one foot up in the air so they could all get a good look at the hiking boots she had on. "But here goes."

"Wait!" Sally hollered. "Would you like some accompaniment?"

"Uh, sure," Justine said uncertainly.

"You and Chaz can demonstrate your hidden talents together," Sally said, turning to her partner guide. "Waddya say?"

"All right," Chaz said, and got up and headed toward the tent she and Megan were sharing.

In a minute, she returned carrying a rectangular waterproof case about the size of a breadbox. It had already piqued Megan's interest. Sally had seemed to treat it with respect, placing it carefully among

Chaz's gear in the corner of the tent, after they'd set it up.

"So is there anything in particular you'd like me to play?" Chaz asked Justine as she regained her seat by the fire.

"How about a few bars of 'Me and My Shadow'?"

"I can do that." Chaz unfastened the twin latches that held the case shut and flipped open the top. Inside lay an antique concertina, protected by thick eggshell foam that had been custom cut to conform to its shape. The instrument was made of leather and rosewood, and the decoratively filigreed plates on each end that held the forty-eight button keys were sterling silver. It looked as though it had been well played but lovingly tended.

"Is that an accordion?" Linda asked, as Chaz removed the instrument and put her hands through the leather hand rests on either end.

"A near relative. It's a concertina," Chaz said. "Or squeezebox."

"I think I've only ever seen one of those in the movies, usually in an organ grinder's hands, or some guy singing on a gondola," Megan said derisively, but she was smiling as she said it.

Chaz merely smiled at the challenge. "Ready?" she asked Justine.

"As I'll ever be."

Justine surprised all her friends with a more than passable time step. Then she launched into a soft-shoe routine that had to have been memorized long ago, for some childhood recital.

They were also all pleased with Chaz's accompaniment, a four-part rendition of the popular tune played flawlessly. When the number was over, they all applauded and whistled.

"I will never call you a klutz again," Megan promised as Justine took a bow and settled back beside her in her camp chair.

"And very nice playing, Chaz," Pat said.

"Yeah, not half bad," Megan conceded with a smile.

"Why don't you give them an idea of what you can really do with that thing?" Sally said. "You know—like that around-the-world medley you did that time."

"Yeah! Play some more," Elise urged.

"If you insist," Chaz said, her eyes on Megan as she launched into a rousing Irish jig, her hands flying over the buttons at an astonishing speed.

After a minute or so of that tune, she transitioned skillfully into a French café song that sounded vaguely familiar, then, from there, into "La donna e mobile," the familiar Verdi piece Megan had been thinking of when she'd made the gondola crack. After Italy, Chaz segued into a German biergarten song, another lively piece with impressive fingering, then into a Polish polka, and, finally, to a Cajun Zydeco strain that took them all to New Orleans.

Megan would never have guessed that the unusual instrument had such versatility. And it was obvious Chaz had spent a lot of hours with the concertina, for she didn't miss a note in the impromptu concert.

There was a rousing chorus of applause and whistles when Chaz finished with a flourish.

"Bravo!" Yancey called out as the clapping died down. "That was marvelous!"

"Great going!" Justine agreed.

"Yes, very nice, indeed," Megan said. "How long have you played that thing?"

"Since I was ten. My father gave it to me when we moved to Alaska—something to keep me occupied during the long winters."

"Where did you move here from?" Elise asked.

"Oregon. I grew up on a commune. We moved to Alaska when it kind of disbanded."

I guess that explains why she's so nonchalant about nudity, Megan thought. The word commune to her evoked images of Woodstock and the hippie generation of the 1960s and early '70s—men and women parading around naked or half-naked as they grew their own vegetables and lived off the land. She imagined them as promiscuous and uninhibited about sex. *Wasn't 'free love' one of the big slogans of that era?* She found the knowledge that Chaz had grown up in that environment most encouraging.

"I don't think anyone should have to follow Chaz's playing," Linda complained good-naturedly. "That was definitely real talent."

"No getting out of it," Pat said. "Besides, I'm very curious to see what you're going to claim as your hidden talent, since the one I know about can't be demonstrated in public."

Linda blushed bright red as everyone laughed. "I can't believe you said that," she grumbled.

"It's a compliment!" Pat said.

"I'll get you for that," Linda promised. "We'll see how long before you get to experience *that* talent again."

That prompted another round of laughter.

"Okay, this isn't really a talent, but it's unusual, anyway," Linda said. She stood and bent over as if to touch her toes, but instead she pushed her foot into an unnatural angle, until it looked as though her shoes were facing in opposite directions.

"Eeewww!" Pat said. "I'm never sleeping with you again!"

"Oh, my God, how are you doing that?" Elise asked.

"Doesn't that hurt?" Yancey added, craning her head for a better look.

"Nope. Double-jointed in that ankle." Linda swiveled the ankle back to normal and sat back down, giving Pat a playful punch as she did. "Okay, so what are you going to do for us, Miss Smart Aleck?"

"We'll see who laughs," Pat promised. She got to her feet and walked around the circle of friends, collecting a small assortment of items—a metal mug, a water bottle, a large tube of sunscreen, and a flashlight. She returned to stand beside Linda before she set them in motion, juggling with practiced skill, dazzling them with constant switch ups in height and direction and speed.

"The lady is good with her hands, what can I say?" Linda conceded admiringly, as the others laughed.

"What about you, Sally?" Megan asked. "Any predilection for something other than practical jokes?"

"I can't compete with the rest of you," Sally said. "My only hidden talent is this." She stuck out her tongue and touched the end of her nose with it.

"Your husband must love that!" Pat said, which touched off another round of laughter. "Who have we missed? Elise?"

"I was going to say I didn't think I had a hidden talent," Elise answered. "But Sally's reminded me that I've won a bar bet or two with the ability to tie cherry stems into a knot with my tongue."

"I bet that comes in handy," Yancey said, to a chorus of laughter.

"Speaking of which," Pat said, pausing to whisper something into Linda's ear, "I think we'll say good night at this point. We're suddenly very...uh, sleepy. Aren't we, honey?"

More laughs.

Pat got to her feet first and offered a hand up to Linda. They strolled arm in arm toward their tent, talking in low whispers.

"Where the heck do they get their stamina?" Yancey complained. "I can hardly move after all this paddling."

"I know they do this kayaking stuff a lot," Justine agreed. "But they are the oldest among us, too. It's not fair. I'm ready to drop." She stretched and yawned. "I think I'll turn in, too, I guess. Any chance I can coerce a friendly masseuse to give me a nice back rub?"

"Well, I'm sore, too, you know," Elise admitted. "How about we work out a trade. Ten minutes for ten minutes?"

"Deal," Justine said.

They got up and took a step or two toward Justine's tent.

"Hey, wait. Can I get in on some of that action?" Yancey called after them.

"Sure," Elise said. "Anybody else?" she added, looking directly at Chaz in a way that made Megan want to punch her again.

Chaz and Megan shook their heads, while Sally responded with a wave and a "No, thanks."

"Maybe tomorrow, then," Elise said.

Or maybe not, Megan thought. *The only person I want massaging Chaz is me.*

"'Night, everybody," Justine called back as the three of them headed toward the tents.

Megan glanced at Chaz, her heartbeat accelerating at the knowledge that they would soon be alone together. "Well, I guess I'll head that way, too."

She felt the same exhaustion as the rest of them, but was pretty sure that when Chaz lay down beside her, she'd get her second wind in a hurry.

Chaz met her eyes but made no move to get up. "Okay. I'll be in there in a while. I'll try not to wake you."

The woman cannot get a clue that I'm trying to flirt with her, Megan thought dejectedly as she made her way to their tent. *Of course it might have helped if I hadn't treated her like a pariah the first couple of days of the trip.*

CHAPTER EIGHT

"Well, she certainly seems to be warming up to you now," Sally remarked as soon as Megan was out of earshot.

"I guess. I haven't a clue why, though," Chaz said. "And don't go getting any more ideas in your head."

"Ideas? Moi? I don't know what you mean." Sally got to her feet. "Are you coming, or are you going to stay out here and avoid her until she goes to sleep?"

"I'm going to stay here awhile and enjoy the fire," Chaz replied.

"You know we can't build a fire every night. What are you going to use as an excuse then?"

"Go to bed, Sally," Chaz grumbled.

"Oh, all right." Sally laid a hand on Chaz's shoulder as she passed by. "Sleep well, hon."

"You too."

As soon as Sally was gone, Chaz fed a few sticks to the fire and settled back in her chair, sipping her wine and recounting the day. Images of Megan filled her mind—especially the way she'd looked tonight, relaxed and at ease by the fire, a smile coming easily to her now. The rough edges she'd arrived in Alaska with had softened a lot. *And she kept looking at me all the time. She's not just warming up to me; it almost seemed like she was flirting with me a little.*

That thought sent a teasing whisper of arousal through her and took her mind back to daydreaming of what Megan might be like in bed. She closed her eyes and imagined slowly stripping off all those brand-new clothes, layer by layer, until she reached Megan's soft ivory skin. She could almost feel it now, beneath her fingertips. In her mind's eye, she could see Megan's breasts as she touched them and roused the nipples to attention with teasing passes. *I wonder what she brought to wear to bed.*

From there, despite her better judgment, she allowed her mind to consider what it might be like to kiss Megan, to feel those soft lips surrendering to her. *Surrendering, hell. She's not the type to surrender*, her rational mind tried to intercede, but by now her body was calling the shots, luxuriating in the imagined pleasures that her conscience was unwilling to allow. A shudder passed through her. It was all she could do not to touch herself.

Time passed; she couldn't have said how much. She had almost dozed, staring into the fire with heavy-lidded eyes, lost in the depths of Megan's kiss.

A scream pierced the silence.

A millisecond later, a loud grunting noise.

Then a roar.

Bear. Chaz scrambled to her feet and grabbed a sturdy burning branch out of the fire. She hurried toward the sounds, fumbling at her belt as another scream rang out. *Megan!*

She had the pepper spray in her palm when she rounded the corner of one of the tents and spotted the grizzly, twelve feet away.

He was a massive brute. Seven or eight hundred pounds, she reckoned. And at the moment, he had his head inside the tent she was sharing with Megan.

Her blood ran cold. *Oh, my God.*

She waved the torch at him and shouted, "Go, bear! Go! Out! Get away!"

The grizzly backed out of the tent and turned to glare at her with small black eyes—pig eyes—set six inches apart. His head was wider than her shoulders, and his mouth seemed disproportionately large at the moment—all sharp teeth. He was drooling a white paste of some kind, and a big glob was stuck to the fur around his mouth.

Chaz shouted some more at the top of her lungs. "Go, bear! Go away!" The fire was nearly gone from the branch she was waving around. Her heart was beating a mile a minute.

He stomped down hard with his massive front paws, stiff legged, and she swore she could feel the earth move beneath her feet. The claws on those feet had to be nine inches long, and she knew they were razor sharp.

She shouted at him once more as the flame gave out on her branch. "Get! Go away!" She dropped the stick and began waving her left arm, as her right arm extended towards him, pointing the pepper spray at his eyes.

He rocked from one huge paw to the other and let out a *woof* that sounded like the bark of a dog. Then he stood on his hind legs, sniffing the air noisily. Frozen in place, she had just enough time to guess his height at roughly nine feet tall, before he dropped to all fours and charged her.

Time slowed.

Chaz stood her ground as she depressed the trigger, determined not to miss. He roared as it hit him, the sound reverberating in her ears, but he kept on coming.

And the wind was not on her side.

The spray came back at her in the blink of an eye, and she sucked in great lungfuls of the stuff as it blinded her. The pain was everywhere at once. She took a great gasping breath for air and began coughing.

She rolled to the ground and curled into a fetal position, head down and hands clasped together behind her neck, trying desperately to suck in fresh air. She felt the enormous bulk of the bear pass her by inches, close enough that she could smell the warm stench of his breath as he went past, bellowing in pain and anger.

Her lungs burned and her eyes were agony. She could hear nothing but her own coughing. Every gasping breath took in more of the noxious fallout. She coughed and coughed until she felt her lungs would come apart. There was no relief from the burning pain. Her eyes streamed tears.

It had all happened in seconds.

Before she knew it, a shaken Sally was at her side, and the rest of the group was not far behind.

"My God, Chaz, what the hell happened?" Sally asked, coughing herself from the remnants of the spray that lingered about the camp. Some of the other women were coughing, too.

"Are you all right?" Pat asked.

"What was that?" Justine asked. "Was that a bear?"

Chaz gasped for air. *Megan,* she wanted to say. *Is Megan all right?* But she couldn't speak; her throat was raw.

"Someone get some water, will you?" Sally asked as she led Chaz back to her chair by the fire. Justine handed her a water bottle. "Lean your head back, Chaz, and let me rinse out your eyes."

Sally poured fresh water carefully into both of Chaz's eyes.

"A bear came into our t...tent," Megan stuttered. In all the excitement, no one had noticed her, standing off to one side, trembling and ashen. "God, he was huge."

As soon as she heard Megan's voice, relief poured through Chaz like a soothing balm.

"A grizzly bear?" Linda asked. Her eyes got wide, and she glanced around as if expecting the beast to return at any moment.

"Are you all right, Megan?" Sally asked.

"Yeah, but he sure scared the shit out of me," Megan said. "I guess I fell asleep. Next thing I know I'm hearing this crunching noise, and I wake up to find this big-ass bear head right next to me."

"Holy shit," Yancey said.

Sally motioned her over. "You look like you need to sit down. Come over here by the fire."

On shaky legs, Megan stumbled to the fire and collapsed next to Chaz.

"Eyes still burning real bad?" Sally asked, after they'd used up the first bottle of water.

When Chaz nodded, Sally made her recline her head again, and she poured another bottle carefully over her eyes.

"How you doing, Chaz?" Linda asked, as Chaz sat up, eyes still streaming tears.

She tried to speak, but her throat felt like she'd swallowed acid. She fumbled for the water bottle that Sally had been using and took a few sips. It eased the burning only slightly. "Man, that stuff is awful," she rasped. Her eyes felt a bit better, but she could hardly stand to open them, even to squint. "Someone have a Kleenex?"

Pat handed her one and Chaz dabbed gently at her eyes.

"My fault," Megan croaked out. She was still shaking.

"What?" Chaz turned to face Megan. Her eyes were tiny slits. Tears ran down her cheeks. "What did you say?"

"My fault," Megan repeated. "I left my kit in my bag. He went right for it."

"What was in it?" Sally asked.

"Toothpaste, deodorant." Megan shook her head. "Hand cream. Lip balm. All sorts of stuff. I'm so sorry. I completely forgot about it."

"Don't beat yourself up," Chaz said. "It happens. Everyone's okay. That's all that matters."

Megan looked at Chaz and laid a hand on her shoulder. "I'm really sorry."

Chaz nearly jumped at the touch. "Don't worry about it, I'll be fine," she said as she dabbed some more at her eyes.

"I doubt very much he'll be back, but we should get your stuff and put it in a bear-proof canister to be safe," Sally said to Megan.

Megan nodded and headed to the tent. She came back carrying the remains of her toiletries, a messy collection of chewed tubes and plastic jars. The nylon ditty bag that had contained them was in pieces. Her minty toothpaste and oatmeal face scrub had been crushed by the bear's powerful jaws and sharp teeth, along with everything else that had been in the kit.

"And he got this stuff, too. It was all together," she said. Her head net, makeshift blindfold, and baseball cap were all in shreds.

Megan's friends gathered around her, staring in horrified fascination at the bear's leavings.

"Oh, man," Linda whispered.

"No lie," Justine seconded.

"There are a couple of huge tears in the side of the tent," Megan told Sally.

"I'll get the repair kit," Sally said, getting to her feet. "While I'm fixing that, will someone get Megan a big Ziploc to put all that stuff into, and make sure it gets put in a canister with the rest of the bear-proof stuff?"

"Sure," Pat volunteered. "I'll take care of that."

"I'm coming with you," Linda said.

The two of them took Megan's mangled items and departed to carry out the task, while Justine accompanied Sally to see if she could help repair the tent.

"Do you want me to pour some more water in your eyes?" Elise asked, sitting down next to Chaz.

"No, I'll be all right. Thanks." Chaz kept sipping at the water; it was helping her throat. She still couldn't open her eyes more than a fraction, though.

"Can we get you anything at all?" Yancey asked.

"Thanks, no. You all can stop fussing, I'll be fine," Chaz insisted. "And you really shouldn't worry. I think I got him pretty good. He won't be back."

"I can't believe I was so stupid," Megan said, dropping into the camp chair opposite Chaz.

"Megan, it could have happened to any of us," Yancey said. She walked over to Megan and stooped to give her a reassuring hug.

"It's late," Chaz said after Pat and Linda returned. "Why don't you all try to get some rest."

"Sure there's nothing anybody can do for you?" Elise asked.

Well, maybe not just anybody... The thought flashed through Chaz's mind that she really didn't want Megan to leave, but she pushed the feeling away. "No, I'm just going to stay here a while. You all go on."

Elise leaned toward Chaz. "Let me know if you need anything." She said it with deliberate flirtation, in a voice only Chaz could hear.

You are *persistent*. "Good night, Elise," Chaz replied, with a trace of a smile.

Elise snapped her fingers in disappointment and got up to leave. "Coming?" she asked Megan.

"In a minute," Megan answered.

Sally walked up as the other women drifted away after exchanging good nights. "I patched up the tent for the night with some duct tape. I'll do a more permanent fix tomorrow. How are your eyes?" she asked Chaz.

"I'm fine, quit worrying."

"Can't help it. How about you, Megan? You okay?" Sally asked.

Megan nodded. She had stopped trembling, and her color was back to normal. She stood a few feet away from Chaz, staring off at the horizon.

"Well, I'm going to turn in, then." Sally yawned. "I'd advise you both to do the same."

Low murmurs of conversations could be heard from the tent area, but an uncomfortable silence descended on the pair at the fire.

Finally Megan sat down beside Chaz, about the time Chaz's eyes recovered enough for her to see without squinting. Megan was chewing on her lower lip, and this close to her, in the soft golden light of the midnight sun, Chaz forgot about the bear and even her own discomfort. She was struck by Megan's soft, full lips and silky hair, her delicate pale eyelashes, and the blush of color in her cheeks from all the excitement.

As if she could feel Chaz's eyes on her, Megan turned to meet them with her own. They looked at each other a long moment. Something passed between them, but Chaz couldn't put words to what it was. Something powerful, though. An unspoken understanding of some sort. Maybe it's only the shared near-death experience, she considered, the reaction of two bodies pulsing with adrenalin.

Whatever it was, it was there and suddenly gone, broken when Megan looked away.

A long moment passed in silence before Megan spoke. "I've been kind of a jerk since I got here," she admitted sheepishly. "And I'm sorry for that. As well as being sorry for the stupid mistake that could have gotten us both killed." She looked at Chaz, then, with such vulnerability that it made Chaz's heart clench in her chest, and said, "I hope you're okay."

"I'll be fine." Chaz found she was unable to tear her eyes from Megan's face. "Truly. Don't think any more about it."

Megan moistened her lips. "Thanks, Chaz," she said in a low voice. "I really mean that. I don't know what he would have done if you hadn't reacted so fast to stop him. You risked your life for me."

Chaz could think of nothing then, but how much she wanted to kiss Megan. *What's happening to me?*

"No problem. I'm glad you're okay." She knew her voice sounded husky. She forced her attention back to the fire. "You should turn in. Lots of paddling tomorrow. I'll be along shortly." *If I go back to the tent with her now, I'm not sure I'd able to stop myself from kissing her.*

Megan nodded and got up from her seat. "Whatever you say. Good night." She briefly laid a hand on Chaz's shoulder before retiring to their tent.

The touch lingered long after Megan had gone. *You got it bad, girl,* Chaz admitted to herself. She built up the fire again, too keyed up to sleep and in no hurry to subject herself to the experience of lying beside Megan, unable to touch her. *How will I get through the next week?*

❖

Megan's nerves were on edge, and she felt as though she might jump out of her skin at any moment. The whole episode with the bear had completely unnerved her. It still seemed unreal, like a 3-D movie. She started at every small noise from outside the tent.

But what had left her even more unsettled was the look—the feeling—that had seemed to pass between her and Chaz. There had been a totally unguarded moment between them that had spoken volumes, though she doubted either of them could really explain what it was and what it meant.

It was as though she had briefly glimpsed a sixth sense she never knew she had. *Did Chaz feel it too?* She wondered. *She didn't act like she did, sending me off to bed.*

Whatever it was, it fascinated her—she had never felt more *alive*.

It scared the hell out of her, too. *What was I thinking?* She berated herself as she stared at the ceiling of the tent, waiting anxiously for the sound of Chaz's approaching footsteps.

Pick about the most remote spot on earth for your vacation, where you have absolutely no control over anything. Oh, and make sure you pick somewhere where you can get eaten alive while you sleep. And while you're at it, develop a serious lust for some gorgeous guide who will hardly give you the time of day. Smart. Real smart.

❖

Megan dreamt of the bear.

She was, frankly, surprised that she'd fallen asleep at all, but when the adrenalin rush had worn off, she had crashed big-time, her body finally succumbing to the sleepless nights and the exertions and excitement of the day.

Sometime around three in the morning, she'd awakened in a cold sweat, thrashing furiously in her sleeping bag, desperate to escape the dream bear's clutches. She was instantly enfolded in the comforting arms of a sleepy Chaz, who held her and murmured reassurances until they both fell back asleep.

When she awoke the next morning, she was alone.

CHAPTER NINE

Chaz was grateful the clients all wanted to talk about the bear. Between their requests to hear her retelling of last night's encounter and her duties preparing breakfast, she was too distracted to think much about waking up with Megan in her arms.

But the memory did surface every time she got a moment to herself, and she couldn't help glancing in the direction of the tents. Everyone was up and eating except for Megan, who had been out cold when Chaz had gotten up an hour and a half earlier. They were all loath to disturb her, after the fright she'd had, and there was no need to rush to get on the river, anyway. Their next campsite was not far downstream.

How the hell do I react when I see her? What do I say?

Chaz had awakened slowly that morning and had briefly felt as though she must still be dreaming, so unaccustomed was she to waking up next to someone. Especially quite like this. She had found herself wrapped protectively around Megan, hugging her from behind, one arm loosely draped around her neck, the other around her waist and... *Oh, my.* Her right hand was inside Megan's T-shirt, pressed against the warm, soft flesh of her stomach, which moved slightly with each slow, deep breath.

She was spooning Megan as though they did this every night.

Initially, she was shocked to find herself thus, but then she vaguely remembered that Megan had had a nightmare. She'd had them herself— nightmares of being chased—the summer that a grizzly followed her for miles during a solo backpacking trip near Denali. She'd wanted Megan to feel safe. She remembered that much, but not much else. *I certainly didn't intend to sleep like that all night.*

Once the initial shock had worn off, and she realized that Megan seemed to be deeply asleep, Chaz had pushed her nagging conscience aside and allowed herself a few totally self-indulgent minutes just to...

relish where she was. A moment to memorize the feel of Megan's skin against her palm. Her hand ached to go exploring, but she refused to allow it. It took every ounce of her willpower to remain still.

She closed her eyes and inhaled the delicate herbal scent of Megan's shampoo, delighting in the press of their bodies against each other. Their legs and lower torsos were separated by their sleeping bags, but during the night, they had somehow managed to unzip the tops of the bags so they could snuggle closer together.

Her breasts were pressed up against Megan's back, and she was all too suddenly aware that her nipples were achingly hard. *Uh, oh. She better not wake up when I'm like this.*

With excruciating slowness, she had extricated herself from their embrace, trying desperately not to wake Megan. Only once did Megan show any sign of rousing. When Chaz's body separated from hers, she let out a soft sigh, a moan of disappointment that made Chaz's heart skip a beat.

She kept hearing that sigh.

Don't go there, she tried to tell herself. *She's a client. Just a client. Just a client.* She kept saying it over and over, trying to imprint it on every fiber of her being, but her body was having none of it. It had had a taste of Megan, and it wanted more.

❖

Megan joined them just before nine, looking relaxed and rested. Chaz caught sight of her as soon as she left their tent, and Megan sought out her eyes, too, and held them, as she approached the eating and cooking area.

Before she had a chance to say anything, Pat and Justine corralled her with questions.

"How are you?" Pat inquired. "Still shaken up a bit?"

"Did you get some sleep?" Justine asked.

"Actually, I slept pretty well," Megan replied with a half smile. She looked in Chaz's direction and her smile got bigger. "All things considered."

Chaz could have sworn she saw a twinkle in her eyes. *Oh, shit. Well, that answers that. She apparently remembers me holding her. So the question now is, does she also know how much I enjoyed it?*

Chaz was blushing, Megan realized. Her spirits were buoyed by the sight. She'd felt a jarringly unexpected sense of loss when she'd awakened alone, and the sight of the huge rip in the tent did nothing to cheer her. But Chaz was a balm to her frayed nerves this morning, just as she'd been last night.

"Get yourself some breakfast," Sally said, coming up behind Megan and putting a hand on her back. "We saved you some. We've got fruit and granola, and Chaz made some blueberry muffins."

"They're awesome," Yancey threw in. "If you don't want yours, we've decided to draw straws for them."

"Not a chance," Megan declared, stealing another glance at Chaz, who was drying some of the breakfast dishes. "I haven't held us all up, have I?"

"Oh, no, not at all," Sally replied. "We only have a short ways to go today. We aren't going to leave until after lunch."

"I'd like everybody to practice wet exits and Eskimo rolls this morning," Chaz said. "We're going to start hitting some of the rougher water soon. Are you up to it?"

"Sure," Megan said.

As soon as she'd eaten both of her muffins, which were every bit as good as promised, everyone donned their dry suits and took to the water in their kayaks.

Chaz first spent an hour or so conducting a seminar on river currents, describing the way the speed of the water changed as it flowed around curves and through narrows, and she briefed them on the different types of eddies they would encounter—pockets of calmer water that form in the downstream sides of rocks and boulders—and how to deal with them.

After that, they took turns tossing the rescue throw ropes that she'd issued them, until all were fairly good at it, at least in the calmer water.

As they practiced, the weather began to deteriorate. The temperature dropped twenty degrees as a low ceiling of clouds swept over the land, obliterating the sun and dumping a steady drizzle of rain that showed no sign of stopping.

"All right. I'd like to see everyone do at least a couple of wet exits and two or three rolls," Chaz said. "Sally is going to watch Pat, Linda, and Yancey, and I'm going to work with Elise, Megan, and Justine."

They divided into two small groups and took turns practicing wet exits first, with no problems. When it came time to do the rolls, Chaz beached her kayak and waded out into the current, to help them as needed as she had back at the lodge.

"Let's be perfect at this, so we can all go in and get warm, what do you say?" Chaz encouraged them as they lined their kayaks up in front of her, paddling to remain in place against the current. She went briefly over the fundamentals again, then they took turns: Justine first, Elise second, Megan last.

Justine managed to do three rolls in fairly quick succession with little help. Elise needed assistance on the first couple of tries, but then got it on her own. Then it was Megan's turn.

Everyone else had gone in. She and Chaz were alone. And Chaz was looking as sexy as hell, with her face pink and eyes shining from the cold. Megan was having a very hard time focusing on all the details that she needed to remember to do the roll right.

Chaz moved into position at the front of Megan's kayak, all businesslike. "Ready?" she asked.

Nothing at all in her demeanor suggested that she had any recollection of the hours they'd spent wrapped in each other's arms. It was time to remind her.

"Thank you for last night," Megan said, with exaggerated provocation. She said it as though they had spent the night having mind-blowing sex.

She was thrilled to see the look that passed over Chaz's face at her words. Chaz went crimson in embarrassment and looked shyly away, as a smile tugged at the corners of her mouth.

"Yeah, well, uh…" Chaz stuttered, tapping her fingers nervously on the end of Megan's kayak. "No problem. I've had nightmares before, too."

Oh, this is good. Very good. Last night was something to her, too.

"Chaz?" She said her name, very deliberately, because she really wanted Chaz to look at her right then.

Finally, after a very long moment, Chaz did, and Megan fell into the depths of those hazel eyes, a mere five feet away, that were gazing at her with such…*heat*. That was the word for it. *She wants me. I can see she wants me as much as I want her.*

"Last night…" she began, searching her mind for the right words, suddenly wishing she'd thought about what she was going to say. Normally she had no problem seducing women, but she felt tongue-tied half the time with Chaz, and she really didn't want to screw this up.

She didn't bother analyzing why this felt different to her than any relationship she could remember. Too much time passed, and Chaz looked away—she could see that Chaz was struggling to regain the professional demeanor that was her trademark.

"Chaz, I can't tell you how much what you did last night meant to me." The words poured out of her in a rush. "Risking your life with the bear, and then…then…" *Making me feel safe*, she wanted to say, but she couldn't admit feeling vulnerable, even to Chaz.

"Helping with your nightmare," Chaz finished for her. "Like I said, no problem. Are you ready to try a roll?"

The heat was totally gone now. The woman who had held her in her arms had changed back into the professional guide. Megan wanted to say something that would put that look back in Chaz's eyes, but perhaps now was not the time. She was freezing, and so was Chaz. There would be time enough later, at their next campsite.

"I guess I'm ready," she said, forcing her mind back to the details of the difficult maneuver. She wanted Chaz to be proud of her.

She got it on the first try. It looked a bit ungainly, to be sure, but she did it all by herself. And three more times, before they went in.

"That was really great, Megan," Chaz complimented her as they walked back to join the others. "You should be really pleased with how well you've taken to this."

She *was* pretty proud of herself, at that.

❖

After a hot lunch, they packed up their tents and headed downriver to their next campsite. It was only a three-hour paddle, and the current carried them along at an ever-quickening pace as the river narrowed and deepened. They had to be more alert to obstructions—rocks and boulders of various sizes were scattered everywhere, and here and there, a branch or log had stuck on something.

They were still in a forest of spruce and alder and cottonwoods, alive with birdsong and the scattered sounds of other small animals, but the mountains on either side were closing in, the river leading them into a narrow valley.

The stopping point that Chaz selected looked very much like the place they had camped the night before. There was a nice flat spot for the tents, surrounded by a spruce forest where there would again be ample wood for a fire. And a fire would be most welcome; though the drizzle had stopped, it was decidedly colder than it had been thus far in the trip, with temperatures falling into the forties.

"We have vegetable lasagna on the menu tonight," Chaz announced to the group as they unloaded the raft. "Would anyone like me to supplement that with some fish again, provided they're biting, of course?"

Several hands shot up, and Linda enthused, "That was fabulous last night."

"Yeah, prepared so simply—and so fresh. It was probably the best fish I've had in a long while," Yancey said.

Megan smiled. "I think you better catch enough for all of us, again."

"I'll do my best," Chaz said, reaching for her fishing gear. "Oh, by the way," she said to Megan, "Don't bother to put up the tent. Sally's going to take a look at it after dinner and try to do a better repair job."

"Okay. Well, if I don't have that to do, is there anything I can do to help you?"

Chaz shook her head. "No, thanks. I've got this. You can gather up some wood for a fire, if you like."

"Sure."

As Megan walked away, Chaz followed her with her eyes. She thought back to the presumptions she'd made about Megan from her registration form. *She's certainly no Muffy.* She hadn't complained about the food or the primitive conditions. She offered to help out and pitched in eagerly. And Chaz had the impression she really did appreciate the pristine surroundings and adventure she was on.

You were wrong about her, she admitted. *What else are you wrong about?*

❖

Chaz's fishing acumen landed them each another fine grayling filet for dinner, in addition to the lasagna and garlic bread they had planned. They divvied up the chores, and so by seven p.m., they were all stuffed, the dishes were done, the garbage and leftovers safely stowed away from bears, and a nice campfire was blazing.

One by one, as they finished their tasks and changed into warmer clothes, the women regrouped around the fire bowl as they had done the night before.

Sally spread the torn tent out next to her and began to sew it up. "I hope we don't get a bad storm. Even with seam seal, this probably won't be watertight any more, and the rain fly has a big tear in it, too."

"More probing questions, anyone?" Elise asked as she pulled up a camp chair and joined the rest. Only Chaz was absent.

"I'm game. That was fun," Pat said.

"But we should wait for Chaz," Megan put in. *Her answers are the ones I'm most interested in.* She started thinking about what question she would ask, when it was her turn. *I could do "What turns you on?" That's not bad.*

"Here she comes now," Sally said, and, sure enough, Chaz was just cresting the low rise that had hidden her from view.

"Are you up for some more probing questions?" Elise called out as Chaz got within earshot.

"If you like," Chaz answered agreeably. "Although I have an alternative that some of you might like to try."

"Do tell, we're all ears," Elise prompted, in a flirtatious way that Megan found really annoying.

"When I was here last year, I stumbled on a very nice feature of this particular place," Chaz said. "About a three-minute walk downstream…" she pointed in the direction she'd just come from, "there is a really nice hot spring, big enough for two, right next to the river."

"A hot spring?" Elise repeated with interest.

"Dibs first!" Linda jumped to her feet and reached down to pull Pat up with her.

"Hey, not so fast! We're all going to want to go," Justine protested.

"Yeah, I sure want some of that," Elise added. "Hey, Chaz, want to pair up with me?"

Oh, no, you don't, Megan thought, jumping in before Chaz could reply. "We should draw straws or something to see who goes when. That would be the fair thing to do."

"My thinking exactly," Chaz said, reaching into her pocket and pulling out a bunch of small pieces of paper. "There are eight slips here," she said, cupping them in her hand. "Each has a number from one through eight. One and two get the first shift, three and four the second, and so on. Trading is allowed. Does that work for everyone?"

They all nodded agreement, so Chaz went around the circle and let them each choose a slip of paper.

"Is this ever going to feel good on my aching back and shoulders," Yancey said, as she selected her number.

"My replacement is going to have to pry me out of there," Justine agreed. "We should set a time limit. Half an hour or something?"

"That sounds good," Megan said, reaching up for her slip when it was her turn to choose. *Please please please let me be paired with Chaz.*

"Okay, who's got what?" Chaz said when the slips had all been distributed.

"I'm number one!" Justine said.

"I'm with you, then," Yancey said, holding up her slip. "Number two."

"I've got three," Linda said.

"Damn. I'm five," Pat said. "Who's got four?"

"That would be me," Elise said. "And yes, I'll trade so you can be with your honey. Never let it be said that I stand in the way of hot tub luuuve."

They all laughed.

"I have six," Chaz said.

Shit. Just my luck. Though Megan couldn't help but notice that Chaz didn't seem entirely happy about being paired with Elise. Or was that wishful thinking?

"Then that leaves Megan and me last," Sally said. "Which means you all better not exceed your time limits!"

"Come pry us out of there when our half hour is up," Yancey called out, as she and Justine headed to their tents to get their towels and swimsuits.

The six who remained by the fire made small talk about the things they had seen that day and what was ahead of them, while Sally worked on repairing the tent, and Chaz kept the fire stoked. After a while, Linda and Pat departed for their turn at the hot spring.

"That was unbelievably wonderful," Justine reported when she returned to the campfire a short time later, her skin pink and glowing. "It's not only great on the sore muscles, but what a setting for a soak!"

"Yeah, the river is kind of dreamlike in this light," Yancey agreed, reclaiming her seat. "It's all salmon-colored, with soft edges."

"I can't wait for our turn," Elise said to Chaz.

I bet you can't. Megan suddenly had a flashback of Chaz sunbathing nude on the rock after her swim. *Maybe she never wears a swimsuit if she's only got women clients. She's so cavalier about it.* Her irritation grew. *She better not get naked with Elise, or Elise will be all over her. She probably will be, regardless.*

She began to regret that she didn't make a try sooner for Chaz. *Sally said she doesn't like to make the first move. If you wait for her, you'll wait forever...or Elise will beat you to the punch.*

"Well, this is done, as best as I can fix it," Sally said, holding up the tent and rain fly, both of which bore neat rows of stitches along the rips the bear had made. Over the stitches, she had liberally applied seam sealant. "I think it's dry enough to put up."

"I'll take care of that," Chaz said, getting to her feet and gathering up the tent. "Then it'll be about time for our turn," she told Elise. "I'll meet you there in a few minutes?"

Oh, I'll be there," Elise said, with such delight in her voice that Megan cringed.

Count to ten, Megan, just count to ten.

❖

Chaz set up the tent in a couple of minutes and went inside to put on her swimsuit, a navy one-piece. When she exited for the hot spring, she could hear Elise in the next tent getting changed, but she didn't wait for her. Elise wasn't taking the hint that she wasn't interested in her flirtations. Perhaps, she thought, it was time to be a tad more direct.

At least she wasn't paired up with Megan. That might have been awkward. The hot springs setting *was* pretty romantic, she had to admit, and she didn't know what seeing so much of Megan's body might do to her self-control. She had never before felt an attraction like this for a client.

She heard laughter through the trees as she approached the hot spring, then voices. She stopped in her tracks when she heard her name and then Megan's. Curious, she edged forward until she could make out what Linda and Pat were saying.

"No way. It's Megan or neither one of them. She hasn't looked twice at Elise." Linda's voice.

"Yeah, but Elise can be persistent," Pat argued. "You know she'll try to seduce Chaz when they get in here together. And not many can resist Elise when she's determined."

"Well, it's obvious Megan has the hots for her, too. She can't keep her eyes off her."

She can't, eh? Chaz knew she shouldn't be eavesdropping, but this conversation was one she didn't want to interrupt.

"I can't understand why Megan hasn't made a play for her yet. She's certainly no wallflower," Pat said.

Linda laughed. "Yeah, I wondered the same thing. She usually moves right in for the kill when she spots a good target. Doesn't take her ten minutes to find someone at the club and leave with them."

"I don't know that I've ever seen Elise and Megan go after the same woman before," Pat mused. "They're both so competitive. I wonder if they have a bet going as to which one of them will get her?"

"I wouldn't be surprised. Megan sure isn't used to hearing no," Linda said.

"Elise, either. I hope this doesn't cause a problem between the two of them after this trip," Pat said.

"Nah, that'll never happen. They'll both have moved on to someone else within a week, anyway."

Pat laughed again. "Too true."

Chaz felt a bit sick to her stomach. *That's what you get for eavesdropping.* But perhaps it was all for the best. It was yet another reason she couldn't, and wouldn't, get involved with Megan.

She took a moment to compose herself, then stepped out of the trees. "Hi, ladies. I think your time is about up."

"Hey, Chaz," Pat greeted her. "This has been glorious. I don't suppose we have time for another soak in the morning before we leave?"

"Not unless you get one in before breakfast," she said. "Tomorrow's destination is a pretty good distance downstream, and I want to get an early start. It's the stop where we'll have the best chance of getting a good view of the caribou herd."

"I can't wait for that," Linda enthused. She and Pat got out and dried themselves off.

"Can't wait for what?" Elise appeared out of the trees.

"We'll see the caribou tomorrow," Pat said.

"We hope." Chaz stepped gingerly into the hot water. "You can't really predict where they'll be, but I was watching them before we left. They've radio-collared a bunch of them, and you can track where they are on the Internet."

"Okay, guys, shoo! Our turn," Elise said, dropping her towel to reveal a skimpy black bikini that left very little to the imagination.

"We can take a hint," Pat said, chuckling, as she and Linda headed back to the others.

As she watched Elise slip into the water beside her, Chaz had to admit that the woman was way above average in the looks department. Her body would certainly make anyone look twice, but it wasn't the body Chaz wanted.

"So, finally, I have you alone," Elise purred, leering at Chaz like she wanted to eat her alive.

"Down, girl," Chaz rebuked gently with a smile. She leaned her head back against the smooth rock side of the hot spring and closed her eyes. The water was roughly chest deep, so she relaxed with her knees slightly bent to keep only her head above water.

"Aw, don't be a wet blanket. You don't mean that, now, do you?" Elise pouted slightly.

Chaz cracked open an eye. "Believe me, I'm flattered, but it's not going to happen." She closed her eyes again in an effort to end the pursuit.

"Can I ask why not?"

"A lot of reasons. First and foremost, you're a client, and I don't go there," Chaz drawled lazily. The hot water really did feel amazing on such a cold and dreary day. She'd stayed at this stop a couple of days the year before, primarily because of this special feature.

"Why don't you go there?" Elise persisted. "What's wrong with two consenting adults having some fun?"

"I don't think it's ethical for a guide to sleep with a client. This is a dangerous place, and I have a responsibility to all of you," Chaz said seriously. "I can't have my judgment compromised by personal feelings. And I can't favor one client over another. There are a lot of other reasons why not."

Chaz thought she'd finally gotten through to Elise, for a long quiet fell between them. In fact, she nearly dozed, lulled by the heat and the steady cascade of water from the river beside them. Her mind wandered back to that morning and the thrill of waking up holding Megan.

The next thing she knew, she felt a touch—so light it was almost a whisper—run slowly up her leg from calf to thigh. She reached down and gently intercepted Elise's hand before it got any higher.

"Somehow I think I'm not getting through to you," she said, opening her eyes to find Elise poised to pounce, her lips inches away from her own. "Elise, I—"

But Elise was not going to let her make any further objections. She closed in for the kill. Her right hand shot out and wrapped around Chaz's neck, and she pulled their faces together for a searing kiss.

For a brief moment, Chaz was too startled to respond at all. Then her mind registered that *Oh, man, her lips are so soft*, and it had been a long while since she'd been kissed like that, and she really *liked* kissing, and Elise sure did know *how* to kiss, oh, yes, indeed she did, and she couldn't kiss the woman she really *wanted* to kiss, so…

"No!" she said, breathless, as she pushed away from Elise and held her at arm's length. It was only then that she realized that Elise had taken off her bikini.

Elise frowned. In a sexy half whisper, she said, "Now, I know you were enjoying that as much as I was." She inched closer as though she was going to take another shot as soon as she saw an opening.

It was a very small pool, and there wasn't anywhere for Chaz to go. "Look, Elise, I'm not going to deny you're a great kisser. But it's still not going to happen."

"I bet I can change your mind," Elise predicted.

"No, Elise." Chaz injected a note of finality into her voice that was unmistakable. "I'm sorry, but no means no. If you're going to persist, I'm going to get out right now."

Elise's expression changed and she backed away. "There's no need to do that," she said dejectedly.

Sensing Elise's feelings were bruised, Chaz said, "I'm sorry. I don't want this to be awkward, and I don't want to hurt your feelings. You're a beautiful woman, and like I said, I'm very flattered. But I'm not into one-night stands, even if you weren't a client."

Elise let out a big sigh. "Oh, well. Can't blame a girl for trying."

Just then, Sally's voice rang out, "Time's up! Everyone out of the pool!"

Chaz turned to see Sally and Megan approaching through the trees. Megan had the oddest expression on her face. She looked as though she'd just lost her best friend.

CHAPTER TEN

After Chaz and Elise left for the hot spring, time had seemed to slow to a crawl for Megan. She kept glancing at her watch and wondering what the two of them were up to. She was certain Elise would try to take advantage of the situation, and the pictures that formed in her mind were not at all welcome ones.

After fifteen minutes had elapsed, she excused herself and went to change into her swimsuit, telling Sally she wanted to make a pit stop before their turn and would meet her there. In reality, she wanted to satisfy her curiosity about what was happening, so she intended to get to the hot spring a little early, alone.

She'd approached through the trees as silently as possible, grateful for the soft cushion of spongy moss beneath her feet. She strained to hear voices, but the only sounds she heard were the soft ripples of white noise from the river, and the chorus of bird songs that seemed to accompany them everywhere.

Her first glimpse of the two of them through the trees had confirmed her worst fears. Chaz had her head leaned back against the side of the pool, eyes closed with a hint of a smile on her face, the picture of contentment, while Elise loomed close, watching Chaz with a dreamy expression. Beside them, tossed haphazardly on a rock, was Elise's bikini. *Shit. Shit. Shit.*

Megan couldn't tear her eyes away, and neither could she move or announce her presence. She had to see what happened next.

Her heart sank when she saw Elise move in even closer to Chaz, so close that she was certain their bodies had to be touching beneath the turbulent surface of the water. Then Chaz opened her eyes and said something—but it was too far for her to make out the words. Whatever it was, it made Elise smile and reach for her.

A moment later, they were kissing.

She couldn't watch any more. *That's what you get for being so damned curious.* The image of the two of them locked in each other's arms was burned into her brain.

Megan retreated soundlessly a few dozen yards back into the trees where she could no longer see them. A turmoil of emotions welled up in her—anger, disappointment, longing, lust, envy, jealousy. She was furious that she was upset at all, that being with Chaz seemed to matter so much to her.

She didn't know what to do. Sally would be along any moment. How would she explain the fact that she was just standing here, all by herself, shaking in rage and frustration?

She took several deep breaths and told herself it didn't matter. So she'd been beaten to the punch. Big deal. She'd go home in a week, find a new bed partner, and forget all about this in no time at all.

No time at all. It sounded good, but she had a hard time believing it.

When she glimpsed Sally approaching through the trees, she'd willed herself to be calm and composed. She could put on a mask better than anyone. Royal Ice Bitch. She'd had lots of practice.

"Hey, Megan," Sally hailed her when she got nearer. "Couldn't you find the hot spring?"

"I got waylaid here watching some birds," Megan lied. "Then I heard you coming and thought I'd wait for you."

"Well, let's go. They've had their thirty minutes." Sally had led the way. "Time's up! Everyone out of the pool!" she hollered as they neared the hot spring.

Megan wanted to look anywhere but at Chaz, afraid she might not be able to disguise her tumultuous feelings over what she had seen. She didn't want Chaz to know what effect she was having on her. Chaz made her feel vulnerable, and at the moment, she didn't like that one bit.

She glanced at Elise as Elise got out of the pool and reached for her towel. She did have a great body, Megan had to admit. All lean and tanned, and Elise was apparently just as comfortable with nudity as Chaz was. *No wonder Chaz couldn't resist her.* Fury poured through her, though she knew she was being unfair. Elise was her friend, and she had no right to be ticked off just because she'd been first to take advantage of a great opportunity. *I had my chances.*

Tears sprang unexpectedly to her eyes, and she looked away, out at the river. She was aware that Chaz was getting out of the water—she could see movement out of the corner of her eye—but she didn't dare turn around.

"That half hour passed much too quickly," Elise sighed, from behind her. "Have fun, girls." Her voice trailed away as she headed back toward the fire.

"Well, if anyone wants another round, they can come replace us," Sally called out as she got into the water.

Megan blinked back the tears as she unwrapped the towel she had around her and turned to join Sally. She thought Chaz had departed with Elise, so she jumped when she discovered Chaz standing behind her, watching her with interest.

"Are you all right?" Chaz asked.

She felt a sharp jolt of joy bounce through her when she saw Chaz's eyes travel south to check out her swimsuit. She involuntarily sucked in a breath, her chest expanding to emphasize how well the skimpy fabric of the bikini top barely held in her ample breasts. She could have sworn she saw Chaz's eyes dilate.

But then Chaz looked away.

"Yes, I'm fine," she said, with as much nonchalance as she could muster. Having Chaz's eyes on her breasts, however briefly, had stirred her blood and made her feel warm despite the chill in the air.

She stepped around Chaz and got into the pool, her mind replaying the kiss she'd witnessed, her body wishing that she'd been the one who had put that contented half smile on Chaz's face. Heat enveloped her as she sank into the water up to her chin, and she floated, swiveling slowly around to find that Chaz had gone.

"I don't mean to pry. Or belabor the point," Sally said. "But are you sure everything is okay? You seem a lot more...I don't know, subdued...than you were by the fire."

"Just...preoccupied, I guess." Megan tried to relax. "Nothing to worry about. But thanks."

Nothing to worry about. She breathed slowly in and out, trying to dispel the whole business from her mind. She sought out the familiar, so, for the first time in days, she thought about work and wondered how the newsroom was faring. *You're needed there*, she told herself, and it brought a small measure of comfort to her state of unsettled frustration.

But it was short-lived. *What does that say about you, that the only thing that needs you is your job?*

She had accomplished a lot and had money, respect, prestige, connections. But she had always dreamed of achieving something truly meaningful, and she wasn't at all certain she'd managed to do that. And in getting to where she was now, she'd given up a tremendous amount, too, she realized.

Suddenly her life felt like it didn't fit quite right, like a pair of shoes she'd outgrown. It wasn't nearly as comfortable as it was when she'd arrived in Alaska. And she wondered whether it was the vastness of the landscape itself that was responsible for her discontent, or a certain dark-haired guide.

The hot spring managed to act as one dandy natural sleeping pill, with all the clients retiring early to their tents. When the last pair had finished their turn and returned to the campsite, only Chaz remained by the fire.

"I'm going to turn in, too," Megan told Sally, detouring toward her tent as soon as she spotted Chaz. "Good night."

"Good night," Sally replied. "Sleep well."

Megan kept trying to dispel the mental image of Chaz and Elise kissing as she readied for bed and snuggled into her sleeping bag. It wasn't easy with Chaz's things in the tent beside her.

Giving in to an impulse, she reached for Chaz's small camping pillow and pressed it against her face, inhaling the faint smell of wood smoke from the fire and a subtle trace of something else—shampoo, probably, since Chaz didn't seem the perfume type. It was earthy, like the woman herself, and it took her back to the night before, when Chaz had held her in her arms.

It does no good to think about things that cannot be, she reminded herself, setting the pillow reluctantly back at the head of Chaz's sleeping bag. But as soon as she relaxed and closed her eyes, she remembered the way it felt to be enfolded against the long length of Chaz's body, and despite her better judgment, she wished for it to happen again.

❖

Chaz noted with disappointment that Megan went directly to their tent from the hot spring. She had rather hoped to get another opportunity to talk to her, to ask her why she'd looked so troubled and sad. But Megan was apparently either too tired, or determined to act as though nothing was wrong.

"What a wonderful find that hot spring was." Sally sank into a camp chair beside Chaz. She had changed into warm clothes and hung her towel and swimsuit on a line they'd strung between two trees. "Why didn't you tell me about it?"

"Because if I had, I'm sure the clients and I would have found all sorts of hidden surprises in there, knowing you. Fake water moccasins or something."

Sally had to chuckle. "Oh, it's all in fun. You're such a wet blanket, sometimes, Chaz. You need to lighten up."

"Someone has to be the adult."

"Speaking of lightening up…What's wrong with Megan? She was acting kind of funny, wasn't she? Not that she hasn't been kind of hot and cold since we got here."

"I noticed that, too," Chaz said. "She seemed to be okay here at the fire. Did something happen after I left? Somebody say something to her?"

"No. She was kind of quiet after you and Elise left, but she seemed fine. You know what was kind of odd? We didn't walk to the hot spring together—she left before I did and was just kind of hanging out in the trees between here and there when I found her. She said she was bird-watching, but come to think of it, that's really when she first seemed kind of…I don't know, distracted, I guess. Maybe upset, too, though she was hiding it well. I asked her about it while we were soaking, but she said she was just preoccupied."

The wheels began to spin in Chaz's mind. "Where exactly was she when you found her?"

"Oh, not far at all from the hot spring. A couple dozen yards into the trees, probably. I was kind of surprised to find her there."

"Oh, shit." She hadn't meant to say it out loud. *She saw us kissing, didn't she? And she was upset about it. Why would she be upset?*

"What?" Sally asked. "What is it?"

"Oh, nothing."

"C'mon, you can't do that. Spill. Do you know why she was acting funny?"

Chaz sighed. *I just can't catch a break. Why did she have to see that?* "Maybe she saw Elise and me kissing."

"*What*? You want to repeat that? I've got to be hearing things."

"You heard me. Maybe she saw Elise and me kissing. And no, I didn't kiss *her*, she kissed *me*. It only lasted a second. Well, maybe a few seconds. I was kind of in shock when she did it. But I set her straight, and it won't happen again."

"I thought Megan was the one you were interested in."

"She is," Chaz said, before she realized what she was admitting. "I mean, she *is* the one I'm attracted to, not Elise, but nothing is going to happen with either of them."

"So Megan was ticked off that you were kissing Elise," Sally recapped. "That's an interesting development. Sure proof that she's interested in you, or she wouldn't be jealous."

"What makes you think she's jealous?" *Could she be? Or is that just wishful thinking? There are certainly other possibilities.* "Maybe she was embarrassed that she nearly walked in on something she thought was a private moment."

"Yeah, right," Sally guffawed. "You keep telling yourself that. I think this is proof she's as hot for you as you are for her, not that I didn't suspect that already."

"Would you stop with this matchmaking stuff?" Chaz replied, exasperated. "It's giving me a headache."

"No, your headache is from your conscience telling you that maybe you shouldn't be turning away from an opportunity like this," Sally said. "C'mon, Chaz. You like Megan and she likes you. I think you'll regret it if you don't see where this might lead."

"Enough."

"Oh, all right." Sally relented. "For now." She got to her feet. "Coming to bed?"

"Later," Chaz said. "Good night."

"Don't sit up too late. You really don't have to—I think she'll be asleep soon, anyway."

Just to be sure, Chaz stayed up another hour, watching the light change as the midnight sun rolled along the horizon. Was Megan really jealous? Or was she ticked off? Pat's words rang again in her ears. Maybe Megan and Elise *did* have a bet going. Maybe they had wagered on who would kiss her first, and Megan had lost. Either way, it was doing her no good to worry and obsess about it, so she extinguished the fire and returned to the tent.

Despite the dim light, she could see that Megan was fast asleep. She looked so adorable, lying on her side in a half-fetal position, that Chaz couldn't help but take advantage of the chance to spend a few moments watching her. Her shoulder-length brown hair was tousled, and a strand near her face moved with each gentle exhalation. It was all Chaz could do not to reach down and smooth it away, caress the cheek it rested against. She couldn't remember the last time she'd wanted to touch someone quite so much.

Quietly, she got into her own bag and ignored an overwhelming urge to cuddle closer, to spoon their bodies together as they had the night before.

CHAPTER ELEVEN

The next morning Megan awoke alone again, with no memory of Chaz having been in the tent at all. But obviously she had been, because her sleeping bag was unzipped, and her things had been moved around.

She reached for Chaz's pillow almost without realizing she was doing so, and this time when she brought it to her face, that same scent was stronger, like Chaz had been lying on it only moments before. An ache passed through her as she set it back down. *Why does it matter so much?* she asked herself, but she didn't allow herself to think about it too closely or too long. *Get over it. Get up and get dressed and enjoy the rest of your time in Alaska.*

She slithered out of her mummy sleeping bag like a snake shedding its skin and reached for a new set of clothes.

"Knock, knock," Sally's voice hailed her from outside the tent. "Megan, you awake?"

"Yes," she responded. "Getting dressed. I'll be out in a minute."

"Do you mind if I have a word with you? It's kind of personal."

Megan went to the door flap, unzipped it, and stuck her head outside. "Sure. What's up?"

Sally came over and stooped until they were roughly at eye level. "Well, I, uh…I talked to Chaz last night." Megan's ears perked up. "Look, this is really none of my business, I know." Sally looked at the ground. "And if I'm out of line, I apologize in advance."

"What it is, Sally?" Megan was intrigued.

"Well, I only wanted to say that if you *were* upset about something last night…" Sally looked at Megan then. "And that something involved Chaz…"

Her heartbeat sped up. *Oh, shit. Is it that obvious?*

"Then I thought you should know that maybe you didn't see what you thought you saw."

It took a moment for the words to sink in. "Excuse me?"

"If you got to the hot spring early and saw something that upset you, I think maybe you misunderstood what you were seeing."

Megan's mind raced. She wanted to deny that she knew what Sally was talking about, but if what she was saying was true..."Let's say you're right," she said. "How do you know I misunderstood?"

Sally bit her lip like she didn't really want to answer. "Because Chaz told me that Elise kissed her last night...and she thought you might have seen them." Her eyes found Megan's. "She also told me that it took her by surprise, and she told Elise not to do it again."

"Really?" Megan's funk lifted instantly.

"Really," Sally confirmed with a smile. "She's not attracted to Elise. She's more interested in someone else." She winked at Megan and left.

Well. Well. Well. This is certainly an interesting development, now, isn't it?

❖

Chaz first suspected something was up when she spotted Sally approaching from the direction of the tents with an impish grin. When their eyes met, Sally began whistling tunelessly as though the picture of innocence.

"What are you up to?" Chaz asked.

"Nothing. Nothing at all," Sally replied, as she set to work getting out utensils and plates for breakfast.

Chaz was busy cooking omelets and hash browns over a pair of stoves and didn't have time to put Sally under the third degree, but she suspected some kind of plot was being hatched.

The clincher was the happy smile on Megan's face and the glimmer in her eyes when she appeared a minute or two later.

Something's going on.

"That smells wonderful," Megan said, choosing the chair beside her. "And I could eat a horse! Can I help?"

"No, thanks," Chaz said, relieved that Megan's dark cloud had disappeared, but in a quandary about why. *Sally better not have said anything to her.*

She had decided, after lying awake next to Megan for nearly two hours last night, listening to her breathe, that it probably was just as well Megan had cooled toward her again, regardless of the reasons why. It would make it a lot easier to get through the next week.

But now things had flip-flopped again. Megan certainly was looking friendly at the moment. Entirely *too* friendly. Every time Chaz glanced in Megan's direction, she found Megan watching her. Watching her like a cat watches a bird in a cage, with heavy-lidded eyes and this bemused half smile on her face...*like she has definite plans for you, later on.*

Feeling Megan's eyes on her was getting her way too distracted and way too excited. The hand holding the spatula began to shake.

"Chaz?" Megan said softly.

She loved hearing her name said like that. She turned her head to look at Megan and found that Megan was grinning from ear to ear and looking incredibly sexy, her shoulder-length hair tousled from sleep. "Yes?" she managed, her voice sounding a lot lower than usual.

"I think those are done." Megan gestured toward the pan that held the hash browns. The way she said it gave Chaz a sneaking suspicion that Megan was suppressing snorts of laughter.

Sally, standing a few feet away, started chuckling.

The pan was smoking. The hash browns were burnt to a crisp.

"Shit!" Chaz dumped that batch onto a plate. "Those are mine," she grumbled.

Sally and Megan both erupted into mirth.

"Wise guys. You two..." Chaz pointed to Sally with the spatula and then Megan. But before she could say anything more, the other clients began to amble up, and she let it drop and started more hash browns cooking.

"Coffeeeeeee. I need coffeeeee," Pat groaned, bleary-eyed.

"Sit," Linda said. "I'll get you some, honey."

"Hash browns!" Yancey peered into one of the fry pans. "And omelets, too! I can't believe how well we're eating on this trip."

"I'll second that," Justine said. "I'm glad we're getting so much exercise or I'd really be gaining weight."

"So today is caribou day, right?" Elise asked.

"No guarantees," Chaz said. "But yes, our best chance of seeing a good group of them is at our next campsite."

"I can't *wait*," Megan said, and the tone of her voice made Chaz wonder if she was taking about the caribou or something else.

❖

They had a long paddle to get there, through more gloriously breathtaking scenery. There were fewer and fewer trees as they went along, and finally the river curved out of the valley they'd been in and cut through a pass between the mountains, then emerged onto a wide sweeping landscape characterized by low rolling hills of emerald green tundra, surrounded by distant, snowcapped peaks.

The water was getting swifter all the time as the river dropped in elevation, cascading over rocks and split in channels by boulders bigger than cars. Three times, in the more turbulent water, Chaz pulled them over briefly so that she could scout ahead. So far, there had been no stretch so bad that she made anyone portage, but she reminded them to closely follow her line of travel through those areas and not to bunch up too much.

It was late afternoon when they arrived at their next campsite, a flat stretch of gravel surrounded by hilly terrain that partially obscured their view of the distant mountains. "Where are the caribou?" Justine asked Chaz with disappointment as they beached their kayaks.

"We have to hike to higher ground to see them," Chaz said. "I thought we'd grab a quick dinner first, unless you all would rather wait and eat late?"

"I'm starving," Pat said.

"You're always starving," Linda replied.

"Yeah, well," Pat embraced her lover tightly and raised both eyebrows suggestively, "I've been burning up a lot of calories."

"Where do you two get your energy?" Yancey grumped. "If my husband was here and wanted to do the deed, he'd be sorely disappointed. I'm whipped from paddling."

"Oh, I suppose I could find some hidden reserves if there was a good reason to," Elise remarked, looking hopefully at Chaz.

Megan was delighted that Chaz seemed to ignore the comment. All day long, she'd been thinking about the night to come, about lying beside Chaz. About kissing her, *finally*, and more. Her thoughts had kept her in a mild state of arousal, energized and expectant. She certainly wouldn't be too tired when the moment arrived.

❖

Setting up the campsite had become a familiar routine, and they were all anxious to see the caribou, so they split into groups and had the tents up and dinner prepared in about an hour and a half. They wolfed down big plates of pasta primavera, washed down with merlot, and assembled with their cameras and binoculars about the time the setting sun began to paint the world around them with tinges of gold, and pink, and amber.

Chaz led the way over spongy, boggy tundra and around grassy tussocks, some a foot high. It was difficult walking, and in no time Megan's calves began to protest.

"My legs are killing me," Yancey complained in a low voice from behind her.

"Join the crowd," Justine agreed. "This is tough going. We're going to sure sleep good tonight."

"It'll be worth it if the caribou are there," Pat said. "But I'm going to be really bummed if we're doing this for nothing."

They went up and down several small rises, scaring up a lot of small birds, whose nests were concealed amid the tussocks—and an arctic fox, who was digging after some small prey when they interrupted him. Cameras clicked as he froze, watching them, then ambled away to try for dinner somewhere else.

After an hour of solid walking, they faced an enormous hill, etched by ancient game trails.

Chaz paused at the base to address them. "Okay, we're here. On the other side of this is one of the main routes the caribou use. Cross your fingers."

They scaled the hill, tired legs protesting the steep elevation. But at the top, all weariness evaporated in the most awesome spectacle any of them had ever witnessed. Every woman stood motionless, mesmerized.

In the long, flat valley below them tens of thousands of caribou moved like a wide, living brown river. Megan was speechless. The picture on the brochure didn't begin to do the scene justice. She had no idea something like this still existed in the modern world. It reminded her of what the Great Plains must have been like, before the buffalo herds were decimated by hunters.

"There are more than a hundred and fifty thousand animals in the herd," Sally said. "I'd say that's a good bit of them down there, maybe two-thirds."

The wind changed slightly and carried the sounds of the herd up to them. Grunts, and bellows, and snorts, and a persistent clicking noise.

"What's that weird sound?" Yancey asked.

"Their leg tendons do that when they walk," Megan answered automatically.

"That's very good. You really did your homework."

Chaz's voice, so near, startled her. She had been so intent on the caribou she hadn't realized Chaz was standing just behind her left shoulder.

"What do you think? Was it worth the trip?" Chaz looked into her eyes.

Her expression was so serious that Megan somehow knew her answer meant a great deal. "Absolutely," she answered honestly. "I'll remember every detail of this day for the rest of my life."

She had turned slightly to face Chaz, and they stood looking at each other, while the others began to spread out over the hillside, some taking pictures, others finding a comfortable place to sit and watch the herd through binoculars. Chaz's lips were so close that Megan couldn't take her eyes off them. They were wonderful lips, full and rosy red with the cold.

"I won't forget you, either," she whispered without really thinking.

Chaz lifted a hand and gently touched Megan's chin, tilting her face up until their eyes met. The touch shot through her like a charge of electricity. Chaz's eyes were dark and endless and drew her in, and for a moment—just a moment—Megan was certain Chaz was going to kiss her right then and there.

Instead, Chaz took a deep breath and let it out, as though she was struggling for control. "And I won't forget you," she said, dropping her hand. She turned to look back at the herd.

Megan's body shook with disappointment, but when her eyes followed Chaz's to the valley below, she decided she couldn't really complain. Seeing the caribou was a once-in-a-lifetime opportunity, and she didn't want to miss a minute of it. There would be plenty of time for kissing later.

Yup. Seducing her is going to be a walk in the park. She might even beat me to the punch.

❖

Chaz gazed out over the herd, trying to still the butterflies in her stomach. Dear God, she had almost kissed Megan. What the hell had she been thinking? She was just so caught up in the moment and the look of sheer bliss in Megan's eyes. Something was happening between them, that was for sure. She had never felt so out of control in her life.

The tent was going to be torture tonight.

Unless…the clients wanted to stay here until very late. After that long, tough trudge through the tussocks and back again, everyone would be absolutely exhausted. Even Megan.

She could only hope.

They watched the caribou for two hours, the gangly calves, thousands of them born within days of each other, trotting along beside their mothers, who were finally shedding their bleached winter fur. The bulls already had their dark coats and velvet-covered antlers, the enormous racks swaying slightly as they grazed. In front of the herd, the land was alive with summer greenery and wildflowers, but behind it was only a vast brown plain, like it had been freshly tilled. The caribou stripped the tundra of every blossom, lichen, cotton grass shoot, and other hint of vegetation.

By the time the women trekked back to their campsite, it was truly the hour of the midnight sun, when the landscape fairly glowed—the diffuse light making colors unbelievably vivid.

They walked in silence, except for the occasional alert to something moving on the tundra and worthy of particular notice. As they arrived back at the tents, a snowy owl with a five-foot wingspan soared over them and then downriver. It was as dark as it would get, with shadows from the surrounding hills shading the tents in a suggestion of dusk.

"Good night, everyone," Sally said, "We can all sleep in tomorrow."

"Great news," Yancey said, stifling a yawn. "I'm beat."

There was a chorus of "good nights" all around, followed by the sounds of tent zippers and low voices.

Megan felt like she had voltage in her veins. The current of restless anticipation had been building all day, until every nerve ending in her body sang, until all she could think about was kissing Chaz and touching that magnificent body. She had put up their tent alone while Chaz cooked, and she had deliberately picked a spot as far from the others as possible to afford them at least a little privacy.

Turning as she stooped to unzip the tent, Megan was disappointed that Chaz was not behind her—she had apparently diverted off somewhere, probably to make a pit stop.

No excuses tonight, she thought. She'd begun to suspect that Chaz's habit of staying up late might have something to do with the growing attraction between them. But there was no campfire to keep Chaz outside, and it was already very late. She had to come in soon.

Sally's words came back to her. *I think it's hard for her to make the first move when she's interested in someone.* And...*She's not attracted to Elise. She's more interested in someone else.* Sally couldn't have drawn her a clearer map, and her goal was within reach.

❖

Chaz surveyed the area around where they cooked one more time to make sure they had taken care of all traces of food and garbage before they turned in. She had checked it thoroughly before they'd gone to see the herd, but she needed some reason not to retire right away, and it was the best one she could think of off the top of her head. *Can't stall much longer.*

Though it was nearly midnight, she was not in the least bit tired. Quite the opposite. Megan had walked directly in front of her as they followed their path back to the campsite single file. She hadn't planned it that way—Megan had taken a couple of quick steps as they all set off, to position herself there.

So she had a full hour to watch Megan's way-too-cute ass sway back and forth as she strode along. After the first ten minutes or so, Chaz was convinced she was deliberately exaggerating the movement of her hips to maximize the impact. *She knows damn well what she's doing to me. Talk about hitting below the belt.*

So by the time they got back, her whole body was thrumming with desire in a way that shocked her.

Can't avoid this forever. Might as well get it over with. Just go in there, get into your bag, and try to go to sleep. Don't look at her and don't talk to her, except to say good night. She knew she was on the verge of losing control, and it was a very unfamiliar place to be. It had always been clear to her, where to draw the line. But then, she'd never been tempted like this before.

She took a deep breath and headed for the tent.

CHAPTER TWELVE

Chaz bent to untie her laces beside the entrance to the tent, so she could slip her boots off before she went inside. Peering through the insect netting, she found Megan wide-awake, lying half within her sleeping bag but propped up on one elbow, watching her intently. The V-necked man's T-shirt she was wearing exposed a hint of cleavage. As their eyes locked, Megan licked her lips in a deliciously enticing way.

Chaz's heartbeat sped up, and her hands shook slightly as she removed her boots and unzipped the tent to slip inside. She didn't dare look at Megan as she piled her gear into a corner by the door and shed clothes—her coat first, then fleece pullover, insulated pants, and socks. She got halfway into her own sleeping bag, wearing navy cotton boxers and a loose-fitting, long-sleeved navy T-shirt. The attraction between them had flared into a hot and undeniable living, breathing entity, and she had no idea how to deal with it except to try to ignore it.

She lay down on her side, facing away from Megan, stuffed her pillow under her head and closed her eyes, struggling to keep her body and voice under control. "Good night," she whispered, praying those words would be enough to stop anything from happening.

For a very long minute or two, Megan said nothing. Chaz, waiting on pins and needles, felt relief and disappointment in equal measure.

When Megan did speak, her voice was soft and intimate, the voice of a lover after a long night of passion. "You almost kissed me, up there on the hill. You wanted to." Not a question. A statement.

"Did I?" Chaz didn't move. *Oh, God, here it comes.* She held her breath. Her skin tingled in anticipation.

"Yes. And I wanted you to. But then, you know that, don't you?" Megan said.

Chaz shook her head. "Megan, I can't—"

"Yes, you can." Megan cut her off. "And you will. You know we have to."

The words sent a sharp current of arousal through her, dulling her conscience, making every single argument against it seem small and insignificant. *You can't! You can't!* But she had lost the battle almost before Megan reached for her.

She felt a hand around her waist, turning her, insistent, and she had only a moment to look into those green eyes, pupils large and dark and full of need, before Megan was kissing her, as she had never been kissed before, and God help her, there was not a thing she could do but kiss her back.

When Megan's tongue thrust into her mouth, Chaz answered with a passion she feared would consume her, her tongue exploring the welcoming warmth with an unquenchable thirst. And when Megan's hand entwined itself into her hair and roughly caressed her scalp, it sent her jangled senses into overdrive. Megan stirred something wild and primitive in her, and touching her was an elemental *need*, like the clean air of the wilderness.

The pressure in her chest made it hard to breathe. The pressure building between her legs made it impossible to think. Kissing wasn't nearly enough. Desire took control and obliterated the last vestiges of reason. She wrapped her arms around Megan and pulled their bodies together, breaking the kiss to roll until Megan was on top of her.

As Megan's smaller frame settled against the length of her body, and their curves and valleys melded together like puzzle pieces, she was rewarded with a long, sensual groan of approval. The sound reverberated through her skin and fueled the fire raging within. Megan's mouth reclaimed hers for another long, deep, scorching kiss, and just as her brain hazily registered that the sleeping bags had to go, she felt the shock of cool fingertips against the warm flesh of her abdomen and realized Megan's hand had found its way under her shirt.

Her stomach muscles contracted, and her heart began hammering even harder in her chest, in anticipation of where that hand was headed.

She didn't have long to wait.

Megan's cool palm slid over the flat plane of her belly; then the back of her fingers traced the bottom curve of her breasts, teasingly close, maddeningly distant. As Megan's fingertips neared their destination, Chaz's hands sought their own reward of soft skin. She caressed Megan's back, grazing her fingernails lightly down the length of her body and into the confines of her sleeping bag until she felt the warm expanse of flesh between cotton shirt and silk panties.

She slipped a hand beneath the silk and cupped Megan's ass roughly. The ass that had taunted her, teased her, driven her mad.

Megan gasped and retaliated with a firm squeeze of Chaz's right nipple between her fingertips. It was instantly hard. She raised her head to look at Chaz. "What do you like?" she whispered, her breathing fast and unsteady, as her hand found Chaz's other nipple and gave it equal treatment. "Tell me what you want."

It was as though someone had thrown cold water on her. The question, the look in Megan's eyes, the momentary pause in the fevered kisses that had overpowered all sense of reason—she wasn't sure what it was. But it made her remember Pat's words and realize that she would only be a notch on Megan's belt—one in a long list and forgotten tomorrow. The thought was enough for her to regain some small sense of control over her runaway libido.

"I…I'm sorry," she stammered, disengaging herself from their embrace. Abruptly, she shifted her weight so that Megan's body was off of hers and deposited unceremoniously on its own side of the tent.

The rejection happened so quickly that it took Megan a moment to register what had happened and raise a protest. She sat up. "What's wrong?" she asked, reaching for Chaz as though she'd lost her mind.

"I'm sorry," Chaz gently intercepted Megan's hand as it headed for her breast, "I can't do this."

"Sure you can," Megan persisted. She leaned toward Chaz to kiss her again, but Chaz stiffened and turned her head away.

"No, Megan."

Megan withdrew her hand as though she'd been burned. "What are you, a tease?"

Chaz shook her head. "I'm sorry," she said again. "I shouldn't have let it go that far."

"You want me as much as I want you," Megan argued. "You can't deny that."

The words sent another rush of arousal through her. "No. I can't deny that." She couldn't look at Megan, or she knew she might lose her resolve again. Flipping onto her back, she stared up at the ceiling of the tent. "But nothing can happen between us."

"Care to tell me why the hell not?" Megan's tone was confused.

"You're a client. I don't think it's ethical."

"Screw that. I don't care about that. We're both adults."

"It's not that simple."

"Sure it is." Frustration seeped into Megan's voice. "It's very simple. You want me, and I want you. What's wrong with having some fun?"

"What's *wrong* is that's all it *is* to you," Chaz retorted, then wished she could take the words back. She sounded like a high school kid upset to find she wasn't the first to kiss her girl. Feeling exposed, she tried for a more reasonable tone. "I'm not like that. I don't do one-night stands."

"You're kidding me, right?" Megan was getting angrier by the second. "If we hadn't had clothes on and these damn sleeping bags between us, we'd be fucking right now."

Chaz tried to ignore the picture that appeared in her mind at Megan's words, but she could not. She was still hopelessly turned on, and she had to admit that Megan was probably right about what they'd be doing. *Damn it all to hell.* "I'm sorry I let it go so far. It was unfair to you."

"No shit, Sherlock." Megan spat out the words and then turned on her side, facing away.

She lay there fuming in silence for two or three minutes, jaw clenching and unclenching, her body stubbornly refusing to relinquish the buzz of arousal that Chaz had lit. *Hell, no. No way. I'm not going to let her do this.* Her heart continued to pound as though their bodies were still pressed together. *God, I can't believe how she makes me feel. And she wants me, too. She admitted it. No way can she kiss me like that and not be just as hot for me as I am for her. I bet I can make her change her mind. Not that I have anything to lose by trying.*

She unzipped her sleeping bag and peeled it back, then turned over to face Chaz.

Chaz was still on her back. She had her eyes closed, but opened them at the movement beside her and looked over at Megan just as Megan began to unzip her sleeping bag. "What are you doing?"

"Seeing if my powers of persuasion are as good as I think they are," Megan said seductively as she opened Chaz's sleeping bag and scooted over next to her until their bodies were just touching. "I'm not buying your bullshit excuses. I could feel in your kiss how much you want this. Need this. Just as much as I do."

Chaz didn't move. *You can't tell her she's wrong.* Her body was still so overheated from arousal that the cool air on her exposed legs was welcome. "Megan, please..." Her voice was honey thick. She meant it to sound like a protest, but it came out like a plea.

Megan looked her in the eyes and smiled knowingly, as though recognizing the desire she could not hide. *Why was it again we shouldn't do this?* Chaz wondered.

Before her mind could regain enough sense to answer, Megan's face was descending toward hers. It paused just before their lips met. "Let me touch you, Chaz. I want to make you come," she whispered, then kissed her hard.

As her tongue pushed into Chaz's mouth, Megan's hand cupped her sex, and Chaz's body involuntarily rose to meet the contact. *Oh, Jesus, God.* She could feel how wet she was, and she knew Megan could feel it too; it quickly saturated the thin material of her boxers.

Megan's own excitement doubled when her fingers told her how aroused Chaz was, and she pressed her body tighter against Chaz's with a moan.

You can't do this. Chaz had no idea how her conscience had resurfaced at this moment. Or was it pride? Her professional ethics were losing their grip. And she hardly cared whether it was just for one night, any more. She wanted Megan so much. *But what if this is all part of a bet?* She didn't want to believe that was true. *God damn it.*

She pulled Megan's hand away as she forced their lips apart. "Please stop." Her voice broke with emotion.

Megan was breathing hard. She backed away slowly, just enough to separate their bodies. She could tell Chaz was upset, and that was what finally penetrated her determined efforts and haze of arousal.

"I want to," Chaz admitted, staring up at the ceiling. She couldn't look at Megan. She'd give in for sure, if she looked into those eyes. "God, I want to. I'm so sorry. But not like this. Please, Megan."

Megan shifted back onto her own sleeping bag and turned away without a word, fighting the urge to say something impulsive she knew she might later regret. Her anger was mitigated slightly by the sincere regret she heard in Chaz's voice.

Not like this. The words echoed in Megan's mind. *She wants you. Just* not like this. *If she has reservations you really don't want to push this right now, do you? She might regret it if you do. And you don't want her to.*

Chaz wished to hell she could think of something to say. Or that Megan would say something. Anything. *Nothing like silence after a rejection to make you feel like a complete ass.* She hated hurting Megan, or embarrassing her. She knew she shouldn't have let them go so far.

After a time, Megan's anger subsided enough for her to realize that it was up to her to ease the tension between them. It had been she, after all, who had started all this in the first place. But it was a difficult apology. She still felt humiliated, and she couldn't face Chaz when she spoke the words. "I'm sorry. I should have heard no the first time you said it."

"I'm sorry, too, Megan," Chaz said. "I don't want this to...make things uncomfortable or anything. I mean, can't we just put tonight behind us and enjoy the rest of the trip?"

"Sure. No problem."

It was an awkward, uneasy truce.

Chaz's mind and body were so keyed up that it was a very long time before she fell asleep, and she knew from Megan's frequent, restless shifts in positions that she wasn't faring any better. But no more words were spoken between them.

❖

Megan was relieved to wake up alone the next morning. She hoped that a few minutes alone in the stark light of a new day might help her make some sense of what had happened. And why what had happened had hurt so much.

She wanted to say it didn't matter. It was only that she wasn't often turned down. And certainly not right in the middle of things like that. *Your ego is bruised, that's all. You'll get over it.*

But it *did* matter. Chaz's rejection stung. And part of the reason it hurt so much was that she had to admit that she herself *couldn't* have stopped what was happening. She had totally lost control. She had been more turned on than she could ever remember, more lost in the sensations pouring through her body than she'd imagined she could be.

It was somehow...*more* with Chaz. More passionate, more sensual, more arousing. More even than with Rita. *But apparently it's not more for Chaz. She doesn't want you enough to let it happen.*

The sense of loss she felt was overpowering. Tears came to her eyes, but she brushed them roughly away. *Damn you, Chaz.*

She was certainly not going to let Chaz see how humiliated she felt. She needed some distance. The first thing she had to do was get a new tent mate.

CHAPTER THIRTEEN

C haz wasn't really surprised that it was the Royal Ice Bitch who came to breakfast. She knew she had hurt and humiliated Megan, and she regretted it with every fiber of her being. But she could think of no way to make things right. She just hoped the awkward truce they'd agreed upon in the end would make it possible to continue the trip without inflicting tension on everyone else.

They were off to a great start.

Megan avoided looking at her, talking to her, or interacting with her at all. She sat off by herself with a cup of coffee, staring at the river, while the rest of them had wild blueberry pancakes. Justine went over to talk to her, and the two moved into a huddle, speaking in hushed tones. Chaz tried not to imagine what Megan must be saying about her "performance."

"What happened between you two?" Sally asked Chaz when they stepped away from the others to wash the morning dishes.

"I don't want to talk about it," she said, not meeting Sally's eyes.

"Megan made a pass at you, didn't she?" Sally guessed. "And you turned her down and hurt her feelings."

Worse. I got her all turned on, and then I said stop. "Something like that."

"That was dumb. Really dumb." Sally shook her head. "Then I'm sorry that I encouraged her."

"What did you do?"

"Let her know you were interested in her, but not likely to make the first move."

Shit. I bet she's incredibly embarrassed, then, in addition to everything else. "You shouldn't have done that."

"Silly me, I thought I was doing you a favor. I don't think I've ever seen you this way with anyone. And she seems to be nuts about you, too. I don't see the problem here."

"She only wants one more in a long list of conquests," Chaz said. "And you know I'm not like that."

Sally was silent for a moment. "Sorry, then." She put one arm around Chaz's shoulders and gave her a brief hug. "I guess I shouldn't have interfered."

Chaz sighed. "You mean well."

A short distance away, Justine poured another cup of coffee and studied Chaz as she took a sip. Slumped shoulders. Dejected expression. *Just like someone else I know.*

She returned to sit beside Megan, determined to get her to open up about what was going on.

It had grieved Justine to watch Megan put up walls around herself after Rita left, to see her never let anyone too close, harden herself against hurt, and work herself to death in the process. But something had changed in her here in Alaska. There was a vulnerability about Megan now, a softness to her. "Still not hungry?" she asked her brooding friend.

"Not much of an appetite this morning," Megan said evasively.

Justine could see that Megan hadn't slept well. She had dark circles under her eyes, and she seemed edgy and restless. "Want to talk about it?"

"I hate the way you can read me like a book," Megan griped, not unkindly.

"Chaz, right?"

Megan blew out an exasperated breath. "Well, I sure made a fool of myself last night. I really thought she was interested. So I…you know…let her know *I* was. I kissed her."

"And? She wasn't receptive?" Justine's voice registered her surprise.

"Well, she sure as hell kissed me back," Megan said, a bit of her embarrassed anger resurfacing at the memory of Chaz's rejection. "But then she backed off and said it wasn't going to happen."

"Did she say why?"

Megan didn't answer immediately. "She said she wasn't into one-night stands," she finally admitted.

"Ah." Justine nodded her head. "So it's not that she wasn't interested in *you*…just what you could offer her."

Megan looked up at her angrily. "What's that supposed to mean? We're only here for another few days. Couldn't be anything more, anyway."

"Would you like it to be?"

Megan opened her mouth to answer, but the quick retort she had planned died on her lips. The answer to that question should certainly have been *no*. It had been no for so long…no strings, no commitments, no promises, no entanglements…that the sudden realization that she might indeed want more with Chaz caught her so off guard that she felt a little shell-shocked.

"I thought so." Justine laid a hand on Megan's shoulder. "Girlfriend, I think you need to think seriously about this one. Maybe it *isn't* possible, but…I've seen a change in you these last few days. You seem a lot happier and more relaxed out here than I've seen you in…gosh, *years*, I guess."

"Justine," Megan said wearily. "We live hundreds of miles apart."

"Funny but I thought it was you who once told me…never say never." With that, Justine walked back to the group, leaving Megan to consider her words.

It's just not possible, she repeated to herself, over and over. *You have a nice comfortable life. Better stick with the plan and switch tents and just try to forget about her and get through the next few days.*

There was no way, however, she was going to take the obvious route. Although she was anxious to put some distance between them, she didn't want to give Elise any prime opportunities with Chaz. So if she wanted to switch tents and still get a good night's sleep, there was only one alternative.

She got her opportunity after breakfast when the group dispersed to pack up their gear to leave. Yancey was beside their kayaks, braiding her long blond hair into a pigtail, when Megan joined her. It was a routine she followed every time they set off, so she could keep her hair out of her eyes when they were paddling.

"Hey, there," she greeted Megan. "You were awful quiet this morning. Everything copasetic?"

"That's kind of what I wanted to talk to you about," Megan said. "I have a favor to ask."

"Shoot."

"Would you mind bunking in with Chaz the rest of the trip?"

Yancey stopped what she was doing and studied Megan's face. "Sure. Fine with me."

"Great."

"You know that Elise volunteered to stay with Chaz?" Yancey reminded her.

"I'd rather that you did."

Yancey's brow furrowed in confusion. "Mind telling me why?"

Megan sighed heavily and looked away, out at the distant mountains. "Because Elise has the hots for her. And so do I. And she's made it clear she's not interested in either one of us."

Yancey frowned in sympathy. "That's rough. Well, if you're certain that's what you want, I don't mind switching."

"I appreciate it." Megan forced a smile. "I'll talk to Elise about it later. Would you mind telling Chaz?"

"Sure," Yancey said. "I can do that."

❖

They had finished loading their gear into the raft and were putting on their PFDs, spray skirts, and helmets, when a thick cloud of mosquitoes descended on them from out of nowhere. They had no tents to escape into this time, so there was a mad scramble into their kits for head nets and repellent.

"Damn it!" Pat cursed, swatting at her neck as a half dozen of the tiny tormenters bit her simultaneously. "Get off of me!"

"Where did they come from?" Linda complained. "How can they all appear at once like this?"

"The wind died down," Chaz explained, as she sprayed herself. "It tends to keep them at bay. That's why we've been so lucky this whole trip—there's been a nice breeze with us most all the time."

"Can I borrow someone's repellent?" Megan asked no one in particular, furiously swatting at her neck, hands, and face. "The bear ate mine." She gagged as she inhaled several of the bugs. "Yuck!"

"Here, I have a spare net," Chaz offered, stepping toward Megan with a head net in her outstretched hand.

Megan hesitated for a moment. Taking anything from Chaz was the last thing she wanted to do. But the high-pitched buzzing in her ears was about to drive her insane. "Thanks," she mumbled, grabbing the head net and putting it on.

Chaz held out her can of repellent, and she took that, too, and sprayed her hands.

When she handed it back, she met Chaz's eyes and saw a look of remorse there. Her anger about their encounter melted just a little. If she was really being honest, she had to admit that she herself was mostly to blame. She had pushed herself on Chaz and continued to after Chaz had said stop. *That was sure some class act, all right,* she berated herself. *What must she think of me now? Probably that I don't care about anyone but myself.*

Soon they were underway, and the river's growing challenges were enough to keep her distracted. The Odakonya sped up as they paddled along, demanding more and more of their attention by the mile. The river kept dropping in elevation, and there were numerous rocks and boulders scattered about that they had to be careful to avoid. Once or twice, Megan was so busy watching something—an eagle soaring past, or a small animal trotting along in the distance—that she nearly crashed into some obstacle in the river that seemed to loom up at her without warning.

Shortly before they were to stop for lunch, the river took them into a narrow canyon, with steep cliff walls rising sharply on either side. On the right bank, there was nowhere to walk at all—and on the left, only a six-foot-wide strip of rocky terrain guaranteed to twist an ankle if you weren't paying attention.

Chaz motioned the clients to beach their kayaks. "As I recall, our first potentially tough stretch is up around the next bend," she announced as she got out of her boat. "I'm going to scout ahead, and I'd like everyone to come with me."

They all got out of their kayaks and picked their way downstream single file, until they came to a vantage point where they could see the most difficult section of the rapids ahead. Chaz pointed out the route they would take, explaining the tricky parts and how the current would act around the boulders and eddies.

"These don't look too bad, and I don't think any of you will have any problems if you follow my line," Chaz said. "Everybody feeling good about that?"

The clients all nodded.

"Okay, then. We'll go through one at a time, and be sure to space yourselves out. I want to alternate the more experienced people with the lesser. So Megan will go behind me, then Pat, then Elise, Linda, Justine, Yancey, and Sally last. Let's go!"

They returned to their kayaks and got back underway.

Megan gripped her paddle tighter. She was feeling pretty confident about her abilities and really looking forward to the challenges ahead. Every bit of whitewater they hit energized her with a burst of adrenalin. Her body was buzzing with it.

All the women made it through that stretch without difficulty, Sally bringing up the rear in the raft.

After a quick stop for sandwiches, they came to three more places where Chaz pulled them over to scout ahead. Each time, she pointed out the route and told the women that it looked very doable for all of them, but she gave them a chance to choose to portage around it. None of them took it.

At one point Megan seemed hesitant, and Chaz wanted to suggest she take the easier option, but she felt certain her suggestion would be rejected, and she was reluctant to single Megan out in front of the others. She knew she was on thin ice, and Yancey's quick word about the new tent-sharing arrangements had driven that point home.

It's probably all for the best, she told herself yet again. She could do without the temptation of Megan lying beside her. And Megan obviously wanted nothing more to do with her after their stressful night. *She'll go home and find another conquest and forget all about me.* That realization depressed her much more than she thought it would, and she had to force herself to focus on their fifth stop.

"That area could be tricky." Chaz pointed to a section beyond the curve that was crowded with boulders.

The only way through was a narrow channel of swift water that dropped at least three feet. "It's a straight shot through if you line up carefully. And from seeing how all of you are doing today, I think everyone's certainly capable of this. But if you have any reservations whatsoever—and I mean *any*—you might want to portage here." She cast a pointed look at Elise and Megan.

"I'm good to go," Elise said immediately.

"So am I," Megan agreed. This next stretch did look rather intimidating, but she was not going to be the only one to walk it. Though she tried not to let her nerves get to her, she allowed them to distract her more than she realized. When she returned to her kayak and put her helmet back on, she meant to fasten the chin strap securely but, in her haste to take her place, forgot.

They proceeded forward in the same order as before, with Megan directly behind Chaz. In no time, they came to the narrow channel they'd viewed from the bank. "Here we go. Careful here," Chaz hollered back as she lined up and floated through.

Megan was next.

Her approach was nearly perfect, but the current swept her kayak sideways right as she neared the gap. *Oh, shit. Oh, shit.* A burst of adrenalin surged through her bloodstream, and her heart felt like it was going to explode in her chest.

"Reverse sweep on your left side!" She heard Chaz's voice above the roar of the water but couldn't manage to get her paddle in position quickly enough.

She entered the gap all wrong, and she knew she was done for. It looked as though both the front and back of her kayak were going to hit the boulders on either side. She tried to brace herself at the last second for the impact, but she was so intent on doing that, she paid no attention to the position of her paddle.

The paddle blade hit the left boulder and threw her off balance. A millisecond later, the kayak slammed into the other boulder with a loud *thwack* and finished the job.

She went over.

Everything from there happened in slow motion. She managed to suck in a great big breath, but her heart was beating so loud and so fast she wasn't sure she could hold it very long.

When the cold hit her it was like a sharp slap in the face, a shock that made her want to cry out and lose that precious, precious air. She found herself spinning in a maelstrom of churning water. In a flash, her helmet and her paddle were carried away by the current. She couldn't keep her eyes open, couldn't see a damn thing, and she didn't know which end was up. All was a chaos of whitewater, and she had no way and no hope of righting herself.

Oh, fuck. This is bad.

Her lungs were ready to burst. She tried not to panic as she grappled for the release tab on her spray skirt.

CHAPTER FOURTEEN

Chaz watched in horror as Megan's kayak slammed against the boulders and overturned. The current was so strong she had to paddle furiously in order to stay in place. She was trying to position herself to intercept Megan's kayak as it was swept downstream, when the worried chorus of the others reached her ears.

"Megan's gone over!"

"Watch out!"

"Don't bunch up!"

"Back paddle!"

"Oh, shit! Does anybody see her?"

Chaz's breathing accelerated with every second that passed without Megan reappearing. She kept her attention on the overturned kayak as she stroked powerfully toward it, but risked glances around her, hoping to spot Megan in the water.

She saw Megan's red helmet float past her, out of reach, and felt a stab of fear.

Somehow Pat suddenly appeared beside Chaz, skillfully maneuvering her own boat into a position to help. They reached the bright yellow kayak at the same time from two sides and managed to get it turned partially over—enough to see that Megan was out of the cockpit.

"She's out!" Chaz yelled to the others as she desperately scanned the water around her.

"There she is!" Yancey cried, pointing toward a car-sized rock in the middle of the river farther downstream.

Megan was hanging on precariously with one hand, her head barely above water. Her face was contorted in pain. She had her PFD on, but there was a deep black hole of churning water downstream of the rock, and its sucking whirlpool was pulling her down.

"Hang on, Megan!" Chaz screamed. Her heart thudded in her chest as she dug in her paddle and raced toward the rock.

Megan looked right at her then, with such terror in her eyes that Chaz's own fear rose, the taste of it sour in her mouth. She was only four feet away when Megan's hand slipped from the rock, and her head disappeared beneath the surface as she was sucked into the hole. Chaz lunged after her, almost overturning, but her groping hand found nothing but water.

Megan bobbed to the surface several yards downstream, coughing violently.

"There!" Several voices yelled at once.

Chaz sped toward Megan as first Pat, and then Linda, tried to toss Megan their rescue lines. Pat's fell short, and Linda's landed several yards to the left, and the current took it downstream and away.

Megan glanced off another large rock. There was a sickening *crack* as her head impacted the hard surface. She lost consciousness and bobbed downstream with the current, as limp as a rag doll.

"Oh, my God!" Justine cried out.

Chaz's blood ran cold as she closed the distance to Megan with power strokes and absolute focus of purpose. *I can't...*won't *miss her this time.* Six feet away. Four. Two.

Gotcha! She clamped onto the collar of Megan's PFD with one hand.

"Sally!" she bellowed, desperately trying to keep Megan's face above water as the current propelled them toward a sharp overhang of rock thirty feet downriver.

Sally was right behind her, already maneuvering into position. She scooted the raft next to Chaz's kayak, and Chaz tossed her paddle in, then grabbed hold of the sturdy rope that ringed the inflatable. As Sally towed them away from the outcropping with long pulls at the oars, it was all Chaz could do to maintain hold of both the raft and Megan, while keeping Megan's dead weight from overturning her kayak. Megan wasn't moving, and Chaz couldn't immediately tell if she was breathing.

"Come on, Megan. Stay with me," she urged, holding so tight to the vest that her knuckles were white. "Stay with me." *Dear God, please be all right.*

Sally got them to shore and laid Megan gently on the gravel bank at the river's edge. She had a gash in her forehead that was bleeding profusely, but she was breathing on her own.

"Grab the first-aid kit," Chaz cried hoarsely as Sally rushed to help her, and the other women converged on the scene.

A few seconds after Sally dropped the first-aid kit at Chaz's feet, Megan came to and immediately began coughing and vomiting up water. Chaz held a compress of gauze against her head to stop the bleeding. When the worst had passed, Megan stared up at Chaz and Sally, who were kneeling on either side of her.

"Where do you hurt?" Chaz asked.

"Left shoulder." Megan grimaced and coughed up some more water. "And head, where you're pressing."

"Do you have any pain at all in your neck? Or anywhere else?" Chaz asked.

"No. Just shoulder and head. My helmet came off somehow."

"We need to get your PFD off," Chaz said.

Megan's eyes got wide. "Can't," she croaked. She coughed again.

"We have to," Chaz said. "You may have dislocated your shoulder."

"Can we wait a while? I mean, I don't want to be a baby about this. But I just want to lie still for a minute. It's only just stopped absolutely killing me."

"We have to do this soon," Chaz said. "If you've dislocated it, the sooner we get it back in place the better. We want to do it before you start having muscle spasms." She couldn't stand the look in Megan's eyes. So scared. "Look, I'll dress your head wound first. We can wait on the other until I do that."

Megan took a deep breath. Let it out. "Thanks," she said, just above a whisper.

"Sally, I think I can handle this at the moment," Chaz said. "Will you take a look and see if you can spot Megan's kayak?"

"We can do that," Pat offered. "Linda and I will take the kayaks down and portage back." Glancing at Elise, she suggested, "Maybe you could walk alongside with a rescue line and look for the kayak."

"Sure," Elise agreed, but her eyes were on Megan. She looked stricken. "Is she going to be okay?"

"Yes," Chaz said grimly.

Elise looked like she wanted to linger, but Pat tapped her on the shoulder and she hurried away.

"Don't go so far you'll kill yourself walking back, okay?" Sally called after them. "And be careful, please."

Chaz finally got the bleeding stopped and gently bandaged Megan's head wound, which was turning into a good-sized purplish goose egg. The lump concerned her, although Megan seemed perfectly lucid. When that was done, it was time to check her shoulder.

"I'll be as gentle as I can," Chaz said. "You ready?"

"As I'll ever be, I guess."

Chaz leaned over Megan and looked her in the eyes as she unhooked the vest. She could see how much Megan was already hurting, and how terrified she was of what they were about to do. She hated causing her even more pain. But she knew she would probably have to.

"Okay," Chaz said. "Try to relax."

"Easier said than done." Megan's eyes remained locked with Chaz's, as if for reassurance. Something to hold on to.

"See if you can pull your other arm out of the vest," Chaz said. "Then I'll slip it off you."

Megan accomplished that part with another loud groan, and the vest was quickly off.

Chaz unzipped Megan's dry suit top and pulled it back. Megan was wearing a black, two-piece swimsuit beneath. The top created a mesmerizing display of cleavage that Chaz couldn't, for a moment, bear to tear her eyes from. In the middle of this crisis, all she could think about was touching Megan's breasts. *I should be ashamed of myself.*

She forced her eyes away, to Megan's shoulder, and steered her mind firmly back to the task. She gently palpated the joint, trying not to think about how soft Megan's skin was under her fingers.

"The good news is, I don't think it's dislocated." She looked into Megan's eyes. "Tell me where it's tender." She continued to gently probe, and Megan indicated with a grimace when she hit a sore spot.

"There. Ow."

"Can you wiggle your fingers?"

Megan did so, without moving her arm. "Hurts in the muscles in my upper arm when I do that."

"Any loss of feeling?"

"Nope."

"Does it hurt when I try to move it?" Chaz asked. With one hand supporting Megan's shoulder, and the other her arm, she slowly and gently moved the arm outwards and up.

Megan grimaced. "Ow, yeah."

"Okay, that's enough, I think." Chaz felt a surge of relief. Megan seemed more alert than she was a few minutes earlier, so her head injury was probably not serious. But Chaz couldn't take the chance that there were factors invisible to her. "I'm not a doctor, but I've had first-aid training, and I don't think you've broken any bones. A bad sprain or strain, I think, in your shoulder. Your head is another matter."

"What's it look like?" Megan asked.

"I put a couple of butterfly bandages on it and got the bleeding stopped. But you'll need medical attention. That cut will probably require stitches, and you took a pretty good knock on the head. I think a doctor will want to run some tests and make sure you don't have a concussion. Head injuries can be serious."

"Shit." Megan blinked. "You mean the trip is over for me? I might be all right in a day or two."

"I'm sorry, Megan." Chaz zipped up Megan's dry suit so she'd stay warm. *And so you can stop staring at her breasts. Get hold of yourself, already.*

"We can't take any more risks with you. We're going to need to airlift you out."

"Damn."

"Oh, what a tough break," Justine said, coming around to stand where Megan could see her. "What can I do for you? Anything?"

"Can't think of anything that would help," Megan told Justine, then looked at Chaz. "The trip goes on, right? I haven't screwed this up for anyone else, have I?"

"Stop that," Justine said.

"Yeah," Yancey said. "You're what's important right now."

"I don't want the rest of you to miss out because of me," Megan repeated.

"It shouldn't be a problem to continue the trip." Chaz took a long look at Megan, in part checking for signs of shock, but also…just looking. Megan's skin was pale and clammy from her long immersion in the frigid water, her hair was wet, and she was shivering slightly. "Cold?"

"Yeah. A little."

"Justine, can you get her bag and pull out a hat and gloves for her?" Chaz asked. She reached into the raft, grabbed a sleeping pad, and laid it beside Megan. "See if we can scoot you over onto this and keep you off the cold ground."

Megan accomplished that with a little help and a muted groan.

Justine got her gloves and a hat on, and Chaz located a thin survival blanket from her bag and tucked it around Megan.

She leaned down until her face was close to Megan's. "Better?"

"Yes. Thanks." It was all Megan could do to answer. She felt exhausted, barely able to stay awake. The adrenalin rush from capsizing was gone, and her arms and legs seemed to be made of stone, like she had fought a few rounds with a much larger opponent.

Chaz stood. Addressing Yancey and Justine, she said, "I need to talk with Sally while we wait for the others to get back. You two mind keeping an eye on her a minute?"

"You got it," Justine answered for them, and she and Yancey crouched down next to Megan and started making awkward conversation.

Chaz could tell they were nervous. No one was going to feel confident until they got Megan to a doctor. She walked a short distance downstream with Sally.

"Couldn't have happened in a worse place," Sally said under her breath as soon as they were out of earshot.

"Yeah, no chance of a plane getting in here." Chaz studied the steep canyon walls on either side of them. The terrain was too steep and narrow for a helicopter rescue, but they couldn't stay here. Any kind of rain or big melt in the mountains and they'd be in trouble in a heartbeat. "We can't get a signal out here, with these rock walls, and we can't wait for a rescue by river. Much as I'd like not to move her, we gotta keep going."

"So, what are we looking at?" Sally asked. "How much farther before we can call for help?"

"The river leaves this canyon soon and crosses some tundra before it heads into another one. We could set up camp there. It's got a nice flat spot for the tents, and I'm sure we can get a clear communications link out."

"How long to get there, do you think?"

"Maybe another half hour. We'll have to take her in the raft." Chaz glanced back toward Megan. She knew the jarring ride downriver was going to be painful on her shoulder, and she really hated moving her with that head injury. "We'll have to lash her kayak and mine to the raft. I'll ride with you."

"What's the river like between here and there? Do you remember?"

"It's not too bad," Chaz said. "We'll lead in the raft, take it slow, and have Pat take up the rear. She's certainly capable."

They spotted Elise, Pat, and Linda returning from downriver, each carrying a kayak. All three looked weary and anxious to be rid of their burdens.

"Hey! You found it!" Sally waved. "Great!"

"How's Megan doing?" Linda asked as she set down her kayak and stretched to relieve the soreness in her back.

"The trip is over for her," Chaz said. "Although I don't think her injuries are too serious, she needs to see a doctor."

"I was afraid of that." Linda plopped down onto the nearest big rock and frowned as she surveyed the steep rock walls all around them. "How you going to get her out of here?"

"We're going to take her downriver in the raft a ways, then radio for help," Sally said. "We can't get a signal out, here in the canyon."

"Is she all right to travel?" Pat asked.

"No choice," Chaz said. "We can't stay here. It's too dangerous. If we get bad weather the river could rise and flood us out in no time. Don't worry, we'll take it real easy with her."

While the others tied the two kayaks behind the raft and prepared to get underway, Chaz efficiently fashioned a sling and secured Megan's arm against her body with an Ace bandage. "It's not going to be a comfortable ride, with that shoulder," she warned.

"Peachy." Megan watched Chaz work on her, admiring the musculature in Chaz's arms and her long, strong fingers. It helped distract her from the pain in her head and shoulder.

"The sling will immobilize it as far as possible. That should help. And I'm going to ride with you."

"All right." Megan stared down at the sling and felt thankful to be alive.

Sally redistributed the gear in the raft to make an area for Chaz and Megan that was as comfortable as possible.

"Okay, I think we're ready for you," Chaz said, stooping down and leaning over Megan again. "Can you walk there, or would you like me to carry you?"

"I can make it with some help," Megan said. So Chaz and Sally got on either side and gently helped her to her feet.

Chaz took off her helmet and gently set it on Megan's head.

"No, Chaz," Megan protested.

"I'm afraid you don't have a choice," she said, fastening it securely.

Chaz settled her long frame into the space they cleared in the bottom of the raft, with her back against one of the inflated sides, then stuck out a hand to assist Megan. "I want you to sit here, in between my legs, with your back against my chest, so I can try to cushion you."

Megan hesitated, scoping out how she was going to get into the raft without falling right on top of Chaz. She felt clumsy and unbalanced with her arm in the sling. "You don't need to do that," she protested.

"Please?" Chaz asked. *Still pissed at me. And now, even needing help, doesn't want to be anywhere near me. Not that I blame her, I guess.* She continued to extend her hand, waiting patiently, and finally Megan succumbed and allowed herself to be led carefully into the welcoming circle of Chaz's embrace.

As soon as she sat down, Chaz enfolded her in her arms, careful to avoid the sore shoulder. Megan's body was rigid and tense. "Try to relax against me," she whispered in Megan's ear as they got underway. "It'll make the ride a lot easier on you."

Megan could feel the warmth of Chaz's breath against her neck as they headed downriver, and it helped immeasurably to distract her from the pain that every bump and jolt of the whitewater sent through her body.

The sudden change in circumstances was only still sinking in. *I'm leaving.* The thought depressed her. She had seen all she was going to see, at least for now, of this magical wilderness that had captivated her and made her forget entirely about work, and home, and everything familiar. She missed it already.

You miss her already, Megan thought, unconsciously relaxing into Chaz's arms.

Thankful to feel Megan relax at last, Chaz cradled her protectively and absorbed the bumps as best as she could as they floated downriver. All the while, she had to make a conscious effort not to let their positions and proximity do what it was doing to her body.

God help her, it apparently didn't matter that Megan was injured and in pain. Or that she'd had her chance and passed it up. Megan just plain flat turned her on, in a way that completely mystified her. She was helpless to prevent it. With every bump, every roll of the rapids, their bodies came together, and the contact was beginning to manifest itself in a warm, moist pulse of arousal between her legs. She was damn glad the PFD she was wearing hid the fact that her nipples were as stand-up-at-attention sensitive as she'd ever felt them to be.

She said nothing for the first ten minutes, not trusting her voice, allowing herself to relish the closeness of their bodies, despite her best intentions. But when they hit a particularly bad bit of rough water and Megan groaned, the sound shot through her and allowed her to regain her sense of professional responsibility.

"How are you doing?" she whispered into Megan's ear.

"I feel like crap," Megan said drolly. "Thanks for caring."

Chaz couldn't help the laugh that escaped her lips, and that got Megan laughing, too.

"I haven't said thank you," Megan said, in a voice low enough that only Chaz could hear. "First the bear. Now this. That's twice you've saved me."

"No problem," Chaz said.

"Have you started thinking of me as the trip Jonah yet?"

Chaz laughed again. "No, but Calamity Jane did occur to me."

"Funny."

"Well, let's just say, I know we billed this as an adventure trip, but I'd like a bit less adventure from now on, if you please."

"I'll do my best." Megan's voice grew serious. "When will they come to get me?"

Soon. Far too soon, Chaz wanted to say. Barely realizing she was doing it, she tightened her hold around Megan's waist. "Today, probably," she said, glancing up at the thickening clouds overhead. "Unless we get some bad weather."

She found herself hoping for a nice low ceiling of clouds, or one of the sudden fog banks that frequently materialized this time of year.

Today. Megan slowly processed the idea. She could be picked up and taken away today, and that would be the last time she would clap eyes on Chaz. Her stomach churned, and it wasn't about the rolling motion of the raft. This might well be her last opportunity to talk to Chaz without the rest of them overhearing.

"Chaz?" Her voice was just above a whisper. Intimate.

Chaz cradled her head beside Megan's, her chin on Megan's shoulder, so she could hear her over the roar of the water. "Mmmhmm?"

"I really am sorry about the way I acted last night. I mean, I'm not sorry I kissed you," she amended. "But I lost my temper. And I should have respected your asking me to stop."

"You don't need to apologize. I shouldn't have kissed you back and let it go so far."

There was a hesitation. "I'm glad you did."

Another brief pause. "I couldn't help myself."

Chaz held Megan a little more tightly and sensed that they were on the same page. It was as though they had both suddenly become aware that their time together was nearly over, but they each had things that needed to be said.

"I think we're almost there," Sally said.

Chaz looked back over her shoulder. They were nearing the end of the canyon. She could see a patch of hilly tundra beyond. She settled against Megan once more and resumed their whispered tête-à-tête. In light of their admissions, and with time so short, there seemed little need for further restraint.

"I'm sorry you're leaving," she said.

"I can't imagine why," Megan murmured. "I've pretty much been nothing but trouble since day one."

"That's not how I'll remember you."

"No?"

"Nope."

"So how will you remember me?" Megan asked.

"I'll remember you with great fondness," Chaz said honestly. "And...as a very tempting opportunity missed."

"Thank you for saying that." Megan felt a pang of regret run through her over what might have been. "I won't forget you, Chaz. I can't tell you what this trip has meant to me."

The raft scraped up against the gravel bank. "Okay, ladies," Sally said. "We've arrived."

Chaz gave in to the impulse to hug Megan good-bye while she could, but before she pulled away, she planted a brief kiss on Megan's cheek. "It's been nice knowin' ya, Megan," she whispered.

It could have been a flippant remark, but the shaky timbre to Chaz's voice revealed the sincere emotion behind the sentiment, and Megan was slightly shocked by it. *She really has feelings for me. And I find this out now?* She felt a rush of panic, like this was a critical moment and she should say something else, but what?

"Need some help getting out?" Sally said, stepping onto the shore. Justine was there too, and the others were pulling up their kayaks.

Megan craned slightly to see Chaz's face. Her expression was impassive. Their moment of intimacy had passed.

CHAPTER FIFTEEN

Chaz radioed for help while Sally and Justine set up a tent for Megan so she'd be more comfortable, especially if the bugs picked up. Right now a pretty stiff breeze from the north was keeping the winged piranha at bay, but it was bringing with it cooler temperatures and an ominous darkening of the low clouds above them. Chaz figured the rescue would be at least a couple of hours away, so they planned to have an early dinner here. Once Megan was picked up, they could proceed downriver to their campsite only a bit behind schedule.

Chaz had described Megan's symptoms to a doctor they'd patched her through to and had given the Alaska State Troopers their GPS position. Now she was on hold, awaiting an ETA for the rescue team. The steep mountains surrounding them and the hilly terrain made it a dicey place for a plane to try to land. It would have to be an extraction by helicopter.

"Hello, Chaz, are you there?" the female dispatcher said into her ear.

"Yes, I'm here."

"We've just gotten a weather advisory that's grounding all planes and helicopters where you are. A nasty front is building north of you and is headed your way."

What else can go wrong?

"The choppers north of you are already grounded, and the ones to the south are too far away to reach you before things really go bad," the dispatcher continued. "It will start as rain, but turn to sleet and maybe snow."

"Any idea when all this will hit?"

"On radar it looks like two or three hours. This may last awhile. Doesn't look like we'll be able to get to you until sometime tomorrow at the earliest."

"Understood. Thanks for the advisory. I'll be in touch."

"What do you want to do?" Sally asked, drawing her own conclusions from the content of the conversation and the expression on Chaz's face.

"Well, I'd rather get the group through the next stretch while the weather holds and the light is still good. The river goes into another long, steep canyon, and it will be awful dark in there once the sun gets low. There's a much better campsite beyond it with room for all the tents, and a cooking area and everything."

"You want us all to go?" Sally asked dubiously.

"No. We can't move Megan anymore. The raft is just too rough on her. I think you and the others should go on ahead. You lead, Pat takes the rear again. The river isn't too bad between here and the campsite— it's the next clear patch of tundra, you can't miss it. Two hours, tops."

"Okay. And you?" Sally asked.

"I'll stay with Megan until the chopper gets here. Then I'll catch up with you." She glanced over at the tent. The rest of the women had made Megan comfortable inside, in her sleeping bag, and were gathered around talking to her. "Shall we make sure this plan is okay with everybody?"

"You got it," Sally said.

Once Chaz had explained the plan and everyone had agreed, there was a frenzy of activity as the women, minus Chaz and Megan, prepared to get underway again to beat the weather.

The rest of the Broads in Broadcasting all took turns poking their heads in the tent to say good-bye. Last one up was Justine.

She gave Megan a conciliatory frown. "Sorry you gotta go home, Meg." She glanced around and her eyes fell on Chaz's gear—sleeping bag, personal items, the case that held her concertina. "But this might not be all bad. Am I wrong, or did it seem like you two seemed a lot chummier in the raft?"

Megan smiled. "Well, I got her to admit she *is* interested in me. And we're here overnight, so I may work on her again."

"Work on her? I know what *that* means. You're joking, right?" Justine stared at her incredulously. "Look at you! You can't seduce her! You're hurt! You're being airlifted out of here!"

"Well, I may have somewhat limited mobility, but I'll manage, wait and see."

"So did you decide that maybe you *did* want something *more* with this one? What about that no-one-night-stands thing?"

Megan shrugged. *Yeah. What about that?* It was a question she'd avoided thinking about. But if she wanted Chaz, perhaps she had to think about it, and fast. She didn't really have to think very long, before she realized she very much wanted Chaz for more than one night.

Their earlier admissions, when they thought their separation was imminent, were impossible to take back. It was out there, now—the fact that they both felt this tremendous attraction. And now they were going to be trapped together for at least several hours.

"I should get going," Justine said before Megan could work up a reply. "Good luck. I hope the weather doesn't get too rough."

Megan thanked her and, as soon as she was alone again, shifted around to make herself more comfortable, which was at best a relative concept. Her friends had cushioned her head, neck, and sore shoulder with some extra clothes, and Chaz had gotten the okay from the doctor to give her ibuprofen from the first-aid kit. It was beginning to kick in. She was warm, and dry, and as long as she didn't try to move around too much, it wasn't half bad.

On her back, her sleeping bag tucked up to her neck, she began thinking about what she would say. By the time Chaz crawled into the tent, she was ready.

Chaz lay down on her side, facing Megan, propped up on one elbow. She was still fully clothed except for her boots and her jacket, which she'd tossed into a corner.

"I'll make us some dinner in a while," she said. "Before the weather hits. How are you feeling?"

"Fit as a fiddle and ready for love. Isn't that the expression?"

That got a smile out of Chaz.

"So did you mean it when you said you view last night as a missed opportunity?" Megan asked.

"When I said that, I thought you'd be leaving in a couple of hours, and I wouldn't get the chance to talk to you again."

"Does that make a difference?"

Chaz hesitated. "Not really. No."

"You have an opportunity now."

"Megan, you're injured."

"We can work around that."

Chaz laughed. "With the way this trip has been going? No. No way. You'd end up paralyzed for sure."

"Funny girl," Megan huffed. "At least kiss me. You have to kiss me."

"You're a shameless hussy," Chaz said.

Megan laughed. "And from your smile, I'd say you like that in a woman."

"Apparently, I do indeed."

"I've had the hots for you for days," Megan said. "And from the way you kissed me back, it was kind of clear the feeling was mutual. You're a great kisser, by the way."

Chaz blushed. "I didn't...and *won't*...deny I am really attracted to you. I've been...unprofessionally preoccupied with thoughts of you since day one." She ran one hand absently through her hair, brushing it back out of her eyes. "And that kiss certainly didn't help matters."

"In that case..." Megan closed her eyes and pursed her lips for a kiss.

"Megan," Chaz groaned. But she leaned toward her, all the same. "You're injured. I mean it. It's not happening."

"So you mean if we could, you would?" Megan said.

"Probably. Yes. You're very hard to resist."

"You've resisted so far," Megan reminded her, her face in a pout. "And left me in a pretty...frustrated state, to say the least."

"Welcome to my world." Chaz smiled. "You have only yourself to blame for last night. You were deliberately flaunting your ass at me as we walked back from seeing the herd."

"Was I?"

"You're going to make this a very difficult evening, aren't you?"

"Not if you kiss me," Megan said. "Then I'll go easy on you."

That got another laugh. "You're incorrigible. I think I should go and fix us some dinner before you get me into trouble." Chaz grabbed her boots and jacket and headed for the door of the tent.

"You're only delaying the inevitable, you know," Megan called after her. *At least I sure hope that's the case.*

❖

Not long after, Chaz returned to the tent and crawled inside. "Much as I hate to move you, we can't risk having any food in here," she said, kneeling over Megan. "I'll help you outside, and we can eat and take care of anything you need to, before we turn in. All right?"

"Okay." Megan started to try to raise herself up, but immediately a burst of pain exploded in her shoulder, taking her breath away. "Damn," she complained, sinking back against her pillow.

"Wait. Let me help you." Chaz leaned down and wrapped one arm beneath Megan's shoulders. As she helped Megan sit up, she put Megan's good arm around her neck.

Megan's cool hand anchored itself right at the pulse point where Chaz's neck met her shoulder. Chaz's heart started beating faster, stronger, pounding away in her chest. Surely Megan could feel it through her fingertips.

Their faces were only inches apart, and there was a moment, the two of them frozen in suspended animation, gazing into each other's eyes, that seemed to go on forever. Chaz was lost. *Kiss her, you fool,* every fiber of her being screamed. But she feared that once she started, she'd never stop. It no longer mattered whether they had an hour, a night, or a lifetime. Were it not for Megan's injuries, they would most certainly make love tonight.

With a shaky breath, she looked away and broke the spell. Without a word, she unzipped Megan's sleeping bag and put her boots on for her, then helped her out of the tent and to her feet. Once they were both standing, Chaz released her grip and stepped away one foot, then two.

"You almost kissed me again," Megan said.

"You have to stop flirting with me," Chaz protested. But it was evident from the tone in her voice she was enjoying the exchange.

"Flirt? Me? I never flirt," Megan said with complete seriousness.

Chaz laughed.

Megan took two steps until they were standing nose to nose. "I *seduce*, yes. But I never flirt."

She leaned up to give Chaz a long, teasing kiss on the sensitive skin of her neck, just at the very place where it hit her the hardest, and she felt it to her toes. She clenched and unclenched her fists, struggling for control, trying desperately to keep her arms from wrapping around Megan like they so ached to do.

"God, Megan," she stuttered, trying to catch her breath. "What are you doing to me?"

"If you don't know then I must not be doing it right," Megan said, leaning up for another one, this one longer, sexier, wetter, her tongue a brief caress. Their bodies were only an inch or two apart.

Chaz felt her knees begin to give out from under her. "Jesus, God, please stop," she said, in a voice she didn't recognize. "I have a responsibility to take care of you, and you're making it completely impossible for me to do that."

"I think you're taking excellent care of me." Megan made no move to either increase the distance between them or close those maddening final inches. "I have no complaints whatsoever, except for that whole you-won't-kiss-me-again-yet thing."

"Dinner," Chaz muttered weakly, retreating another step, unable to bear the sweet torture of Megan's warm exhalations against her neck any longer.

Megan rolled her eyes. "Yeah, keep telling yourself it's not going to happen, Chaz. Maybe you can get someone to believe it." A low rumble of thunder could be heard far off in the distance. "I guess I can hold off until after dinner," she said playfully, and headed toward where Chaz had set up their cook stove.

They sat beside each other in their camp chairs and ate pasta with sun-dried tomatoes and artichoke hearts in a light parmesan sauce, both of them warily watching the northern sky and an ominous wall of dark gray clouds that stretched as far as the eye could see.

Chaz was beautiful under any circumstances, Megan decided. But sitting there, with the snowcapped mountain peaks starkly outlined against the stormy sky behind her, she was breathtaking. *You'd think that after a week out here roughing it, the woman might look disheveled or something.* Without makeup, hair dryer, and all the other usual beauty accoutrements she was used to, Megan certainly didn't have her usual confidence about her own presentability.

But she doubted Chaz could look any more stunning than she did at this moment, her chestnut hair slightly tousled, hazel eyes moist from the stinging wind, cheeks flushed, and that melt-your-heart smile. She was beautiful in the way that the Alaskan landscape was, rugged and independent. Unadorned and untamed.

"You look like you belong here," Megan said aloud without meaning to, wistful wonder in her voice.

"I do belong here." Chaz's eyes swept the landscape. "I don't feel whole...fully *alive*, in the city. It seems like such an artificial existence to me, in many ways."

"Where do you live?" Megan asked. "Don't you work in Fairbanks?"

"Yes, I teach biology at the university. But I live forty miles outside the city. I'm pretty isolated. My nearest neighbor is six miles away."

"I live in a condo overlooking Lake Michigan. There are probably four or five hundred people in my building."

There was silence as the differences in their worlds sank in.

"Do you miss it?" Chaz asked, in a way that suggested there was significance to the answer.

Megan pursed her lips and thought about that for several moments. "Yes and no." One side of her mouth twitched upwards in a half smile. "I'm surprised at how much I actually enjoy this camping stuff. But I will admit that the first day or two out here, I did really miss that long, hot shower in the morning. And my nice feather bed. And I would have said my triple-shot cappuccinos, but you've made this trip entirely tolerable on the coffee front, I must say."

"Speaking of, would you like an after-dinner espresso?" Chaz said.

"I'd like that very much, thank you."

"How about your job? Do you miss that? I expect it's pretty exciting to work at a television network." Chaz measured coffee and water and put the espresso pot on the stove.

"I like it, most of the time," Megan said. "It's different every day—you never know what's going to happen. A quiet day can explode in activity at any moment. That's a big plus for me. I get bored easily. And...the money's good, and I get to travel. Meet interesting people."

"You're a vice president, aren't you? Quite a bit of responsibility and stress goes along with that, I expect."

"Stressful is the right word for it. I don't miss that part, for sure. Most of the time, I probably work...let's see, fifty-five to sixty hours a week." Megan could feel her whole body tense up at the thought of returning to her old routine. "Seventy or more, when there's something major happening on a weekend. I'm on call 24-7."

"Ugh. That's awful." Chaz shook her head. "I can't imagine being cooped up in *any* office ten or twelve hours a day, seven days a week, no matter *what* the job. I'd go nuts."

"It can get old," Megan admitted. The long hours wore her down sometimes, to be sure. More often, in recent months, if she dared admit it to herself.

"When do you have any time for yourself? I mean, working sixty or seventy hours doesn't give you much time for anything but sleeping and eating."

Megan pondered the question. It was the same thing Justine had been trying to tell her for months. Maybe it was time to start listening. "I guess I hadn't thought about how hard I've been working in a long time. This trip is the first vacation I've taken in…hmm, I guess it's been more than five years."

"Five years?" Chaz was wide-eyed in disbelief. "Seriously?"

Megan was a trifle annoyed at Chaz's reaction. Like hard work and getting ahead was a terrible thing. "I have a very important position these days," she said defensively. "It's difficult for me to get away."

"Oh, I'm sure it is," Chaz hastened to add. "I just…feel bad for you, that's all. Even if you enjoy your work…which you obviously do…it's got to be tough not to have time for yourself, and the ability to get away now and then to really relax and recharge yourself. Get away to a place like this." She poured their espressos and handed one to Megan. "Mind if I make a personal observation?"

"No. Go ahead."

"If I might say so, you seem—despite your injury—a lot more relaxed and happy now than when you started this trip."

Megan sipped the espresso. "Mmm, this is delightful," she complimented Chaz. "And I guess you could say that's a fair assessment."

"Can I ask you something?"

"Sure."

"It seemed as though you didn't like me very much when you first got here. Or am I wrong?"

Megan sighed. "Yeah, well. That was rather childish of me, and I owe you an apology."

"I really wasn't fishing for one," Chaz said. "And if you don't want to talk about it, that's fine. I was just wondering…what changed. To make you…you know, kiss me."

Megan squirmed a little under Chaz's blunt questions and couldn't meet her eyes. "You remind me…*reminded* me of someone. At first."

There was a long silence. "I take it you don't like this person very much?" Chaz asked gently.

"I liked her very much," Megan said, her jaw clenching as the memories flooded into her mind. "Once upon a time. But not at the end." She looked right at Chaz then. "You're nothing at all like her, Chaz. And I'm really sorry I treated you so rudely."

"I told you, I wasn't looking for an apology. I just hoped it wasn't something I did or said."

Megan smiled. "It wasn't. And thank you for being so understanding. So…you teach biology at the university, you said. Do you like *your* job?"

"Very much." Chaz didn't flinch at the sudden change in subject. "I have wonderful students, for the most part. Bright, inquisitive, motivated. I get to spend my days talking about the things that I'm the most interested in—Alaska's wildlife and ecology, and its future. I have a view of Denali from my office. And my teaching job gives me the opportunity to lead groups like this during the summer."

"And you really *like* this, don't you? Isn't it still *work*, having to take care of everything and everyone?"

"To a certain extent, sure," Chaz said. "But I get to spend three months a year in some of the most beautiful places in the world, and get paid for it, with not a whole lot of real hard work involved on my part." She chuckled to herself. "Of course, some trips are more fun than others."

"You've had to go above and beyond on this trip, that's for sure, because of me," Megan said apologetically.

"Don't worry about it. Except for the bear and the near drowning, I've really enjoyed it."

Megan laughed. Chaz's exuberance for her work was evident in her radiant smile. In addition to the obvious sparks between them, she would miss Chaz's company a lot, she realized. She was easy to be with—bright and funny and with an irresistible charm.

"Honestly, though," Chaz said, "I'm just sorry you have to leave early."

"Me, too. I wasted a lot of time that I should have spent getting to know you better."

A loud boom of thunder sounded in the near distance, and both women jumped.

Chaz turned to look behind her. "We better get into the tent soon. That will hit us before we know it," she said, studying the sky. A solid wall of dark charcoal clouds was approaching fast from the northwest. "I just love storms." A huge grin spread across her face. She always felt energized when a big storm was coming, like her body was one giant barometer. "The power of nature exerting itself. Elemental, you know? And when you're out here, surrounded by it, at its mercy…well, I just love it. Makes me feel *alive*."

"Storms scare the crap out of me," Megan said. "At least they usually do." But she was feeling no fear at the moment, she had to admit. She was feeling it too…the excitement and energy and raw anticipation that were written all over Chaz's face.

"We'll be fine," Chaz said reassuringly, and Megan believed her. So far, leaving it all up to fate had worked out pretty well for her. It had brought her to Alaska and to Chaz. She wasn't going to fight it now.

CHAPTER SIXTEEN

Even Chaz, who had a much better understanding than most of the volatile unpredictability of Alaska's weather, was surprised at the ferocity of the storm that barreled down on them. As the thunder edged closer and the rain picked up, the wind began to increase, pushing and pulling against the thin fabric that surrounded them until it seemed as though the entire tent was breathing in and out.

The sky turned so dark that it appeared as though the sun was going to defy its normal summer path and really sink beneath the horizon this time. The air around them was charged with electricity. But Chaz wasn't sure whether it was the storm, entirely, or the chemistry that was now crackling between them as they lay side by side and only inches apart.

The long rip that Sally had repaired was directly over her head. She raised one arm and traced her finger along the length of it, pleased that the seam seal was keeping out every drop of moisture, at least for now.

"That was a pretty terrifying moment for me," Megan said.

Chaz turned on her side and leaned on one elbow to look down at Megan. "I'm sure it was. I won't forget it any time soon, either."

"You know, I really admire you, Chaz. The courage you showed against the bear. Your calm control over the most harrowing circumstances. The patience you have with everything." She smiled up at her. "Including me."

Chaz grinned back. "Thanks, Megan. That means a lot to me."

"You kind of seem to…have it all together, more than most women. You know exactly what you want."

Chaz looked away, her expression hard to read. "I would probably have said that was very true just a couple of weeks ago," she said slowly. "I *am* absolutely content with where I live. I couldn't imagine being anywhere else." She glanced at Megan with regret in her eyes, then looked away again. "And I love what I do. I feel a sense of passion and purpose about my job, and who could ask for more than that? *But...*" She let out a long sigh. "I have been thinking a lot the last few days about...how content I really am with living alone."

"The last few days?" Megan repeated.

"I have a much better idea of what I might be missing out on."

"Look at me, will you?" Megan asked gently.

Chaz turned her head slowly until their eyes met, their faces two feet apart.

"I wish to God you'd kiss me right now. If you don't, my heart is just going to burst right out of my chest."

Chaz's own heart seemed to skip a beat or two as it accelerated rapidly to match Megan's. As Megan's words repeated themselves in her head, her eyes involuntarily trailed down Megan's body to watch the rapid rise and fall of her breasts. *Sweet Jesus.*

"Now, Chaz. *Please.*"

She looked again at Megan's face and saw a depth of wanton desire that she had never seen before in a woman's eyes. Her body was electrified by it. Her every nerve ending sang. No one could have resisted that look. No one.

And then, Megan's lips became all she saw. Full, and red, and as she watched, Megan moistened them with her tongue in a teasing invitation, and that was all she wrote. Her final conscious thought was to be careful of Megan's injuries, and so she cautiously edged her body closer and leaned over Megan so that Megan would not have to move at all.

"About damn time," Megan whispered with a breathiness that shook Chaz to the core.

She closed the final distance and brought their faces together.

That first touch was only a brief caress; Chaz brushed her lips along the length of Megan's and then retreated for only a moment before descending again, to nip gently at Megan's luscious lower lip. Once, then twice.

Megan moaned, a soft sigh of surrender.

Chaz wanted to take it slow; to make it last, and to imprint it on her mind, every single detail, because she knew she would want to recall it often in the months ahead. But when Megan made that sound, a hunger flared up in her that was unrecognizable, an almost animalistic hunger that made her feel more alive, and more driven for one purpose, than she could ever remember.

She pressed hard against Megan then, devouring her mouth, thrusting her tongue into the warmth. Megan's tongue found hers with equal enthusiasm. And then, oh then…the sounds that came from Megan—a whimper of need, a groan of desire; it was a chorus she recognized because it sang inside her own body.

They kissed and kissed, and kissed, snatching a breath when they needed to, shifting momentarily to nip at each other, until Chaz was so turned on her arousal was almost painful. Much more of this, and she would come right then and there. She broke the kiss and raised up off of Megan a few inches to look at her. Megan's eyes were heavy-lidded with arousal, and their fevered kisses had left her full lips swollen and flushed.

"God, what you do to me," Megan whispered.

Chaz's heart hammered so fast she found it hard to breathe. "Megan, I know that I said I don't do one-night stands, but I want whatever time I can have with you. Even if tonight is *it*, for us. If…I mean, if you think we *can*…make love…with your injuries." She stammered in her nervousness, but she was encouraged by the look in Megan's eyes.

Make love. The words separated themselves from all the others that Chaz had said. Megan was so incredibly, *unbelievably* aroused, that her mind was having a hard time hearing words at all. How could her brain function anyway, when all of her blood was between her legs?

But those words cut through her haze of desire.

That's it. It was the answer to all those questions that had been skimming around on the periphery of her consciousness ever since she'd met Chaz. Why this felt different than all the others. Why it mattered more. Why she'd begun to question so much in her life.

She had had plenty of sex in the last five years. But never once had she made love. After Rita, she wasn't sure she ever wanted to make love to anyone, ever again.

But with Chaz, that was exactly what she wanted. For with Chaz, it could be nothing less, nothing else.

"I feel the same way," she said. "I would like…very much…to have much more than one night with you. But if that's not possible, I want to have tonight to remember."

"You're sure?"

"Never more."

A burst of heavy rain hit the tent, the sound so loud it drummed out any further attempt at conversation. But they were beyond words now anyway. Lightning flashed nearby, as if feeding from the highly charged atmosphere they were creating between them. A moment later, the following boom of thunder seemed to shake the ground beneath their bodies.

Megan was very glad she was lying down. She felt so absurdly light-headed she wasn't sure she could remain on her feet if she were upright. Her entire body seemed to pulse, at one with the primitive and wild forces of nature raging outside the tent. It was exhilarating beyond measure.

Chaz reached between them and unzipped both their sleeping bags, then sat up and slipped off sweater and turtleneck in one easy movement, then sports bra, exposing the naked splendor of muscled arms and back. The smooth, tanned skin was so enticingly close that Megan couldn't help but reach out for it.

When her fingertips touched the warm flesh, Chaz froze, momentarily startled. Then she half turned to flash a smile back at Megan, before resuming the cavalier removal of her clothes. Pants, boxers, socks. Stripped, she turned to Megan and lay on her side, smiling as Megan's eyes traveled the length of her naked body, appreciating every curve and ripple of musculature. From the broad shoulders to the firm, round breasts: not too large, dark areolas, nipples already erect.

Megan sucked in a breath as she felt her own nipples harden in response; then her eyes continued downward to the thick, dark triangle of hair, the rock-hard thighs, the legs that went on forever. She said a prayer of thanks for whatever experiences had contributed to Chaz's total lack of inhibition. Her lithe sensuality was intoxicating.

"God, you have an incredible body," she said, meeting Chaz's eyes.

What she saw there—a fiery heat, smoldering, ready to flare— surprised her. Chaz's relaxed posture belied what Megan could see clearly in the honest depths of those eyes: a coiled, raw sexuality, powerful and barely contained.

"I'm very glad you think so." Chaz's voice was thick with need and want. Her hand trembled as she reached for Megan's unzipped sleeping bag and peeled it back. "I have to see you. Touch you." She shifted position until she lay pressed against Megan, their faces close together. "And taste you," she added, leaning down to kiss Megan again as her hand found the button of Megan's jeans.

The implied promise sent a rush of heat to meet the cool intrusion of Chaz's fingers against her abdomen. In every sexual encounter she'd had since Rita, Megan had always been the one calling the shots. It was all about control. Initiating every touch, orchestrating every position. There were no surprises for her in bed any more. Satisfying releases, yes. But little more. So she found it briefly puzzling that she had no difficulty whatsoever in submitting to Chaz's lead. For some reason she was unable to explain, she was perfectly content to surrender to whatever Chaz might have in mind. Her body told her she would not be disappointed.

Chaz's lips found hers as she felt her pants being loosened. This kiss was as unsettling as the earlier ones. And they were kisses that reached parts of her that had been dormant for years, hidden and forgotten, awaiting the right touch to come alive. She was so lost in the warmth of Chaz's mouth that she barely registered the fact that somehow most of her clothes were gone. She realized it only when Chaz broke their connection to slip her shirt off, so gently her shoulder felt only a momentary twinge of pain, quickly forgotten.

Chaz stared down at her with open approval, unconsciously licking her lips as she surveyed the pale smooth skin she had uncovered, her gaze like a caress, lingering first on Megan's ample breasts, then on the silky patch of light brown hair below.

Megan trembled under that penetrating assessment.

"Cold?" Chaz asked.

She was, if anything, quite the opposite. Her body was on fire. But before she could answer, Chaz was pulling the sleeping bags over them and zipping them together to form a cozy nest for two.

And then they came together as both of them had imagined many times, Chaz covering Megan's body with her own, weight on her elbows, careful of Megan's shoulder but determined to touch skin to skin, breast to breast, pelvis to pelvis.

The same sound—a moan of contentment—escaped them both as Chaz settled her weight against Megan's, insinuating one hard thigh between her legs. Megan's center rose to meet hers, and their mouths met for another warm, slow, wet kiss as their bodies began moving against each other, increasing the friction where it was needed most. Unhurried but insistent, the pressure for release building with each rock and sway of their hips.

Chaz's lips left Megan's to trace a provocative path along her jaw, pausing to nip at her earlobe. Then a wet tongue caressed her neck and tasted the hollow of her throat, where the rapid beating of her heart could be seen and felt.

She sure has a talented mouth. Oh, yes, she certainly does, big points for that, Megan thought hazily. A shudder of anticipation shot through her as that talented mouth headed south. Chaz shifted her weight slightly so that she would be able to feel Megan's right breast with her hand while her mouth claimed its twin.

"I'm so close already, I think I'm going to explode as soon as you touch me," Megan gasped, as Chaz's hand and mouth found their destinations.

Skillful fingers cupped, lightly caressed, firmly fondled, and then pinched—hard—as Chaz's mouth did things that made Megan feel as though her nerve endings had been rewired: lines crossed, direct currents newly running between her nipple and groin.

She heard sounds. Gasps, moans, whimpers, all coming from her. Unrecognizable. Unfamiliar. Their bodies were moving against each other again, more insistent now.

Megan became aware of how wet her thigh was, where it met Chaz's center. Instinctively, she pressed more firmly against Chaz right where it mattered. Chaz groaned and her body stiffened slightly, but she never paused in her tortuous oral seduction. To Megan, it felt as though her mouth was already elsewhere. How was that possible?

I am *going to come,* Megan realized, just a millisecond before Chaz seemed to read her mind and withdraw enough to keep her poised just on the brink. The mouth and tongue and hand returned to teasing caresses, not quite firm enough to finish the job.

"Not yet," Chaz said, her voice much lower than normal, as though freshly roused from slumber.

God, she could drown in that voice. No one had ever been able to see inside of her…and know precisely what she was feeling…the way this woman apparently could. She found out how when Chaz raised her head and looked directly into her eyes.

"So close," Chaz said, and Megan could see in her eyes the joyous strain of acute arousal, orgasm contained by sheer force of will, and painfully so. Withheld, she knew, so that they could come together. Chaz knew what she was feeling because she felt exactly the same.

"Yes," she answered, her breathing erratic. Chaz's was, too. "Touch me, Chaz. Feel how wet you make me. And let me touch you."

Her consent unfettered Chaz, released her from whatever had bound her to a slow and deliberate seduction. It unleashed that powerful and fierce sexuality that Megan had glimpsed earlier in those hazel eyes. Chaz kissed her, hard, as she shifted her weight to allow them access to each other.

She had a moment to think again: *God, you can kiss*. It was almost better than sex itself with all the others she had been with. She felt it in every bit of her, every cell, every inch of skin.

Then her mind became incapable of thought, as Chaz's skilled fingers slipped into the wet, silky folds between her legs. *Jesus*. She arched her back involuntarily to meet the touch, forgetting entirely about her shoulder. A sharp stab ran through it, and she exhaled a grunt of pain as she slumped backwards.

Chaz's fingers paused but did not leave the warmth of Megan's center. "Are you all right?" she asked hoarsely.

"Yes, don't stop," Megan pleaded, spreading her legs wider and reaching down for Chaz.

Chaz's whole body tensed in anticipation, and when Megan's fingers passed through the coarse hairs and sank into the depths of the folds beyond, already soaked and swollen, Chaz made a sound she'd not heard before, a soft, keening cry.

And then they were stroking in tandem, helping each other to prolong the sweet ache, moving in synch, their bodies as one, backing off enough at the moment of eruption to push it still higher, the pressure incredible.

Both of them were gasping for air, their bodies rigid in those excruciating moments just before release, when Chaz's voice, husky, came from close above.

"Open your eyes, Megan, I want to see you," she said.

She had always thought it too personal…too intimate…to let someone into her eyes at that moment. Like they could see all the things that she safely kept hidden all the rest of the time. She never allowed it.

But she did not hesitate this time. She opened her eyes and sank into the depths of Chaz's, and they soared together over the precipice, crying out in unison, and she had never before seen anything more starkly, breathtakingly beautiful than Chaz was, when she came.

And she had never felt the overwhelming rush of heat that poured through her and lit her up from within…than when Chaz brought her to orgasm.

She was still shuddering with the aftershocks when she heard the sound of a zipper and realized Chaz had opened their sleeping bags again so she had room to maneuver, room to slowly descend down Megan's quivering body, kissing every inch as she went, no time to recover.

Megan spread her legs and Chaz slipped down between them, and before she knew it, Chaz's warm mouth was on her, the tip of her tongue playing along her wet folds with a maddeningly light touch.

Chaz looked up at her, eyes dark, pupils enormous, her lips bruised from their kisses. "I can't get enough of you, Megan," she said, breathing heavily in and out, before resuming a slow and tantalizing campaign to bring her to climax again.

Chaz's tongue explored every inch of her at leisure, discovering every place that made her hips rise up for more. Returning often to those strokes that made Megan moan, and gasp, and especially those that made her clench her teeth and cry out.

That accomplished tongue stroked the length of her, nipping, sucking, dancing in tight little circles around her painfully swollen clit, until she could stand it no longer. And somehow, Chaz knew the moment. The precise moment. For it was then that she entered Megan with her long fingers, filling her completely, and Megan roared to climax.

The storm, at its height, raged outside; the wind was howling and thunder boomed all around them, and it seemed somehow perfectly appropriate. The atmosphere both inside and outside the tent was fraught with the same kind of wild energy, elemental and totally uncontrollable.

"This is sure going to be a hell of a hard act to follow." Megan sighed, as Chaz settled beside her, one arm and one leg draped over her protectively.

Chaz raised her head so they could look at each other. "It's never been anything like this for me, either."

She kissed Megan again, a soft, sweet kiss this time that lingered long so they could memorize every second of it. Eventually they were quiet for a long while, cradled together, listening to the rain. As they drifted off to sleep, Megan wondered whether she'd ever again feel quite as content, quite as happy, quite as blissfully whole as she did at that moment.

She prayed the bad weather would continue. Anything to delay her departure.

CHAPTER SEVENTEEN

S ome time later, Chaz was awakened by the sensual caress of fingers running through her hair, languid and soothing. Next she became aware of the naked body she was draped around. Finally, she opened her eyes to find her face pillowed against Megan's left breast.

The heady smell of sex reached her nostrils, reminding her of the way Megan tasted, and she went from fast asleep to fully awake in an instant. She raised her head to find Megan watching her with the same intensity she'd had in her eyes right before she'd climaxed.

"I don't want to waste what little time we have sleeping," Megan said.

Chaz opened her mouth but nothing came out. She cleared her throat. "No?"

"No, I want more images for my mental scrapbook. Photographic memory, remember?"

Chaz really liked the provocative tone in Megan's voice. Her body began to move against Megan's as her hand cupped Megan's breast.

Megan's chest swelled as she inhaled sharply. "Jesus, Chaz," she said shakily. "I swear to God it's like you have electricity in your fingertips when you touch me."

"Do I?" Chaz trailed her hand lower, along a teasing path that skimmed through the hair at the apex of Megan's thighs before returning to her breast.

"But as wonderful as it is," Megan added, as her nipple sprang to attention, "I had something else in mind at the moment."

Chaz's hand stilled and she looked at Megan. "Of course. What would you like?"

Megan's eyes held hers. "I just *have* to taste you. Please?"

The coil of desire in Chaz's belly flared until it threatened to consume her. Her body started to shake. "Damn, Megan, just telling me you're going to nearly puts me over."

"I'll take that as a yes. This shoulder kind of puts a crimp in my style." Megan cocked her eyebrows expressively. "So I could probably use some creative positioning on your part…"

"Oh, I think that can be arranged." Chaz smiled at her, enjoying their easy banter.

"First things first, though." Megan moistened her lips.

"Yes?"

"Have I told you what an absolutely fabulous kisser you are?"

Chaz felt her cheeks get warm as she leaned down and brushed her lips against Megan's, then slowly, almost reverently, claimed her mouth. Every kiss between them had been different, but memorable in its own way. This one had equal parts of the passion of the night before and the sadness of the separation ahead. It was bittersweet, and a harbinger of how much she would miss Megan.

Over the hours that followed, they made love in as many ways as they could think of and that Megan's injuries allowed. Slow, and fast. Gentle, and rough. Playful. Seductive. Cramming every possible experience into their limited time left together.

In the wee hours of the morning, scant moments after Chaz had reached yet another climax, just seconds after Megan, a wolf howled in the distance. Both women froze for a second, mesmerized by the sound, then Chaz howled back—a long, jubilant cry.

It was lifelike enough that the wolf replied, then Megan started up, too, and they all howled together until the howls turned to laughter that went on and on and on.

Chaz wiped tears off her cheeks as she collapsed back against Megan. "Well, that's a first. No woman has ever made me howl before."

"Just one of my many talents. How will you ever get over me?" Megan asked, with a flippancy that wasn't convincing.

Chaz picked up on it and looked her in the eyes. "That's a good question."

"Can we keep in touch?" Megan asked.

"I really hope we do," Chaz said. "Maybe you'll come back and visit one day, and I'll show you some of my favorite places."

"I get four weeks' vacation a year, and I've got a million or so frequent flier miles. I'll come back if you want me to."

"Good. Because I do. Very much." Chaz kissed Megan again and tried not to make it feel like good-bye. But it was already beginning to. Far too much. She couldn't help it. Three or four weeks a year would not be nearly enough.

They lazed back into a spoon without further words, Chaz wrapping her body around Megan's, front to back, always mindful of her injured shoulder. Soon she felt the deep even breathing she could already recognize as Megan asleep, and she had to fight back sudden, unexpected tears that sprang from nowhere.

How is it possible to feel so much for her, so soon? It's not fair. To finally feel something like this and have it be so impossible. It was nothing at all like she'd expected. The women she had seriously dated were all just like her. Wilderness devotees. Monogamous. Perfect fits, all of them, at least on paper. They had the same interests, outlook, priorities in life.

She and Megan, on the other hand, had very little in common on the surface. Sure, Megan appreciated the uncommon beauty of their surroundings with a sensitivity that not everyone possessed. That much was clear. *She picked up kayaking pretty fast and seems to enjoy it, despite the accident. No complaints about the primitive camping experience. She's bright, and funny, incredibly sexy, and...she makes you feel things that no one has ever made you feel.*

But the differences between them seemed insurmountable, distance being only one. They had different priorities. And even though it seemed to her, when they were making love, that Megan was feeling exactly as she was feeling...that this was incredibly *different*, and special...she knew it wasn't so.

For her, it's only an affair. And she has them all the time. You know that you'd want much more than that. If you kept seeing her, it would only make it that much harder to say good-bye when she moved on to someone else.

Yes, it was probably just as well that they had only one night. For every additional hour that she spent with Megan was an hour spent getting closer and closer to her. Already, she could not imagine how she would ever say good-bye.

❖

When next Chaz woke, the light streaming into the tent and the bird calls outside told her that the storm had passed, and it was probably well into the morning. She knew she should find the radio and turn it on; they would be sending a helicopter as soon as possible. But she couldn't bring herself to move right away.

She wanted a final moment to relish what it was like waking up next to Megan, after the most incredible night of lovemaking in her life. She was on her back and Megan on her side, tucked up against her with her head in the crook of her shoulder. Her soft breathing against Chaz's chest felt like brief, airy caresses. Chaz's nipples started to get hard.

One of Megan's legs was carelessly draped over hers, weightless and unmoving but, placed where it was, between *her* legs, still extremely provocative. She could feel herself getting aroused again. *Jesus, get a grip. Aren't you worn out yet?* Apparently not.

Her common sense won out. It wouldn't do for the chopper to arrive with them lying like this. She managed to reach her watch without having to move too much. Megan slept on. 8 a.m. *Shit.*

She glanced outside. There was a touch of fog; that was good, it meant probably that rescue wasn't imminent. But the rain had stopped, and morning fog often burned off by midmorning. She really did have to check in, and in order to reach the radio, she'd have to move Megan off of her.

She tried to slowly extricate herself from Megan's embrace, but as soon as she moved a few inches, Megan moaned, and, still half-asleep, nestled her body even more snugly against Chaz. The languid movement of Megan's body along hers did nothing to help quench Chaz's growing excitement. *I'm just going to have to wake her. Or pretty soon I'm not going to care whether the chopper is coming or not.*

"Megan?" she said gently.

Megan sighed a long sigh of contentment. Chaz knew she was still asleep, but the gentle exhalation sounded so much like the sigh she'd made after orgasm number three that it kicked up Chaz's arousal another notch.

"Megan!" Louder this time, her voice betraying the level of her fear of losing control. "I have to radio in."

She slowly stretched to reach her pack, and her movement made Megan come fully awake. She yawned sleepily and blinked at Chaz. "Hi, there. Good morning."

Her eyes were twinkling at Chaz, and she had a shyness to her voice that in light of what they'd been doing to each other all night, sounded incredibly sweet and endearing. *Why do you have to be so irresistible?*

Chaz did the only thing she could do. The only thing that made sense, when Megan looked at her like that. She kissed her, like she meant it. Like she never wanted to let her go. Damn, she was going to miss those kisses.

"Good morning," she replied some time later when they came up for air.

"I could get used to having that every morning as my alarm clock," Megan said lazily as she relaxed back again Chaz's chest.

The hint of regular domesticity about that statement made Chaz's stomach clench. *If only that was true.* Stoically, she reached for the radio. "It's late enough that I really need to call in and see when they're coming for you. Probably would not be real good to have them come up on us unexpectedly."

"So, what happens next?" Megan asked.

"The air ambulance will fly you to the hospital in Fairbanks. Orion will be contacting you there and will make arrangement for your flight home and anything else you need after you're released."

"I don't suppose I can suggest we postpone getting me out of here another day or two or three?" Megan asked in a quiet voice, not looking at Chaz.

"I wish that was possible. But you need to be looked at. I know they'll be sending someone as soon as the weather allows."

"This sucks. I don't feel bad, considering. Just a sore shoulder. The headache is pretty much gone. I want to spend more time with you."

"I wish we could, too, Megan. But I also have to rejoin the group. I have a job to do and they need two guides." With that, Chaz reluctantly turned on the radio and reported in to the Alaska State Troopers.

The news couldn't have been worse. The chopper was on its way. They roused themselves and got dressed, and Chaz put some water on for coffee, then packed up their gear and took down the tent. They didn't say much to each other as they waited. But they sat side by side, leaning back against a gray boulder, legs stretched out in front of them and their bodies touching.

"You have all my information on the registration forms, right?" Megan asked.

"Yes. I'll copy it all down when I get back to the lodge." Chaz reached into a pocket for a small pad of paper and pen and wrote down her name, address, phone, office information, and e-mail address. "Here's mine," she said, tucking the note carefully into the breast pocket of Megan's jacket.

"Better be careful where you put those hands," Megan kidded playfully. "You don't want to start something you can't finish."

"Damn, woman, don't you ever get tired?" Chaz's comment was offset by the fact that she leaned over to nuzzle Megan's neck as she said it. She would more than happily go again if they had the time.

But there was no time. They heard it before they saw it. Chaz got to her feet as the chopper came into view over a nearby mountain peak. Their alone time was at an end, and she felt it as a very real ache in her chest.

"I guess this is it," she said, leaning down to help Megan to her feet.

Megan gazed up at the approaching chopper. "I hate good-byes anyway. And this ranks up there with the class-A worst ones."

"Yeah, I'd agree with that."

"I know you had reservations about getting involved with a client." Megan lowered her gaze and turned moist green eyes on Chaz. "How do you feel about public displays of affection?"

"What are you proposing?" Chaz asked with a smile.

"I'd about kill for one more of your kisses."

Chaz cradled Megan's face in her hand. Made one last caress of that sun-kissed cheek before she leaned down to claim that mouth a final time. Megan's arm came around her waist and pulled their bodies together.

The sound of the helicopter landing on a small patch of level tundra nearby forced them apart.

"Stay in touch," Chaz said, looking into Megan's eyes while they waited for the air ambulance crew to disembark.

"I will. Thanks for everything." Megan wanted to say something profound and meaningful, but how could she think when Chaz looked at her like that? "I'll never forget last night."

Chaz couldn't keep her eyes from misting up. "I won't either. I'll miss you."

"Me, too."

That was all the time they had.

Five minutes later, Megan was comfortably ensconced in the helicopter. She gave a final wave, and the chopper lifted off and headed south. As she watched Chaz's silhouette get smaller and smaller, an ache began in her chest. It grew with each mile that separated them.

❖

Chaz waited until the helicopter was out of sight and then got into her kayak and on the river, happy to have some time alone before she had to resume her guide duties. She felt unsettled, even mildly disoriented. Megan had turned her world upside down in the space of twenty-four hours, and Chaz couldn't imagine how it would right itself again. She kept telling herself that it was all for the best, but there was no way that her separation from Megan after their night together felt like anything but what it was: a sudden cold and hollow place, where there had recently been an abundance of heat and belonging.

The rest of the group was finishing a late lunch when she reached their campsite two hours later. She briefed them all on Megan's departure and caught up with how they had fared in the storm; then they all set off in their kayaks to resume their trip downriver.

They reached their next stop about seven that evening and fell into the now-familiar routine of setting up tents and getting dinner started. Sally knew her well enough that she sensed something was different, but she gave Chaz some space to think things out on her own. She asked only if Chaz was all right and offered a shoulder if she needed someone to talk to.

Justine was not so easily deterred. At the first opportunity to talk to Chaz alone—which happened to be while Chaz was doing dishes—she corralled her and began peppering her with questions about her night with Megan. "So, Chaz…I know this is going to sound like I'm butting in, but I'm Megan's best friend so I think I'm entitled." That out of the way, she found a flat rock to sit on and made herself comfortable. "So did you two finally admit that you have a thing for each other before she left?"

Chaz felt her whole face get hot as images of her and Megan in various positions of lovemaking flashed into her mind. "Uh…" she stammered. But she couldn't suppress a silly grin at the memory.

"Great!" Justine said. "So I see it went *very* well, in fact, from the smile on your face and that nice shade of crimson you're sporting."

"Well, we did hit it off," Chaz managed finally. Despite the third degree, Chaz developed an immediate respect for Justine. She was direct, and outspoken, and she obviously had nothing but Megan's welfare uppermost in her mind. Chaz felt okay about talking to her. "I really don't…get involved with clients generally, but—"

"I'm glad you made an exception in this case," Justine said. "Are you two planning to keep in touch, I hope?"

"We exchanged addresses and e-mails, phone numbers." Chaz finished the dishes and sat down beside Justine. She missed Megan already far more than she even imagined she would. Here was her best friend—a potential font of information about the woman who had captured her attention, and she apparently wanted to talk about Megan so Chaz was certainly going to let her. "So was it that obvious that we're attracted to each other?"

"Maybe not to everyone. But Megan confides in me more than most."

"You're lucky, then," Chaz said.

"Yes. She's not close to a lot of people. Doesn't volunteer much and doesn't trust easily."

"Do you mind if I ask you a question that I'm curious about? You don't have to answer."

"Shoot."

"How did this Royal Ice Bitch thing come to be?"

Justine laughed. "Well, Megan does have an intensity about her when she's in the newsroom during a big story…calling the shots and directing coverage. No nonsense, for sure. But she got the nickname from a bunch of malcontents she inherited."

"Inherited?"

"There's a running joke at WNC that you have to do something notoriously bad to get fired. The company is so afraid of lawsuits—for age discrimination or whatever—that they make it almost impossible to just fire someone because they do a half-assed job. You pretty much have to be a complete and certifiable psycho, and even then you get two warnings before they let you go." Justine laughed. "Well, before Megan took over, the newsroom ran totally on seniority. The best shifts and perks went to the people who had been there the longest. Megan put everything on a merit-based system."

"And made some enemies," Chaz concluded.

"Exactly. The people who had the primo, nine-to-five shift but who were only skating along and just showing up—suddenly found themselves working overnights. People who worked hard, had great attitudes and innovative ideas…they got raises, better hours, and first shot at being the one chosen to go overseas when a plum assignment opened up. I'm a reporter because of her—I was a writer with on-air ambitions, and she provided me with the opportunity to show what I could do."

"She's good at her job, isn't she?"

"The best. Corporate loves her because ratings across the board are up every year since she took over. And most of the people in the newsroom love her, because hard work and creativity are recognized and rewarded. She's got high standards, sure, but she doesn't ask for anything she won't do herself. She genuinely cares about her staff and feels a responsibility for them. If you need anything—time off for an emergency, a change of jobs, she makes it happen. She's always available to her staff."

"She told me she puts in a lot of hours," Chaz said.

"Workaholic personified," Justine agreed. "Way too much so. I've been worried about her. That's why I think coming here and meeting you was the best thing that's happened to her in a very long while."

"You do?"

"I haven't seen her really come up for air—and take a vacation, where she really relaxed—since Rita. She just goes out once in a while to blow off steam. Did she tell you about Rita?"

"No. She did tell me she hadn't had a vacation in five years."

"I'm not real surprised she didn't tell you about her, but I'd hoped she would. You'd understand some things a lot better."

Chaz's heartbeat picked up. From Justine's tone, it was obvious that this Rita was very important to Megan. *Rita.* Then it hit her. Clients had occasionally told her she looked like a reporter named Rita Thompson. So she'd looked her up on the Internet and had noted the resemblance. That was a couple of years ago; she'd forgotten all about it because she couldn't get WNC on her TV.

Intrigued, she asked, "Will you tell me about her?"

"They were together for five years. Married, at least as far as Megan was concerned—they said vows to each other. She was sure it was forever, until Rita cheated on her and left her for someone else."

Chaz remembered Megan's explanation for why she'd been so cold when she arrived in Alaska. *You reminded her of someone she liked very much, once upon a time. But not at the end.* "I look like Rita?"

"Very much."

"She wasn't attracted to me because I look like her ex, was she?" The possibility depressed her after the evening they'd had.

"Just the opposite. She kind of despises Rita now, I think. Megan likes you *despite* the fact you look like her," Justine said.

"From…well, from something I overheard, I got the impression that Megan doesn't stick with anyone very long. That she isn't into commitments. Kind of surprises me to hear that she was married."

"She's been running from any real emotional involvement ever since Rita was such a shit to her," Justine said. "But something tells me she may have stopped running when she met you. I think you mean a lot to her."

Chaz shrugged. "Well, even if that's true, I don't see how we can have any kind of future. I can't even bear the *thought* of leaving Alaska. Could you imagine Megan leaving her job?"

Justine shrugged. "Maybe not."

"How do you have a relationship when you live hundreds of miles apart?"

"I don't know, Chaz. I don't have any answers for you on that. I just wanted you to be aware that Megan *does* have feelings for you. Pretty powerful ones, I think, even if she's not ready to admit them." Justine got to her feet. "I hope you two can find a way to be together. She's a keeper, and so are you. I think you could be very good for each other."

She walked away and left Chaz contemplating all that she had said. She could think of little else the rest of the trip.

❖

Before she knew it, she and Sally were back at the airfield in Winterwolf saying good-bye to the Broads in Broadcasting. Chaz pulled Justine aside as they waited for the plane to arrive to fly them back to Fairbanks. "I presume you'll see Megan pretty soon after you get back?"

"Sure," Justine said.

"Would you give her this for me?" Chaz held out the envelope containing the letter she'd written the night before. She could have mailed it, or even e-mailed it, but sending it through Justine just seemed more personal, more intimate. She hoped Megan would think so too.

"Of course." Justine took the letter and gave Chaz an impromptu hug. "Thanks for everything—it was the adventure of a lifetime. And think about what I said. Chicago is a great city to visit."

Chaz didn't doubt that, but something told her that if she ever did make it to Chicago, she'd see very little of the place.

CHAPTER EIGHTEEN

Chicago, Illinois

Megan was only in the fourth hour of her first day back at work, and already she missed Chaz, and Alaska, with an intensity that took her completely by surprise.

Her experience had changed her perceptions about nearly everything in her well-ordered routine. She noticed for the first time as she flew into O'Hare that the air over Chicago was a dirty yellow-gray, in no way resembling the vivid blue of the Arctic sky. The bumper-to-bumper traffic from the airport was no different than any other day, but it frustrated and rankled her ten times worse than normal. The noise level in the city was nearly unbearable after ten days of birdsongs.

It was as if she now saw her environment anew through Chaz's eyes. She was amazed to discover she could count the trees in her neighborhood on one hand, and there was hardly a patch of green to be seen in the crowded urban landscape. Nearly every person she saw on the street looked stressed and in a hurry. *She really would hate it here.*

Her condo was claustrophobic after the vast landscape of Alaska, and so was her office, with two weeks' worth of accumulated work piled high on her desk and credenza. She had a list of people who wanted to see her. Her phone rang nonstop—always with something that demanded her urgent attention—and hundreds of e-mails were waiting in her inbox.

I must have been insane to think I could take two weeks off.

Despite the hundreds of distractions, her eyes kept returning to the photo on her desk. Chaz on the hilltop where they'd watched the caribou herd, windblown hair and rosy-cheeked complexion accentuating her rugged good looks. Megan had copied it to her computer and printed it out as soon as she'd gotten home. *God, you're beautiful.*

She'd had no contact with Chaz since their separation nine days earlier. She tried to catch her between trips, but the first time she called the lodge, Chaz had been at the airstrip seeing Megan's friends off. And by the time she called back, Chaz was off on another ten-day trip into the wilderness.

A knock at the door forced her eyes reluctantly away from the photo.

"Bet I know who's in that picture you're staring at. How's the shoulder?" Justine stood leaning against the doorway, a big smile on her face.

Megan got up and gave her a hug, then shut the door so they wouldn't be disturbed. "Shoulder's fine. Kind of stiff. So how was the rest of the trip?"

"Fabulous." Justine took a seat. "Sorry you had to leave early, but everybody took lots of pictures so you'll see what you missed. Speaking of which, we're all getting together at the Cool Breeze Friday night to share photos."

"I'll be there," Megan said. The chance to relive the trip and see new photos of Chaz was something she'd look forward to all week. And she had already decided she'd been working too hard and needed to make sure she made time for her friends.

"Wow, no fight at all? Have you finally learned to relax, or is it the prospect of seeing a bunch of pictures of Chaz, all gorgeous and buff?

Megan couldn't help the smile that spread across her face at the mental image that sprang to mind—Chaz sunbathing on the rock.

"Ah, I *see*," Justine said.

"It was amazing being with her. I miss her like crazy," Megan admitted.

"No kidding," Justine deadpanned. "I think the feeling is mutual, by the way."

"Did she talk about me? Ask about me?"

"You sound like you're back in high school. But yes, she did. And I won't keep you in suspense any more." She pulled Chaz's envelope out of the pocket of her blazer. "She asked me to deliver this."

Megan ran her hand over the envelope reverently, fingertips caressing where Chaz had written her name. "Thanks." She looked up at her friend, anxious to read but mindful of her manners.

"Go ahead, I know you can't wait." Justine got to her feet and headed for the door. "I'll tell Grace to hold your calls for a few minutes and come back later so we can catch up."

"Thanks, Justine."

As soon as Justine had closed the door behind her, Megan carefully opened the envelope and took out a two-page letter written in Chaz's precise penmanship. It began

Hello, Megan. I miss you more than I can say.

Seeing those words first, right off the bat, made her heart flutter in her chest. She ached for reassurance that their time together had meant as much to Chaz as it had to her.

She glanced at the photo again, before returning to the letter.

And it's not just because you are incredible in bed (though you most certainly are, and thank God for your stamina).

That line not only produced a big smile, it started up a slide show in her mind of some of things they'd done to each other during that long, incredible night. She had never been more grateful for her ability to recall events in absolutely perfect, vivid detail, down to the accompanying tastes and smells. *No telling what might happen when we get together and I don't have a bum shoulder to work around.* She glanced at the photo again. *Damn. I've got it real bad for you, don't I?* She returned to the letter.

It didn't take me long after you left, to realize that you already mean more to me than perhaps any woman ever has.

Her heartbeat kicked into high gear at that line.

Megan, I don't know how or when, but I want to see you at the very earliest opportunity. And at every opportunity thereafter. I hope you meant what you said about those million frequent flier miles because I miss you fiercely.

Oh, God. Chaz. You have to have a way with words, too. An ache of longing blossomed in her chest. It was going to be absolute hell not to be able to communicate with Chaz for at least another week.

I've fallen for you. In a big way. I guess there are many who would say that after only one night together, telling you how I feel is jumping the gun. That it's too much, too fast, too soon. But I know how I feel. I just pray to God you feel the same.

I know that making a relationship work when we have such radically different lives, so far apart, seems impossible. Maybe it is. But I want to see where this might lead.

Her heart was thumping hard in her chest now, and it was getting more difficult to read as tears welled up in Megan's eyes. *Oh, yes. She feels it, too.*

I can't stop thinking about our night together, Megan, the next line read. *I miss you, and I need to feel your body.*

Oh, shit, Megan thought. *Perhaps I shouldn't be reading this at work.* The memory of Chaz's hands on her, burned vividly in her mind, flared to life. *Oh, hell.* Her nipples were instantly hard, and she felt a sudden urge to press her thighs firmly together.

I would certainly run out of superlatives if I tried to describe what it was like for me to make love with you. Incredible. Exquisite. Unbelievable. It's like you awakened a part of me I didn't know existed. No one has ever made me feel more alive than I felt that night, Megan. You stir my blood.

More memories flashed through her mind. She could feel herself getting more and more aroused. *Shit. Shit. Shit. This is definitely not appropriate at work.*

I'm sorry it's going to be so hard for us to communicate with each other while I'm leading trips the rest of the summer. I'm especially anxious, of course, to hear how you'll react to this letter. I hate it that it'll be several more days before I can try to reach you. I will call as

soon as I can. Know that you are never far from my thoughts.
Chaz.

The second page of the letter was Chaz's itinerary for the rest of the summer. For the next month and a half, Megan would be able to talk to her only every seven to ten days.

Something tells me these are going to be the longest weeks of my life.

She pulled out a piece of her business stationary, a heavy bond of ecru with her name and title in embossed letters. Everything else could wait. She wanted Chaz to have a letter waiting for her when she got back from her trip.

❖

Megan buried herself in work all week to try to make time move faster. Not that she had any choice; so much had piled up in her absence that she worked twelve-hour days and still wasn't caught up by Friday night.

But she was not about to miss seeing new photos of Chaz. So she locked up her office and actually beat all the others to their regular booth in the back of the Cool Breeze.

"Oh, my God!" Justine exclaimed when she arrived. "You're the first one here? You really are smitten, aren't you?"

"Shut up and pull out your pictures," Megan grumbled good-naturedly. "I can't believe you wouldn't spring for one-hour photo processing. I'm buying you a digital camera for Christmas."

"Hey, there she is!" Pat hailed them as she and Linda approached, Elise not far behind. "How you doing, Megan? No sling, I see."

"I'm fine. They kept me overnight for observation in the hospital, but I flew home the next day and had the sling off not long after."

"Anybody talk to Yancey?" Elise asked. "She coming?"

"Would I miss this?" Yancey said from behind her. "May I see a show of hands of who wants to go back to Alaska tomorrow?"

All hands shot up, Megan's a fraction faster than anyone else's.

"So who wants to go first?" Linda asked, as everyone settled into a seat in the big circular booth.

"I'll start," Elise said, pulling out a thick stack of four-by-six color snapshots, the colors so vivid and the landscape so picturesque that each one could have been a postcard.

"Ah, the one that got away," Elise lamented when she got to the first one of Chaz. She had captured Chaz the day of the rolling lesson, her formfitting wet suit paying sexy tribute to her excellent physique.

You wish, Megan thought smugly as she took the photo from Elise.

"I don't think she got away from everyone," Linda said, looking pointedly at Megan with a grin.

Megan shot a look at Justine that said, *You didn't!*

But Justine shrugged innocently. "Don't look at me. I didn't say anything."

"I'm just perceptive," Linda said.

"What am I missing here?" Yancey asked.

"You're not the only one," Elise said. "Did you and Chaz get something going, Megan?"

Hell, what's the problem? You got the gorgeous woman that everyone wants. And she's crazy about you.

"Well, as a matter of fact," Megan said, "we did get something going. Something pretty great. I think I'm going to be seeing a lot of Alaska."

Winterwolf, Alaska

"Megan Maxwell, please." Chaz settled into the nearest comfy chair as she waited to be patched through to Megan. *Finally.*

She'd come straight to the pay phones in the lobby as soon as they hit the lodge, while Sally and their backpacking clients headed for hot showers and turns in the large outdoor hot tub.

"I'm sorry, Ms. Maxwell is in a meeting. May I take a message?"

Damn. "Yes, please. Would you tell her Chaz Herrick called and will try again later. She is also welcome to call me." She recited the lodge's phone number.

"I'll give her the message," the polite voice replied.

Chaz's heart sank at having to wait any longer to talk to Megan than she already had. She'd been restless for days, impatient to hear Megan's response to her letter.

Sighing, she headed toward her room, but Paul Bartlett, one of the lodge's owners, hailed her from the front desk.

"Hey, Chaz! Got a letter here for you!"

Megan! She hurried to the desk and felt her spirits soar when she saw the Chicago postmark and WNC return address.

"Thanks, Paul." She ripped open the envelope as she headed to her room, her hands trembling in anticipation of what she would find inside. A chance at happiness? Or a polite sorry, but not interested?

She sat on the bed and began reading.

Dear Chaz,

There are many things I really like about you. Foremost, at the moment, having just read your letter, I really like your courage and your straightforward honesty.

I feel the same, Chaz. I'm head over heels in love with you, too.

But I think it probably would have taken me a lot longer to admit it.

I'm buried in work here, but I can't stop thinking about you. (And, yes, most certainly about that night. And you're one to talk about stamina!)

You've shaken up my life a lot more than you know. In a good way.

I can't wait to talk to you. See you. Touch you. Kiss you. Hold you. Taste you.

Uh, oh. Maybe I shouldn't be writing this at work.

Call me.

I miss you terribly.

Megan

Chaz leaned back against the headboard of the bed with a contented smile. *Now we just have to figure out a way to be together as often as possible.* She could access her fall class schedule online. *I'll take a shower and then e-mail that to Megan so she can compare it to hers and see when we can get together. Then I'll grab a bite to eat and try calling her again.* She had to keep busy. The minutes until she could try phoning again would absolutely drag.

At least I can talk to her every day once I get home from guiding. But these weeks until then are going to be torture.

Chaz tried Megan again an hour later. "Ms. Maxwell, please," she said when Megan's assistant answered.

"Ms. Maxwell is in a meeting. May I ask who's calling?"

"This is Chaz Herrick. I tried earlier, and—"

"Oh! Ms. Herrick, yes! Ms. Maxwell left instructions that you were to be forwarded through to her if you called back. Please hold and I'll connect you."

Chaz's heart picked up in anticipation.

"Hello, this is Megan. Chaz? You there?" There was a lot of noise in the background, like Megan was in a crowded room with a lot of people talking.

"Yes, I'm here." *Finally!* "God, have I missed you…" Chaz got half of it out, but Megan was talking over her before she finished.

"I've missed you so much! I was worried I was going to miss your call."

"I caught you at a bad time, didn't I?" Chaz asked.

"No! Hang on! I'm heading to my office so I can have a little privacy, but don't hang up. I don't want to lose you."

"Don't worry, I won't."

The sounds behind Megan diminished. "So…that's better. How are you?"

"Good. I'm good, now that I'm talking to you. This week has just *crawled*."

"Tell me about it." Megan laughed.

"Thank you for your letter," Chaz said.

"Well, thank you for *yours*."

There was a short embarrassed silence, then the two of them began laughing.

"Let's not waste our precious phone time being shy with each other *now*," Chaz said. "I mean, considering what we did to each other…in every conceivable position—"

"Oh, God, you can't do that to me." Megan stopped her. "I'm at work, and I have meetings in a while. I'm supposed to be all cold and bossly, and here you're going to make me all mushy and warm inside. My staff won't know me."

"I can't be held responsible for how your voice enchants me."

"Damn, you're a smooth talker, Chaz Herrick."

"So I take it you're all healed up? Everything's all right?" Chaz asked.

"If you were here, I'd ravish you in all those ways we couldn't in the tent," Megan said, in a breathy, seductive voice.

Chaz felt a sharp twist of arousal at the juncture of her thighs. "Jesus, Megan. Now who's being provocative? I'm in the lobby of the lodge!"

"Oh, am I getting you all hot and bothered?" Megan asked in the same sexy voice. "Does it show? Are people watching?"

"Stop that!" Chaz was really heating up now, and starting to fidget. She glanced around. No one in sight at the moment, but that could change at any time. "You're a cruel woman." But the playful banter and the effect that Megan had on her body, even long distance, only reinforced the growing attraction between them.

"Oh, I think you *like* it," Megan murmured. "In fact, you like it a *lot*. You sure liked it when I teased you that night, remember?"

"You could make a fortune as a phone-sex provider, not that I'm advocating a change of careers for you," Chaz said. She felt light-headed, not surprising since all her blood was traveling south a mile a minute.

"You think so?" Megan said. "Well, maybe as a hobby. Just for one exclusive client."

"Is that an offer?"

"Oh, I think we're going to have to find all sorts of creative ways to get through the long periods when we can't be together. Do you have a webcam?" Megan asked.

"A webcam? No," Chaz answered.

"Get one as soon as you get home," Megan said. "They're really cheap now, and they really are the next best thing to being there. At least then we can see each other when we talk."

"Oh! That would be great."

"Yes, and let me tell you right off the bat I thoroughly encourage you to wear as little as possible when we chat."

Chaz laughed. "Hmm, well, I'm beginning to see the possibilities here."

"Thought you might. So when *are* we going to be able to get together? Have you looked at your schedule?"

"I e-mailed it to you a while ago."

"Great. Hey, I can maybe get away for a long weekend over Labor Day. How about you?"

"Can't. I've got some departmental meetings then—curriculum development for the coming year."

"Damn."

Chaz could hear the disappointment in Megan's voice. "Sorry. How about Thanksgiving?"

"November is sweeps month—our most important rating period. I can't get away that month at all." Megan groaned.

"Christmas?"

"Christmas I can definitely do. But damn! That's so far away!"

"I know."

They both went quiet. Much of the enthusiasm they had built up with their flirting deflated with the realization they wouldn't see each for five more months.

"You sure you want to pursue this, knowing how tough it's going to be?" Megan asked in a quiet voice. "How long before we see each other again?"

"I'm absolutely certain," Chaz affirmed. "I meant what I said, Megan. I know how incredibly difficult it's going to be to have a relationship with you, with all the strikes against it. But I feel something for you that I've never felt before. I *have* to try to see where that can lead. I will always regret it if I don't."

Megan sighed. "I'm glad. It's the same for me, Chaz. I want to do whatever it takes. Even if it's a long while until we can truly be together the way we want to be."

"We're sure going to become extremely patient people, I think," Chaz said.

"Or experts at phone sex," Megan answered wryly.

Chicago, Illinois

Megan had to settle for long, similarly frustrating phone calls every week or so during the next month and a half, while Chaz was leading trips. In between, they exchanged long letters and e-mails, filling the other in on the bits and pieces of their lives: family and upbringing, schools and pets, friends and jobs. They were happy to find they had many more things in common than they knew: politics, movies, books, music. Ethics and morals. A deep concern for the environment.

With every written exchange and telephone call, they further cemented the bond between them. But talking by webcam once Chaz returned to Fairbanks was both a blessing and a curse, because seeing each other without being able to touch was the most excruciatingly frustrating torture.

By mid-September, Megan knew it would never be enough.

It wasn't a startling revelation. She didn't wake up one morning and decide that things had reached critical mass. There was just a nagging discontent with her life as it was, and a growing realization that what mattered most in her life were those long talks with Chaz in the evening.

Something had to give.

CHAPTER NINETEEN

Fairbanks, Alaska

Chaz stared out of the window of her office, in the general direction of Denali. It was a view she never tired of, but her mind was entirely on Megan. It was 3:00 p.m. in Alaska, which meant it was 6:00 p.m. in Chicago, and Megan would likely be headed home about now. Chaz often paused in her daily routine to glance at the clock and imagine what Megan might be doing at that moment. She had also begun to watch the news more often than ever before, because she knew if a major story broke that Megan would be unavailable for a while.

Her last class of the day, Mammology, didn't start for half an hour, and she was restless. It was as though the only time she felt entirely happy now—completely whole and content—was during those moments she was talking to Megan. Swiveling in her chair to face her desk, Chaz picked up a framed five-by-seven photo of the two of them together that Sally had taken. She had a second copy beside her bed at home.

Unbeknownst to either of them at the time, Sally had captured that moment on the hilltop above the caribou herd when she had very nearly kissed Megan. From looking at the picture—their expressions, their faces close together—it would have been hard to believe they *hadn't* kissed a moment after the photo was taken.

Seeing it set off a visceral, involuntary reaction within her body, a warm rush of feeling as it recalled the heat of Megan's kisses. There was just no way she could wait until Christmas to be with her.

"You're sure somewhere else," Gareth Rosenberg said from the doorway. "You have a melancholy look on your face, my friend. Everything all right?"

Chaz leaned back in her chair and didn't answer immediately. *You have to spend some real time with her.* "How upset would you be with me if I asked to take a sabbatical?"

Gareth frowned. "Is something wrong, Chaz? Not sick or anything?"

"No, nothing like that," she hastened to reassure him. "I'm fine. I just have some personal things that need my attention, and I will probably need some time off to do them."

"How long are we talking?"

"I'm not sure. Maybe a year."

"And you'd want to start right away? Next term?" he asked.

"Yes. I think so." *Probably would be wise to get Megan's input on this. I certainly hope she'll be up for me coming to Chicago for a while.*

"Well, of course you can have whatever time you need. I'll just be anxious to get you back. We need you around here, you know."

"Thanks, Gareth." She glanced at the clock. "I'll have a better idea of my plans in a day or so, I think." She gathered up some papers on her desk and got to her feet. "Gotta head to class. Going my way?"

"You bet."

Her last class of the week was her least favorite. Not that she wasn't enthusiastic about the subject; she loved talking about the wildlife of Alaska, and she had some great new photos from her summer trips to show the class. But this was a required class, so it was held in one of the large impersonal lecture halls, and every time she handed out a test she had 168 papers to grade. Her other classes were all small enough that she could get to know each student somewhat during the course of a term.

The stacked tiers of seats were only half filled when she arrived; students were still filing in from two sides so she busied herself getting her materials ready.

Today on the big screen that dominated the front of the room, the students would be treated to 400 or so breathtaking photos that Chaz had shot during her countless trips, alone and as a guide. She had close-up shots of all the major mammals that populated the state, including some of the more reclusive: polar bears and grizzly bears, wolves and wolverines, lynx.

"Hi, everybody. If we can settle into seats, please," she asked to get the stragglers moving. "I'd like to pick up where we left off—chapter

10. Today I'm going to be talking about the magnificent mammals that inhabit this great state."

She flicked the switch that lowered the lights above the students and turned on the digital projector. "First up is *Ursus arctos horribilis…* or our friend the Alaska grizzly bear…"

The ninety-minute class flew. Perhaps she had brought a few too many photos. Or maybe she had paused a bit too long on the ones she'd taken of the caribou herd that summer, because those photos always reminded her of Megan. Before she knew it, the time was nearly up, and she still had pictures left to show.

"I'm going to just let the slide show play out here, to give you all a look at the rest of what I brought," she said. "But I'll stop now…in case anyone has any questions? Comments?"

There were four.

The first was a query about where musk ox could be found.

The second, a compliment of her excellent photography skills, drew a smattering of applause from other students.

The third asked when midterms were.

She thought that was all. In fact, she had already begun to hear that pervasive rustling that was the sound of students gathering up belongings to leave, when a familiar voice rang out from the dark last row.

"Ever come face to face with a grizzly bear?"

She was stunned into silence.

A long moment passed. The rustling had stopped and the room was quiet. The students were all watching her intently.

"Yes," she replied, a smile twitching at the corner of her mouth. "Once."

There was dead silence in the room.

"But there's not time to tell that story today." This elicited a loud groan from at least three-fourths of the class, but she stepped to the wall switch and turned the lights back up, saying, "See you all next week."

Megan was seated in the dead center of the last row. She remained where she was, staring at Chaz with a positively beaming smile on her face, as students got up all around her and filed out. Finally, once they were alone, she rose and made her way forward, her eyes never leaving Chaz's.

Chaz's breath caught in her throat. *Oh, God.* Megan had never been more stunning. Like she stepped off the cover of a magazine. Hair shining, eyes glowing. Lips full and moist. She was wearing a pair of dark gray dress slacks, topped with a red silk blouse and charcoal sweater.

Megan slinked slowly toward her. Until she got to within a few feet—then she flew into Chaz's arms and hugged her with a fierceness that took her breath away.

"You're really here," Chaz said, inhaling the herbal fragrance of Megan's perfume.

"Indeed I am. In the flesh." Megan drew back from their embrace to look her in the eyes. "And very anxious to be alone with you. I think you're done for the day, aren't you?

"How are you here?" Chaz was still in shock. "How *long* are you here, more importantly?"

"I'm here on assignment," Megan answered. "I've got at least a couple of weeks." She pointed to a small suitcase, shoved beneath a row of coat hooks along one wall. "That's mine. Know a place I can stay?"

"Oh, boy, do I ever."

A minute later, they were in the vast parking lot. It was only mid-October, but it was already white as far as the eye could see.

"Didn't you tell me you lived quite a ways out of town?" Megan asked as they climbed into Chaz's big pickup truck.

"Forty miles."

"There is absolutely no way I can wait that long to kiss you."

Chaz started toward her at once, but Megan still managed to meet her halfway.

Their lips pressed together, softly at first—tentatively, reacquainting after nearly four months apart. Then their too-long-denied heat for each other took hold and ignited the kiss into a scorching, hungry exchange.

"Jesus," Chaz said shakily when they parted to breathe. "We'll never make it to my place."

"Yes, we will." But Megan was breathing heavily, too, and her lips were bruised and tender. "I'll be good." She leaned back into her seat and buckled her seatbelt, while she gestured with her head for Chaz to do the same. "Once we really get started, you know we won't be able to stop. So you better get this truck going before I lose my resolve not to touch you until we get there."

Chaz fumbled the key into the ignition and got the pickup moving. For the first time ever, she wished she lived a hell of a lot closer to town. She kept glancing in Megan's direction. "You're going to have to stop looking at me like that, Megan."

"Like what? How am I looking at you?" Megan's sexy tone indicated she knew damn well what she was doing.

"I mean it, now! Stop! It's hard enough to keep my eyes on the road as it is. Be nice!"

"Can't help it. God, I've missed you so much. I can't wait to get my hands all over you."

"That's exactly what I mean. You're looking at me like I've already got all my clothes off."

"Never seemed to bother you before," Megan said with a grin.

"Well, I have absolutely no problem taking off my clothes with you," Chaz said. "But you can't be putting these images into my head when the road is slippery and we have miles and miles to go yet."

"You are such a wet blanket sometimes," Megan griped. "But okay. I'll behave."

"So talk to me. Keep my mind off of where it is right now so I can get us home safely. Tell me about this assignment you're on." Chaz glanced sideways at her and refrained from stopping the truck so they could kiss. "I still can't believe you're actually here. Why didn't you tell me you were coming?"

"I wanted to surprise you. I'm here to do a series of special reports on the refuge."

"No kidding! Was this your idea?"

"Yes. I'm executive producing. My crew arrives next week. I'm here to scout locations and do some research."

"Well, you know whatever I can do…" Chaz said.

"I was hoping you'd say that. We've talked to the university about getting someone to act as our guide and resident expert—I've requested you." Megan grinned at her. "They gave me the go-ahead to see if you're interested. It'd be good exposure for the school and good for the refuge. You know I'll cover it right—really make people interested in helping to make sure it stays a protected wilderness."

"*And* we get to spend a couple of weeks together," Chaz said.

"Sounds like a wonderful plan to me."

"I'm glad you approve."

"You know, the next time we talked I was going to ask you what you thought about my maybe coming to Chicago for a very long visit." Chaz slowed the truck to turn off the main road onto the one that led to her cabin.

"How long are we talking?"

"Maybe a year?" Chaz glanced over to see the reaction. Megan had a very happy grin on her face.

"And how would you manage that?" Megan asked.

"Take a sabbatical. I could probably be there in January. I ran it by the head of the department today, but I wanted to talk to you before I made a formal request."

"You'd take a year off from your job…and leave Alaska for Chicago…for me?" Megan's voice was soft in disbelief.

"Of course. I said I'd do whatever it takes to give us a real shot."

"Yes, you did." Megan was quiet for a long while, staring out the window. "I'd like to tell you about someone, Chaz. From my past. I told you that you reminded me of someone."

"Rita," Chaz answered. "Justine told me a few things about her."

"Did she?"

"Not that much, really. I think she wanted me to know that you weren't really a one-night-stand-only kind of person, at heart. That you had fallen in love and had gotten serious with someone, but she hurt you very badly."

"That sums it up pretty well." Megan's voice was resigned and sad. "I thought it was love. I thought we were happy. But she was cheating on me behind my back, and when she left, she hired an attorney and wanted to make it all very messy. I just wanted to stop the pain, so I let her have everything. The house. Most everything in it. The nice new car. Our two cats. I walked away with nothing much but my clothes."

"I wish I knew what to say," Chaz said. "It's inconceivable to me that someone who purportedly loves you could do such a thing. My heart aches for you, that you had to go through that."

Megan shrugged. "You know, I carried around a lot of…bitterness. Anger. Resentment. Lots of negative shit, from that relationship. For a very long time. I really didn't realize I was doing it…until I met you. But I see now it's what kept me from really getting close to anyone else.

I was just too damn afraid of it all happening again. Making myself vulnerable enough for someone to be able to cut me so deeply." She put a hand gently on Chaz's thigh. "I really trust you. And I have to say…that I feel things for you that I never felt for Rita."

"Thank you for telling me about her," Chaz said.

"I want you to know everything."

"As I want you to know everything about me." Chaz hated that Megan had suffered so in her relationship with Rita, but she felt almost giddy that she had pushed past all of that in order to find her in Alaska. "So does that mean you're up for my coming to Chicago?"

"Well, I think we have another alternative that might be better," Megan said, as Chaz's cabin came into view in the distance.

"Do we?" Chaz asked.

"This assignment could turn into something more long term."

Chaz's heartbeat picked up. "Define long term."

Megan was watching her intently. "Well, it could be permanent, if that's what we both want."

The truck ground to a halt. Chaz turned to her. "Permanent?"

"If that's what we both want," Megan repeated. "You don't have to decide today." She gestured at the road. "Come on. Keep going."

Chaz put the truck into gear. "How is it possible?"

"Well, I pitched an idea to the network president, my boss. I told him I wanted to start up an environmental unit—that it was high time WNC had one—to do documentaries in the public interest."

"And he went for it?"

"Well, I had to threaten to resign first, to show him I was serious that's the only way I would continue with the company," Megan said. "He likes me well enough that he wanted to keep me on the payroll."

"But how can you be here permanently?"

"Well, that was one of my conditions. That I would be based wherever I choose. I'll be on the road some, of course, but it won't be too bad."

Chaz shook her head in disbelief. "I can't believe you'd do all this for me."

"Why? You were ready to do it for me." Megan's staff couldn't believe it at first either, and she knew it appeared to most like a pretty monumental change she was making in her life. But the decision had actually been pretty simple when it came right down to it. "I get to be with you, in Alaska…which I've grown rather fond of, by the way. And I'll get to do something I feel passionate about. Something that might make a difference. Besides, I was beginning to be very unhappy with where I was, without you there."

The truck came to a stop in front of a well-kept one-story log cabin. A matching garage sat off to one side. In every direction were magnificent, snowcapped mountains, and behind the cabin there was a picturesque lake, already frozen over except for a few small patches of open water that glistened in the sunlight. It couldn't have been more inviting.

"We're here," Chaz said, shutting off the engine and turning to Megan. "Welcome. Welcome home."

❖

Megan paused just inside the doorway, her eyes taking in the comfortable and homey great room as Chaz darted about, picking up a sweater she had thrown over a chair, the loose mail on the coffee table, the empty coffee cup from that morning.

"Sorry about the mess," Chaz said. "Please…come on in and make yourself comfortable. I'll get a fire going and pour us some wine. How does that sound?"

"That would be lovely," Megan answered.

A massive stone fireplace dominated one wall. The other walls were crowded with bookshelves, jammed to overflowing with books and with framed photographs from Chaz's travels. Her concertina, unlatched as though it had been recently played, sat on an end table beside the couch.

Everywhere was evidence of Chaz's love of the out-of-doors. Snowshoes hung above the mantel, cross-country skis and poles were propped in one corner. Inuit art and sculptures were scattered about, on bookshelves and in small glass display cases. Megan wandered about the room, taking things in, as Chaz built a fire.

Within a few minutes, a cheery blaze was going, and Chaz lit a few candles to add to the romantic ambience. Then she excused herself to get some wine from the kitchen.

"Join me," she said, when she returned to settle on the couch in front of the fire, with two glasses of Lambrusco.

Megan took one and held it up for a toast as she sat beside Chaz. "To us," she said.

"I'll certainly drink to that." Chaz clinked her glass against Megan's and took a sip. "I still can hardly believe you're here."

"Well, then I guess it's time I start convincing you I'm not only here, but here to stay a while." Megan put her glass on the coffee table, then took Chaz's and set it down as well, before she repositioned herself—facing Chaz, straddling her, one knee on either side of Chaz's lap.

She cradled Chaz's face in her hands and leaned in for a long, slow kiss. They had all the time in the world, now, and Megan wanted to make it last. She kissed Chaz with all the passion that four months of longing had built up inside of her, and Chaz kissed her back in equal measure.

Her body came alive then, teased by Chaz's body undulating beneath her, and her hips began to move of their own accord. Before she knew it, Chaz's hands had worked their way beneath her clothing and were caressing her sides, her back, her hips, her stomach, with increasing pressure and purpose. Soon her heart was pounding so loud she was certain Chaz could feel it, hear it. It sent a warm wave of blood pulsing between her legs.

She gasped for air when Chaz's fingers found both of her nipples at once. Each tweak, firm and insistent, resonated to her core and sent her higher. She ground her pelvis against Chaz and moaned, long and loud, arching her back and letting the sensations wash over her.

The sound seemed to fuel Chaz's purposeful touches—she lifted Megan's sweater and shirt and took one of her breasts in her mouth, sucking hard, while one arm wrapped around Megan and pulled her close.

"I love your mouth on me," Megan whispered, breathless with excitement. "But I need to feel you, Chaz. We have far too many clothes on."

"Your wish is my command." Chaz slipped Megan's sweater off and fumbled for the buttons on the red silk shirt underneath.

Soon she was naked from the waist up, and Chaz followed a moment later with the swift removal of her own fleecy top and turtleneck. They came together then, breast to breast, mouth to mouth, their bodies moving more urgently against each other as the passion between them flared higher.

"Jesus, Chaz," Megan cried out. "You're driving me crazy! Clothes! Off! Now!"

Chaz lifted her, one strong hand beneath each thigh, and shifted Megan until she was lying on the couch. *Thank God for those long hours spent kayaking and backpacking*, Megan thought. *Muscles to spare. And she'll need them tonight.*

She stared into Chaz's eyes as her slacks and panties were stripped from her body. She could drown in those eyes. Dark pools, the pupils enormous, lids heavy with arousal.

She watched as Chaz got to her feet to slowly remove her own jeans and boxers in a seductive striptease. The warm amber glow from the fire lit her skin, casting shadows that accentuated every curve and hollow and taut muscle of that exceptional body.

"Come lay on me," Megan whispered.

"You don't want to move to the bedroom?" Chaz asked, her voice hoarse and unfamiliar. She offered a hand to help Megan up.

"For the next round, perhaps." Megan took the hand and pulled Chaz down on top of her, opening her legs to surround Chaz's body and pull her close.

She felt Chaz shudder as their centers came together, and she couldn't contain an answering tremble of her own body. When they were together like this, nothing else mattered. And everything, *everything*—made sense.

The travel brochure had promised Megan that she would have an unforgettable experience in Alaska. One that would change her life. It had certainly lived up to all of that and more. It had given her perspective and purpose, and for the first time in her life, here in Chaz's arms, she felt truly complete, filled with a sense of belonging she had yearned for all her life. She was home at last, and in the calm that enveloped her as Chaz stole the breath from her body and noisy doubt from her mind, she could hear her heart's truth. This was for keeps. And she wanted it no other way.

"I love you, Chaz," she said.

Chaz drew back slightly and stared down at her with solemn yearning. "I could get used to hearing that. How does every day for the rest of our lives sound?"

Megan brushed her mouth across the soft lips just a breath from her own. "I think I could sign up for that. But I'll need to practice."

Chaz grinned. "Then let's not waste any time. I love you, too, Megan Maxwell, and now I'm going to show you how much."

About the Author

Kim Baldwin started writing fiction in 2001 after a 20-year career in journalism. She has published three novels, including the 2005 Golden Crown Literary Award finalist *Hunter's Pursuit*, and two short stories in the Bold Strokes Erotic Interlude series. She is currently at work on her fourth book, *Flight Risk*. Her interests include kayaking, motorcycling, collecting books, and music. She and her partner live in the north woods of Michigan.

Books Available From Bold Strokes Books

Whitewater Rendezvous by Kim Baldwin. Two women on a wilderness kayak adventure—Chaz Herrick, a laid-back outdoorswoman, and Megan Maxwell, a workaholic news executive—discover that true love may be nothing at all like they imagined. (1-933110-38-4)

Erotic Interludes 3: Lessons in Love ed. by Radclyffe and Stacia Seaman. Sign on for a class in love…the best lesbian erotica writers take us to "school." (1-933110-39-2)

Punk Like Me by JD Glass. Twenty-one year old Nina writes lyrics and plays guitar in the rock band, Adam's Rib, and she doesn't always play by the rules. And, oh yeah—she has a way with the girls. (1-933110-40-6)

Coffee Sonata by Gun Brooke. Four women whose lives unexpectedly intersect in a small town by the sea share one thing in common—they all have secrets. (1-933110-41-4)

The Clinic: Tristaine Book One by Cate Culpepper. Brenna, a prison medic, finds herself deeply conflicted by her growing feelings for her patient, Jesstin, a wild and rebellious warrior reputed to be descended from ancient Amazons. (1-933110-42-2)

Forever Found by JLee Meyer. Can time, tragedy, and shattered trust destroy a love that seemed destined? When chance reunites two childhood friends separated by tragedy, the past resurfaces to determine the shape of their future. (1-933110-37-6)

Sword of the Guardian by Merry Shannon. Princess Shasta's bold new bodyguard has a secret that could change both of their lives. He is actually a she. A passionate romance filled with courtly intrigue, chivalry, and devotion. (1-933110-36-8)

Wild Abandon by Ronica Black. From their first tumultuous meeting, Dr. Chandler Brogan and Officer Sarah Monroe are drawn together by their common obsessions—sex, speed, and danger. (1-933110-35-X)

Turn Back Time by Radclyffe. Pearce Rifkin and Wynter Thompson have nothing in common but a shared passion for surgery. They clash at every opportunity, especially when matters of the heart are suddenly at stake. (1-933110-34-1)

Chance by Grace Lennox. At twenty-six, Chance Delaney decides her life isn't working so she swaps it for a different one. What follows is the sexy, funny, touching story of two women who, in finding themselves, also find one another. (1-933110-31-7)

The Exile and the Sorcerer by Jane Fletcher. First in the Lyremouth Chronicles. Tevi, wounded and adrift, arrives in the courtyard of a shy young sorcerer. Together they face monsters, magic, and the challenge of loving despite their differences. (1-933110-32-5)

A Matter of Trust by Radclyffe. JT Sloan is a cybersleuth who doesn't like attachments. Michael Lassiter is leaving her husband, and she needs Sloan's expertise to safeguard her company. It should just be business—but it turns into much more. (1-933110-33-3)

Sweet Creek by Lee Lynch. A celebration of the enduring nature of love, friendship, and community in the quirky, heart-warming lesbian community of Waterfall Falls. (1-933110-29-5)

The Devil Inside by Ali Vali. Derby Cain Casey, head of a New Orleans crime organization, runs the family business with guts and grit, and no one crosses her. No one, that is, until Emma Verde claims her heart and turns her world upside down. (1-933110-30-9)

Grave Silence by Rose Beecham. Detective Jude Devine's investigation of a series of ritual murders is complicated by her torrid affair with the golden girl of Southwestern forensic pathology, Dr. Mercy Westmoreland. (1-933110-25-2)

Honor Reclaimed by Radclyffe. In the aftermath of 9/11, Secret Service Agent Cameron Roberts and Blair Powell close ranks with a trusted few to find the would-be assassins who nearly claimed Blair's life. (1-933110-18-X)

Honor Bound by Radclyffe. Secret Service Agent Cameron Roberts and Blair Powell face political intrigue, a clandestine threat to Blair's safety, and the seemingly irreconcilable personal differences that force them ever farther apart. (1-933110-20-1)

Protector of the Realm: Supreme Constellations Book One by Gun Brooke. A space adventure filled with suspense and a daring intergalactic romance featuring Commodore Rae Jacelon and a stunning, but decidedly lethal, Kellen O'Dal. (1-933110-26-0)

Innocent Hearts by Radclyffe. In a wild and unforgiving land, two women learn about love, passion, and the wonders of the heart. (1-933110-21-X)

The Temple at Landfall by Jane Fletcher. An imprinter, one of Celaeno's most revered servants of the Goddess, is also a prisoner to the faith—until a Ranger frees her by claiming her heart. The Celaeno series. (1-933110-27-9)

Force of Nature by Kim Baldwin. From tornados to forest fires, the forces of nature conspire to bring Gable McCoy and Erin Richards close to danger, and closer to each other. (1-933110-23-6)

In Too Deep by Ronica Black. Undercover homicide cop Erin McKenzie tracks a femme fatale who just might be a real killer...with love and danger hot on her heels. (1-933110-17-1)

Course of Action by Gun Brooke. Actress Carolyn Black desperately wants the starring role in an upcoming film produced by Annelie Peterson. Just how far will she go for the dream part of a lifetime? (1-933110-22-8)

Rangers at Roadsend by Jane Fletcher. Sergeant Chip Coppelli has learned to spot trouble coming, and that is exactly what she sees in her new recruit, Katryn Nagata. The Celaeno series. (1-933110-28-7)

Justice Served by Radclyffe. Lieutenant Rebecca Frye and her lover, Dr. Catherine Rawlings, embark on a deadly game of hide-and-seek with an underworld kingpin who traffics in human souls. (1-933110-15-5)

Distant Shores, Silent Thunder by Radclyffe. Doctor Tory King—and the women who love her—is forced to examine the boundaries of love, friendship, and the ties that transcend time. (1-933110-08-2)

Hunter's Pursuit by Kim Baldwin. A raging blizzard, a mountain hideaway, and a killer-for-hire set a scene for disaster—or desire—when Katarzyna Demetrious rescues a beautiful stranger. (1-933110-09-0)

The Walls of Westernfort by Jane Fletcher. All Temple Guard Natasha Ionadis wants is to serve the Goddess—until she falls in love with one of the rebels she is sworn to destroy. The Celaeno series. (1-933110-24-4)

Change Of Pace: *Erotic Interludes* by Radclyffe. Twenty-five hot-wired encounters guaranteed to spark more than just your imagination. Erotica as you've always dreamed of it. (1-933110-07-4)

Honor Guards by Radclyffe. In a wild flight for their lives, the president's daughter and those who are sworn to protect her wage a desperate struggle for survival. (1-933110-01-5)

Fated Love by Radclyffe. Amidst the chaos and drama of a busy emergency room, two women must contend not only with the fragile nature of life, but also with the irresistible forces of fate. (1-933110-05-8)

Justice in the Shadows by Radclyffe. In a shadow world of secrets and lies, Detective Sergeant Rebecca Frye and her lover, Dr. Catherine Rawlings, join forces in the elusive search for justice. (1-933110-03-1)

shadowland by Radclyffe. In a world on the far edge of desire, two women are drawn together by power, passion, and dark pleasures. An erotic romance. (1-933110-11-2)

Love's Masquerade by Radclyffe. Plunged into the indistinguishable realms of fiction, fantasy, and hidden desires, Auden Frost is forced to question all she believes about the nature of love. (1-933110-14-7)

Love & Honor by Radclyffe. The president's daughter and her lover are faced with difficult choices as they battle a tangled web of Washington intrigue for...love and honor. (1-933110-10-4)

Beyond the Breakwater by Radclyffe. One Provincetown summer three women learn the true meaning of love, friendship, and family. (1-933110-06-6)

Tomorrow's Promise by Radclyffe. One timeless summer, two very different women discover the power of passion to heal and the promise of hope that only love can bestow. (1-933110-12-0)

Love's Tender Warriors by Radclyffe. Two women who have accepted loneliness as a way of life learn that love is worth fighting for and a battle they cannot afford to lose. (1-933110-02-3)

Love's Melody Lost by Radclyffe. A secretive artist with a haunted past and a young woman escaping a life that has proved to be a lie find their destinies entwined. (1-933110-00-7)

Safe Harbor by Radclyffe. A mysterious newcomer, a reclusive doctor, and a troubled gay teenager learn about love, friendship, and trust during one tumultuous summer in Provincetown. (1-933110-13-9)

Above All, Honor by Radclyffe. Secret Service Agent Cameron Roberts fights her desire for the one woman she can't have—Blair Powell, the daughter of the president of the United States. (1-933110-04-X)